From the Gulf of St. Lawrence to the Golden Gate, America's destiny followed trails blazed by forgotten heroes — lonely figures in homespun and buckskin. This book tells the stories of some of those daring men of the BUCKSKIN BRIGADE

BY JIM KJELGAARD

BUCKSKIN BRIGADE

Illustrated by Ralph Ray, Jr.

HOLIDAY HOUSE · NEW YORK

FOREWORD

This book is a tribute to daring men whose names are forgotten, but whose deeds and spirit illuminate every page of American history. As the westward march of civilization made its slow way over and through successive barriers of forest and prairie and mountain until it had spanned three thousand miles from ocean to ocean, it followed the moccasined paths of nameless men in buckskin. Always, beyond the towns, the settlements, the log-cabin clearings, were "the adventurers of the far side of the hill."

Woods runners, rivermen, long hunters, scouts, fur traders, and mountain men, these trail blazers were bound by no frontiers and limited by no horizons. Let the homesteader and land speculator and politician follow them; their world was illimitable and their only law the law of survival. By moccasin and snowshoe, by canoe and horse, protected only by their wits and their long rifles, they led the way into the unknown. They starved, froze, drowned, and were murdered by beast and Indian. But they lifted the veil of secrecy from the North American continent and showed other men the way to security, wealth, and fame.

The chief characters in these stories are real, although few will be familiar. Each one is representative of a period and a type—if such rugged individualists can be typed. Known facts have been used wherever possible, and the fiction which supplements and gives life to those facts has always been governed by a sense of probability. The stories have been arranged chronologically, and historical perspective maintained by brief factual introductions.

CONTENTS

1506	THE TREE	1
1588	CROATAN	33
1615	THE MEDICINE BAG	63
1661	SAVAGE TREK	91
1753	THE OPENING GATE	125
1780	WILDERNESS ROAD	161
1791	CAP GITCHIE'S ROOSTER	183
1808	THE FIFTH FRIEND	213
1833	FREIGHT FOR SANTA FE	243
1844	END OF THE TRAIL	281

THE TREE

1506 *The importance of John Cabot's explorations in 1497 was not the discovery of a "New Found Land," but his report of seeing vast numbers of cod in the region now known as the Grand Banks. Fish were a staple article of food in the Catholic countries of Europe, and French, Portuguese, and Basque fishermen lost no time in tapping this new source of supply. Within ten years the sturdy little craft from the French channel ports and the Bay of Biscay were making regular runs across the dangerous North Atlantic, and bringing back more and more reports of the lands that lay about and beyond their fishing grounds. Hardy Breton and Norman seafarers established a proprietary interest in these distant shores that lasted for a hundred years. It is singularly fitting that the oldest surviving European name on the Atlantic coast of North America is Cape Breton Island.*

THOMAS AUBERT relaxed on the coil of rope, contemptuously watching fussy little Captain LeJeune. Nobody but a Basque from St. Jean de Luz would stand at the prow of a ship, holding a glass to his eye and trying to peer through a fog that you couldn't cut with a scaling knife. But what could you expect from a Basque, anyway? God knew that the only true sailors, those really weaned on salt spray, were Bretons—preferably from St. Malo. No doubt Captain LeJeune and his five funny sailors were very good oyster shuckers, and certainly they were un-excelled as garlic eaters. But it took men from St. Malo to sail a ship.

Aubert cast his eye down the deck to where Baptiste LeGare and Hyperion Talon, two other St. Malo men crazy enough to sail under a Basque captain, were standing unconcernedly. They, too, had known for some days that the *Jeanne* was off her course. But, naturally, Captain LeJeune knew everything and certainly didn't intend to take the advice of any St. Malo men. They recognized none of this sea. Thirty-two days out of St. Malo, they should have been on the Grand Banks six days ago. But where were the hordes of waterfowl that hovered over the Banks? Where were. . . .

Aubert braced himself instinctively, anticipating the shock a second before it came. Out of the sea loomed a great, shapeless mass, and the *Jeanne* quiv-

3

ered like a woman in pain. There was a tortured scream, and the crack of rending timbers. Aubert saw Hyperion Talon go down, and shook his head angrily. If there was one floating object in all the North Atlantic, you could trust a Basque captain to find and hit it.

Then the floating iceberg passed on and the *Jeanne* righted herself. But there was a dangerous list to starboard, and with that innate knowledge of ships which generations of seafaring ancestors had instilled in him, Aubert knew that she was mortally wounded. He made his way toward the stern, and bent over the recumbent Talon.

"Are you badly injured?" he asked.

Hyperion shrugged. "I have a pain in the side. It will pass."

"Wait here," Aubert commanded. "I will return."

He joined Baptiste LeGare, who was scornfully watching the frantic efforts of Captain LeJeune and his five men. You could rely on Basques to panic every time. They were acting as though they had less than half a minute to launch their fool boat, when, as a matter of fact, they had a full half hour. Maybe more. The *Jeanne* was a stout little craft, and would take a lot of water in her hold before she finally settled.

The boat struck the water, and the five Basque sailors pushed into it. Captain LeJeune sputtered at them and ran back into the cabin. He emerged a moment later with the ship's log under his arm. Aubert's brown eyes twinkled, the wind-etched wrinkles in his face deepened, and his black beard jerked as he suppressed a chuckle. LeJeune had launched a boat without water, without food, without anything except oars. But he had to save his precious log. Aubert laughed outright.

"What's so funny?" Baptiste LeGare demanded.

"The little captain," Aubert grinned. "He has taken his log with him. Can you not imagine it, Baptiste? One hour from now, if it has also occurred to him to take a goose quill and ink, he will be making some such entry as, 'June 5, 1506: The *Jeanne,* somewhere off the Grand Banks of the New Land, struck an uncharted reef and foundered. The three men from St. Malo were carried overboard by heavy seas.' Bah! Basque sailors!"

Lying prone on the deck, his head pillowed on his sea cloak, Hyperion Talon turned his head to look.

"Where are we, Thomas?" he inquired.

Aubert shrugged. "In the Atlantic Ocean, Hyperion. And that, in truth, is all I know. How is your side?"

"It has felt better; it could feel worse. Are the fools from St. Jean de Luz gone?"

"They are gone."

Aubert gravely regarded his fellow townsman and shipmate. There was blood on Hyperion's mouth.

Aubert liked neither the look of his eyes nor the pallor of his face. He raised his head and watched the little boat, whose sailors were frantically pulling away into the mist. Apparently they were going in no special direction. Well, they'd end up somewhere, if only at the bottom of the sea.

Aubert said, "Our turn, Baptiste."

LeGare followed him, and they broke out the little twelve-foot dinghy that was roped to the side of the cabin. Aubert regarded the dinghy fondly. It was a St. Malo boat; he'd made it himself. He knew what had gone into it and what it would stand. After Captain LeJeune and his men had capsized in their clumsy Biscayan lifeboat, the dinghy would still be floating. Grasping either end, he and LeGare carried it to the settling stern of the *Jeanne*, over which waves were beginning to break.

"Put in three casks of water and a keg of biscuit," Aubert instructed. "We'll need adzes, chisels, knives, mallets—you know the tools she'll hold. One musket, with plenty of powder and shot, should be enough. Also a coil of rope and a pulley."

LeGare began to load the dinghy while Aubert went below. The hold was gloomy and foul smelling from the countless tons of fish the *Jeanne* had carried during her many trips to the Newfoundland Banks. Aubert looked at the soggy heap of salt that was supposed to be thrown over the fish they took this trip,

6

and at the little stack of chests loaded with trade goods for the savages who were sometimes encountered when a fishing boat put into a New Land harbor for water and fresh meat.

Aubert shook his head disapprovingly. He hadn't liked it when they left St. Malo. He didn't like it now, this idea of a captain taking along trade goods to feather his own nest while he was catching cod for the ship's owners. To be sure, there was money to be made so doing. He had known the savages to trade as many as ten fine fox pelts for one tin plate and a few trinkets. But a fishing boat should do nothing except fish, and if anybody wanted to send a trading boat over here it should do nothing but trade. However, there really were not enough of the New Land savages, nor did they have sufficient furs, to justify anyone's sending a ship over just to trade for them. The captains got what there were. But to mix fishing and trading was a breach of propriety that somehow was sure to bring bad luck. Still. . . .

On sudden impulse Aubert caught up a small chest of trade goods and carried it with him when he went on deck. He cast an expert eye the length of the *Jeanne*. She had settled perceptibly since he went below. Aubert stowed the little chest in the dinghy. LeGare stood by, the oars in his hands, staring into the mist-wreathed sea. Aubert inclined his head toward Hyperion Talon.

7

The injured man groaned when they lifted him, and bright blood bubbled from his mouth. They laid him in the dinghy, with his head on a cloak and another over him. Aubert held a bottle of brandy to his lips. The half-conscious sailor took a feeble gulp, and smiled wanly. For a moment Aubert stood over the dinghy, checking its contents. But LeGare had done a good job, both in selecting and packing. Aubert returned, wrenched the compass from its stand by the tiller, and carried it to the dinghy. He and LeGare took their seats.

A few minutes later the *Jeanne's* stern went under and the little dinghy floated free. With a half-dozen lusty strokes of the oars Aubert sent it clear of the deck. He and LeGare turned around. Talon weakly raised his head. There was a swirl of water and for a moment the *Jeanne* stood upward, her bowsprit in the air as though beseeching aid.

The fog closed in.

IT WAS VERY THICK, a sinuously undulating cloud that sent clammy fingers into every nook and corner of the dinghy and touched the backs of the men with cold hands. Aubert raised the compass, gripped it between his knees, took a bearing, and swung the dinghy. Talon had fallen asleep, the cloak pulled up to his eyes and one hand peacefully upraised. Le-

Gare, a mist-shrouded figure on the stern seat, hunched his shoulders.

"What course?" he asked.

"West."

There was a thoughtful silence as LeGare digested this information. A lone gull squawked out in the fog and Aubert stopped rowing to listen. You couldn't tell much about gulls. They might be anywhere. Some followed the fishing boats clear from France. Some, apparently, lived in the middle of the sea. There was one chance in a million that this one presaged the nearness of another ship. Aubert shrugged. It would be impossible to find another ship in this fog, anyway.

LeGare spoke again. "It is a wise plan, Thomas, one that I would expect you to conceive. By going west we encounter a fishing boat on the Banks, eh?"

"We are not on the Banks."

"But we cannot return to St. Malo by going west."

"Consider, Baptiste. Could we reach St. Malo in a twelve-foot dinghy, even this one?"

The gull squawked again, faintly, then only the fog was left. The sea heaved a little, lapped at the prow of the dinghy. A wave splashed over it and Talon muttered sleepily as spray blew in his face. LeGare looked at the injured man as he replied.

"Of a certainty, Thomas, we cannot reach St. Malo. But what lies to the west?"

"I do not know. I have heard men say that the shores of China lie in that direction."

"A long way, my friend, is it not?"

"Perhaps. But which is better, Baptiste? We know that we cannot return to St. Malo. We may reach whatever lies ahead, and if we do we shall find means to survive. Meanwhile, we are on the sea, and what man of St. Malo hopes to die in bed?"

"You are right," LeGare said philosophically. "We may trust the sea."

Talon sat up, and Aubert turned in his seat to look at him. The injured man's face was no longer gray, but red. His eyes were bloodshot, his smile forced. Aubert dropped the oars, broached a cask of water, poured some into a tin dish, and passed it back. Talon drank thirstily, fell back into the bottom of the dinghy, and coughed. Aubert crossed himself, and looked gravely at LeGare as he picked up the oars. He rowed strongly, evenly, taking long sweeps that produced a maximum of forward effort with a minimum of exhaustion.

After three hours LeGare said thoughtfully, "You remember Basil LeSeur, the old man who hung around the docks at St. Malo? He has been to the Grand Banks and the New Land many times, and he himself told me that he thought the New Land might be an island, perhaps many islands. He said he thought there might be other land not far from it.

Perhaps, after all, we shall come to the coast of China."

"Perhaps we shall."

He rowed on into the mist, pushing the little dinghy forward with powerful sweeps that curled the water at her prow and left a wake behind. Reason told him that theirs was a very serious predicament.

But something else within him stirred, something that, had it not been tempered by Talon's suffering, would have been only delight. Starting when he was thirteen, he had come six seasons to the Grand Banks and had helped catch great numbers of fish to take back to a Catholic Europe. Now, at nineteen, the Grand Banks and the bleak New Land had lost their charm, and the long trip from St. Malo had become dreary routine rather than high adventure. But Aubert had looked at the uninviting New Land, and yearned toward what lay beyond. Certainly the fabled Orient must be somewhere to the west. Now, at last, he was going toward it. Even though he had only a dinghy, and probably would never get there, at least he was trying to do so. If he could change his own fate now, he would not.

A wind stirred and the mist lifted for a little while to reveal a gray sea. LeGare took the oars, and night closed in. Aubert slept, with his head pillowed on his knees, and it was still night when LeGare awakened him to resume rowing. Talon muttered in delirium.

Little wavelets rose, and when morning came the fog had again closed in. Talon sat up, and gripped the side of the dinghy with the great strength that sometimes comes to dying men.

"Tell Catherine Minot," he gasped, "that she should not weep for me. There are other good men in St. Malo."

Talon collapsed limply, and his suddenly pain-free eyes seemed to be staring at some happy thing that only he saw. The sea was about to claim another St. Malo sailor. Aubert crossed himself, and in the stern seat LeGare followed suit. But LeGare's simple face reflected fear and doubt.

"How shall we administer the last rites?" he whispered.

"We cannot, Baptiste. We are no priests."

"Well then, how shall we bury him?"

"In the sea."

"But the sea monsters?"

"Fear not, Baptiste. The good God, who marks the sparrow's fall, will let Hyperion be claimed by neither the devil nor a sea monster."

"That is so," LeGare answered doubtfully. "We must have faith."

Aubert turned around, for a moment cradled Talon's limp body in his arms, and slid it over the side. He was no priest, but he murmured a prayer as the gray sea closed in about his comrade and took him to its bosom. Aubert resumed rowing, averting his eyes from his companion's. This was the way things had to be; the living could neither help nor harm the dead. For a long way he rowed furiously, seeking in hard physical labor surcease from mental anguish. Then he changed seats with LeGare, and sat huddled in the stern while the stout little dinghy plied westward. Night came again.

Morning followed it, and another night and another morning until Aubert lost count. They were rowing mechanically now, robot men in an unreal boat on an endless ocean. For days they had not spoken. Exhaustion had laid its heavy hand on LeGare's face. When he rowed, his head drooped, and when he rested, he dozed fitfully. All day the mist followed them, and the nights brought no stars. LeGare held the last water cask up, and the few spoonfuls remaining within it gurgled. He offered it to Aubert, who shook his head and rowed on while he licked parched lips. LeGare looked longingly at the cask, corked it, and put it back of him, out of sight.

Aubert thought that it was about the middle of the night when something grasped the oars. He tried to wrench them away, and could not. All about were splashings and disturbances in the water. Aubert gave all his strength to the oars, and moved them slightly. His hoarse voice cried out, "Baptiste!"

But LeGare was lying in the dinghy, snoring sonorously. Aubert groped for the musket, was unable to reach it. A strong, heavy odor pervaded the air, and the splashings in the water came nearer the dinghy. A loud bell seemed to be ringing in Aubert's ears, red fire danced before his eyes. They seemed to be moving, either in a westward current, or else whatever had gripped the oars was pulling them along. Again Aubert tried to reach the musket, and at last got it in his hands. But he could see nothing, and it would be senseless to waste a shot unless there was something at which to shoot. But when he tried to stand up he stumbled forward in the dinghy. Again and again he tried to rise, and see. But at last he lay still.

He awoke to a hot sun streaming out of a cloudless sky, and looked around in bewilderment. A great herd of dolphins was playing about the dinghy, splashing and diving as they went northward. Aubert blinked, and stared wonderingly at his hands. The dolphins—a good omen for fishermen—were what he had heard last night. There had been nothing on the oars. His hands and his strength had failed him, that was all. Aubert looked behind, and a hoarse shout broke from his parched lips.

"Baptiste!"

LeGare awoke grudgingly, rubbing his eyes with the backs of his hands. Both men stared, fascinated, at a spit that jutted out from a great expanse of land.

In the very center of the spit, a mighty pine stood majestically in the morning sunshine.

A HALF HOUR LATER Aubert beached the dinghy on the stone-studded flank of the narrow spit and stepped into shallow water to pull the little boat farther up. LeGare joined him. The two staggered forward, unable instantly to adjust themselves to the feel of solid earth beneath their cramped legs. Lush green grass covered the point, and ripe strawberries gleamed redly through it. Aubert looked at them, and licked his lips. He glanced at LeGare, who was staring in fascination at the berries' rich redness. Aubert dropped to his knees, solemnly plucked a berry, crushed it between his fingers, and let the red juice stain his hands. He plucked another, almost reverently placed it in his mouth, and very slowly ate it. Then, with LeGare beside him, able to think of nothing else, he ate berries. An hour elapsed before they arose to look about them.

About a quarter of a mile long, the spit jutted from a dark green forest. On the other side was a sheltered bay. At its edge, a number of moose were feeding in the shallow water. Across the gulf, very far away, was the dim outline of more forested land.

"This is not the New Land!" LeGare breathed. "It

has no such great beasts as those. *Sacré Dieu!* It must be China!"

"Perhaps, although I have seen such beasts in Norway. But I never saw them enter salt water."

"Then we cannot be in Norway. But consider the size of those horns!"

Aubert picked up the musket and led the way down the point. The strawberries crushed under their feet. A flock of partridges that had been eating them walked indifferently out of the way. An otter climbed out on the spit, looked at them with beady eyes, and dived back into the water, startling a flock of ducks into flight. A cow moose raised its mulish head and swung to face them. Aubert marvelled. Wherever they had come to, it was a very rich land, indeed. And there was something about it. . . . He turned to look again at the enticing horizon across the gulf. If men had ever been here, he had not heard of it.

They reached the mainland, and circled the bay to

come upon a sparkling little river. A huge trout broke the surface and settled lazily back to lie fanning its fins. Aubert and LeGare threw themselves prone by the river to drink, and rose to smile at each other. A yearling moose, its neck out-stretched, snuffled toward them. Back in the forest a slim doe stamped its foot, uncertainly.

"This is an unviolated land!" Aubert said wonderingly. "No man has yet taken toll from it!"

He squatted beside the bay, looking over the water spread before him. What was the great gulf that met his vision? Did it lap the shores of another New Land, one upon which no man had yet placed foot? Was there a passage or strait that led through it to the fabled shores of China? He had to know, but how was he going to find out? If only the *Jeanne* were here, instead of at the bottom of the Atlantic where the blundering Captain LeJeune had sent her! If only he could explore this gulf, know what lay in it instead of tormenting himself with thoughts of what might be!

His glance roved back to the spit of land, and the great pine in its center. It was a huge tree, tall as any he had seen in Norway, and its massive trunk probably could not be encircled by the combined span of his and LeGare's arms. Aubert leaped erect.

"Baptiste, we shall make a ship!"

"You are mad!"

"No! There is our ship! That pine! We have adzes, chisels, saws, augurs!"

"It will take years!"

"What of it? What is time to us now? See, beasts that will scarcely move aside to let us pass, fish and birds in vast abundance. Can even a lazy man starve here? Can he freeze, with unlimited quantities of wood to burn? We shall start our ship now, and when the season changes build a house!"

"But . . . !"

"We must gain knowledge of this land, much knowledge, and then. . . ."

"But one cannot build a ship on an empty belly," grinned the practical LeGare. "Let us eat first, my friend."

They unloaded the dinghy. LeGare had forgotten nothing. There were most of the tools that a fishing boat carried, as well as fish-lines, hooks, flint and steel, and even tin plates. They dragged their dinghy up on the spit, ·upended it, propped the end with a cairn of rocks, and carefully placed their supplies beneath. Aubert attached a hook to a line, weighed it with a pebble, and experimentally whirled it about his head.

"We saw many fat fish in the river," he said. "They should be honored to provide a feast for men of St. Malo. Build a fire, Baptiste, and your greedy belly shall be filled."

Aubert walked back to the forest, a little faster now and not stopping to look at anything else. Hunger, he reflected, was a demanding master. It was indeed an honor to set foot where no man had ever trod before, but LeGare was right. A fish still in a river took precedence over a tree on the shore. He overturned a rock, plucked a fat cricket from beneath it, and impaled it on the hook. Swinging the line about his head, he cast far out into the river, and almost at once was fast to a fighting trout. Aubert hauled it in, rebaited his hook and cast again. He caught another trout, and another, and marvelled. Even in virgin Norway it was impossible to catch big trout so fast. He carried the fish back on the point, watched LeGare split and clean them, and set them to broiling over the fire he had built. When they were cooked both men ate prodigiously, and Aubert sighed. Certainly whatever coast they had come to was a fine place to be. His curiosity returned.

"There are many duck's nests along the river," he said. "The eggs should be fine eating."

LeGare took the hint and departed. No sooner had he left than Aubert took an adze, stood beside the huge pine, and swung at it. The outer bark chipped away, revealing the orange-yellow inner bark. Sweat began to stream down his forehead as the sun shone hotly. He removed his shirt, laid it on the ground beside him, and continued to work on the tree.

Baptiste had been right. It was going to take a very long time just to fell the tree, much longer to fashion a ship. But certainly they were going nowhere without a ship.

LeGare returned, his doublet laden with duck's eggs. He pierced their ends and put them in the fire to bake while he went about arranging the camp. Aubert continued to work. By nightfall the huge pine that for hundreds of years had stood its lonely guard was well girdled. White chips littered the earth about it. But it was after nightfall when Aubert ceased his labors and crept under the dinghy to sleep.

AUBERT WAS AWAKE very early. Light mist blanketed the bay, lazy smoke rolled from the ash-banked fire. The moose had not yet come to the mouth of the river, but twenty curious deer stood on the spit, watching. A doe stamped her foot and advanced to within a few feet as she smelled at the chips from the pine. Aubert studied her. When cold weather brought assurance that meat would not spoil, he and LeGare must take a number of deer, and perhaps a few moose. Also, when the work of chopping down the pine and fashioning a ship from its trunk became too wearisome, they could catch and dry a number of fish. In the act of prodding the ashes to stir up the fire, Aubert stopped suddenly.

The lightening of the mist under the rising sun revealed a birch-bark canoe with six paddlers coming down the bay. Aubert crawled under the dinghy and shook LeGare's shoulder. Le Gare came awake, and sat up slowly.

"Savages approach," Aubert whispered. "They look not unlike those who visited our ships when we anchored off the New Land. Take up an adze, and stand ready to repel them if they are hostile."

Aubert picked up the musket, put a horn of powder and a pouch of shot beside him, and sat in the grass awaiting the canoe. The paddlers were all men, with well-developed arms and shoulders, and Aubert noted approvingly that they handled their frail craft with ease and grace. Apparently these savages were seamen, not afraid of the water. Their heads were shaven save for a long strip, oddly like a horse's tail, down the center. Their cheeks were painted with some sort of roan pigment.

LeGare, standing beside him with the adze, whispered, "They are not wholly like the savages of the New Land."

"No. Their hair is of a different arrangement. Let us see what they want."

As the canoe hove to in shallow water, the Indians stepped out and waded ashore. A breechcloth flapped about the waist of each, and each had a stone axe and knife thrust into a buckskin belt. Five of them wore moccasins fashioned of deerskin and decorated with stained porcupine quills, the sixth was barefooted. A hawk's wing was thrust into the pierced ear of one, while the rest wore the skins of crows suspended from their belts. He of the hawk's wing, apparently the chief, held up his hand with the palm out.

"The peace sign," Aubert murmured. "They do not have hostile intentions."

Aubert stood up, showed his palm and walked three paces forward. The Indian grinned, childishly pleased, and with his five solemn followers trooping behind him stalked up the bank. They squatted down by the dinghy, and broke into an unintelligible gibberish as they poked inquiring fingers into its side. The chief reached for the musket, and when Aubert snatched it aside, drew sullenly back.

"Break open the chest," Aubert instructed LeGare. "It is well not to anger them. We cannot fight them off if they come in sufficient numbers, and angry. Presents may pacify them."

LeGare opened the chest of trade goods, revealing the shiny red ribbon, beads, cheap little knives, needles, and other knicknacks within. Gravely Aubert picked up a handful of red beads, gave two to each of the men, and four to the chief. Smiles lighted their faces and chuckles rolled from their throats. A tall Indian with two ugly scars running the length of his ribs laid his beads on the grass and watched in childish delight as the sun's ray glanced from them. The chief held his in the palm of his hand, his awed eyes staring from them back to the chest. He gestured toward it.

"Close the chest," Aubert ordered. "We may have much need of what is there."

LeGare slammed the lid down, and the six Indians sat looking from the treasures in their hands to the incalculably greater amount still in the chest. No one spoke. A flight of ducks glided out of the sky, and came to rest on the placid bay. Aubert looked at the sullen savages, now beginning to mutter among themselves. What if they decided to take the chest? Out of the corner of his eye, Aubert saw the ducks, scarcely a stone's throw away. Wheeling suddenly, he levelled the musket and shot over the heads of the Indians. Out on the bay eight ducks either lay quietly or beat the water with dying wings, while the rest of the flock paddled about in confusion. The chief fell backward, and rose to clench his hands to his breast while he looked at the gun with frightened eyes. The rest ran to the water and splashed to their canoe. The chief ran after them, and paddles flashed furiously as the canoe sped up the bay. Aubert gazed thoughtfully after them.

"They have never seen white men nor heard guns," he said. "I did not like to waste the shot, but it is well to have them know that we can protect ourselves."

"They are like children!" LaGare exclaimed. "They are more simple than children! Excited over red beads!"

"Well, they are gone. And I am going to fell this tree."

He picked up the adze and resumed his place beside the mighty pine, patiently hacking out chips, enlarging his cut as it was required to let the adze bite deeper. LeGare removed his clothing, and swam out to retrieve the dead ducks. He carried them up on the spit, and set about skinning them while Aubert continued to hack at the pine. The mysterious horizon across the bay beckoned, and the rippling waters in the great gulf called in a thousand different ways. Aubert swung the adze furiously. It was a hard thing, now that he had at last found some place he really wanted to go, to wait years to get there. But, no matter how many years it took, get there he would. The chopped wedge in the pine's trunk deepened, and chips piled thickly about his feet as he worked on. LeGare rolled the ducks in wet clay, and buried them beneath the fire. Then he went to the river and returned with the water cask filled. Aubert drank deeply, and went on felling the pine.

The sun had passed its zenith and was sinking toward the west when LeGare swung suddenly to look out on the bay. A startled exclamation broke from his lips. "They come again!"

Aubert dropped his adze to look. Eight canoes, manned by from four to six men each, were coming down the bay. Wet paddles flashed in the sun. The paddlers strained forward, as though each were striving to outdo the rest and get there first. An excited, happy yell echoed over the water. LeGare turned questioning eyes on Aubert.

"They are very many this time. What shall we do?"

Aubert studied the advancing canoes, listening to the shouting of the men in them. Men bent on war did not come that way, or openly, but in the dead of night and silently. Beyond a doubt their first visitors had carried word of the strange interlopers back to whatever village they had come from.

"Give me the musket," Aubert said. "We cannot do other than let them come. But I do not believe that they come for war."

Out on the bay one canoe gained a long lead on the rest, and its paddlers hurled taunts and jibes over their shoulders as they sent their flying craft toward the spit of land. But the rest were deliberately holding back, Aubert saw. Not believing all they had been told, they were waiting to see what fortune or misfortune befell those in the leading craft before they themselves came in. The first canoe hove to. The chief with the hawk's wing in his ear stepped into shallow water and stood with his arms folded across his breast while he stared fixedly at Aubert. The paddlers hovered nervously in the canoe, their upraised paddles ready to dip into the water.

"Why do they wait?" the puzzled LeGare inquired.

"They fear the musket," Aubert guessed.

He laid it on the grass before him, and a friendly smile split the chief's face. He waded back to the canoe, bent over it and lifted out a bundle of furs strung on a buckskin thong. Aubert gasped. They were glossy, shining sables, so many of them that the dangling string reached from the chief's shoulders to the earth. The chief climbed up the bank, a wild, stark figure against the bay. He looked suddenly down at the gun, and stopped in his tracks. Aubert nodded, understanding. The musket's power had been demonstrated, and to this ignorant forest prince of whatever land they were in, it was mighty power indeed. Aubert put the gun back under the dinghy, and the chief threw his string of sables on the ground. Aubert looked at them, marvelling. Furs such as these were not known in Europe. Even the fishermen from the New Land brought back nothing like them. The Indians pointed at the chest of trade goods, nodded vigorously, and again spoke in his own dialect.

"He wants to trade!" LeGare blurted.

Aubert shook his head dubiously. "Not for anything in our chest, Baptiste. Even a savage would not do that. Furs so magnificent for trinkets so cheap? He wants another present."

Aubert opened the chest, took out a spool of red ribbon, cut from it a foot-long strip, and gravely gave it to the Indian. The chief snatched at it, muttered in delight, tied it around his left bicep, and stretched his arm to admire the shining cloth. He nudged the furs with his foot, picked up the thong that bound them and placed it in Aubert's hand. Aubert stared, dumbfounded, at LeGare.

"He did want to trade!"

The seven other canoes had arrived during this parley. Now the Indians scrambled out of them, splashing through the water and climbing up the bank as though each had to be first. Every one bore a string of furs: sable, ermine, otter, mink, beaver, lynx, fox. Gravely Aubert snipped off a twelve-inch length of ribbon for each offering, and the spool was scarcely half emptied when all the furs were piled about him. A huge Indian with a scarred face laughed, evidently displaying his contempt of the fools who would trade priceless ribbon for worthless furs that were to be had in endless amounts. Two Indians, with ribbons exactly identical, gravely effected a trade. Finally all sat down in a pleased semi-circle, admiring the bits of ribbon on their own arms and those on the arms of their companions. LeGare stared with unbelieving eyes.

"Thomas, we're rich!"

"True," Aubert agreed soberly. "A king's ransom."

"But what are we going to do with them here?"

Aubert shrugged. "Sleep on them, Baptiste. A ship would be worth a thousand such piles of peltry to us now. I'm still going to fell the tree."

He took the musket from beneath the dinghy and laid it on the grass. The chief pointed to it, and guttural speech rolled from his throat as he spoke excitedly to his assembled comrades. A few of the Indians rose to go farther back on the spit, but most drew their feet a little farther beneath them and remained. Aubert watched closely, and finally turned away satisfied. The Indians were afraid of the gun. Aubert took up his adze and resumed chopping at the pine.

In the background the assembled Indians murmured pleasantly, and exchanged comments as they kept their eyes on this fascinating spectacle of a white man chopping down a tree with a strange instrument of metal. Aubert worked furiously, sinking his adze into the cut and drawing it out for another blow. The chief rose, made a wide circle around the gun, and watched from the other side. Half his warriors followed. A great cloud of waterfowl squawked overhead, and settled down to ride the little waves that a slight wind was kicking up on the bay. The sun, a blazing red ball, hung sleepily over its couch in the west. And it was just at that moment that the tree fell.

A shudder ran the length of its mighty frame, and there was a sudden rending of fibers. The top of the pine swayed toward the water, and the Indians on that side scrambled to get out of the way. A mighty splash of water erupted from the bay as the upper half of the giant fell into it.

For a few minutes more the Indians stood about, greatly admiring this white man who could bring down so mighty a tree for no apparent reason. One by one they took to their canoes and faded into the twilight that hovered over the bay. When the last one had gone, LeGare dug into the pit he had made beneath the fire and brought out the roasted ducks. These they ate with wild strawberries, then for a long while lay watching the dark and silent gulf. The Indians knew some of it, but certainly a frail birchbark canoe had never sailed clear around any water so vast. Only a ship could do that.

It was very late when Aubert finally fell asleep.

HE WAS AWAKENED the next morning by a shout, and lay still, doubting his ears. But the shout was repeated, and this time it came very clearly to him.

"Ahoy the shore!"

Aubert scrambled from beneath the dinghy and looked out on the bay, now doubting his eyes. There was a ship out there, a channel fisherman, riding at anchor with furled sails! Aubert rubbed his eyes and looked again. There was no mistake. It was the *Pensee* out of Honfleur, commanded by Jean Denys. Aubert threw back his head and a great, bull-like roar burst from his lungs.

"Jean!"

"Thomas!"

Aubert watched a boat lowered from the *Pensee,* saw the bearded figure of Jean Denys in the prow. LeGare crawled from beneath the dinghy, clapped happy hands, and laughed. The *Pensee's* boat bumped the spit of land. Jean Denys stepped ashore, grinning.

"You Bretons get lost in strange places, eh? And, of course, Normans have to find them. What are you doing here, my friend?"

Aubert grinned back. "Showing the way to the men of Normandy. Welcome to Cape Breton!"

Denys laughed. "A good name, I admit. But where is your ship?"

"Foundered. It was a Basque ship, so no matter. *Our* ship is there," and he pointed to the great trunk of the pine. "True, it is not quite finished."

Jean Denys whistled in admiration. "It has already earned your passage to St. Malo," he said soberly. "We were about to turn back last night. But I was looking through the glass and saw a tree fall. Such a tree does not fall by itself. *Voilà.* I am here."

"But this is not the New Found Land. What were you doing here?"

"Exploring. Ship's owners gave me permission to spend four weeks doing it and see if I could find new fishing grounds."

Aubert's eyes glowed, but he tried to make his voice casual. "What did you find?"

"It's a vast gulf, Thomas." He swung suddenly to look Aubert squarely in the eyes. "That horizon you see over there is an island. Beyond it is a great expanse of water to a forested shore. And, Thomas, at the far western end of the gulf there is a passage through the land!"

"No!"

"Yes! And who knows where that leads to?"

Their eyes met, understandingly, and together they swung to face the enticing, unknown west.

R. RAY

CROATAN

1588 *Thomas Aubert did come back. Two years later he sailed part way up the St. Lawrence, and thus pointed the way for his fellow Breton, Jacques Cartier, a generation later. New France had begun.*

But during the Sixteenth Century England was too busy watching the rival power of Spain to worry much about the activities of a few French fishermen and fur traders who had capitalized on the English-sponsored expeditions of the Cabots. Not until the end of the century did Sir Walter Raleigh undertake his two ill-fated experiments in colonization, and then he chose a region far south of the St. Lawrence, on the more temperate shores of the Carolinas.

The lost colony of Roanoke was, and remains, the most famous mystery in American history. It was also a complete failure. But it showed the shape of things to come, for its purpose was neither trade nor conversion, like the French settlements to the north, but colonization. *It was to be a new home for Englishmen, and it was no accident that an English child was born on Roanoke Island thirty years before the first French woman sailed up the St. Lawrence.*

FLIGHT AFTER FLIGHT of little green-winged teal dipped out of the sky to settle on the slough. Their flapping wings churned the water into a froth, and those already on the slough scarcely moved aside as others sought to enter. It seemed, Tom Weston thought, that there was no water at all, but only successive layers of teal, with the final row of bobbing heads and restlessly moving wings on top. But newcomers always found a place.

The teal were harbingers of cold weather. Last year their vanguard had arrived on the fifteenth of October, two months after Governor White had sailed to England—supposedly to return within nine months with more people and more things for them to work with. Not that there was any real need of that. If a hundred men and a dozen women couldn't support themselves on an island like this, then only the Lord could help them.

When the colonists had first arrived, they had expected both to be welcomed and to find plentiful stores waiting. But the savages who inhabited this Roanoke Island—or at least came to it whenever they aroused enough ambition to paddle—had destroyed or carried off the stores and killed the fifteen men left to guard them. That had been an unpleasant shock to the men and women who had landed on this island fifteen months ago, in the year of Our Lord, 1587. And that shock was their principal trouble.

Well, maybe it wasn't. Most of them had listened to glowing tales of great wealth and easy living when they had embarked for this new colony of Virginia. Everything, they had been told, would be waiting for them and they had only to lift a hand now and again in order to ensure themselves a richer and finer life than they had ever known before. Because nothing had been waiting for them, and there had been no one to tell them exactly what to do, they didn't even want to lift that hand.

A great horde of teal swooped down and somehow crowded in among those on the slough. There was a mighty quacking gabbling, and Tom rose suddenly from the log behind which he had been crouching. As he did so his right hand was whirling a crude, homemade bolo—four buckskin thongs attached to holes in pierced shells. There was a deafening roar of wings, and an immense splashing of the water. The bolo sailed into a veritable horde of ducks, and when it dropped to the slough five of the little teal were entangled in its serpentine coils. Tom waded out to retrieve his kill, dropped them behind the log on top of the twenty-three he had already captured, and again concealed himself until the settling teal came in closer.

He lay indolently, letting the sun caress his back and warm his legs. Of course that warm sun wouldn't last very long; frost would follow the teal within six weeks. When the great, black-necked, white-throated geese appeared you could be certain that frost would come almost within a day. It didn't make much difference. There were no crops to kill because those who should have been planting had instead passed their time on the shore watching for the ship from England. When that came there would be no need of crops because there would be food in plenty.

What the colonists should have known, but did not, was that the ship wasn't coming. It was impossible to look across the Atlantic Ocean and see that Elizabeth's England was again at war with Spain. John White had said that he would be back and the colonists had been watching for him since spring. Now it was October, and the earliest a ship could come was next April or May. No captain cared to risk his sailing vessel in the Atlantic while it was lashed by storms.

If only the colonists would work, and look to that which was all about them for their own salvation! But they would not, and now their confusion and hopelessness would be multiplied tenfold. Ananias Dare, son-in-law of John White, husband of Eleanor, and acting governor of the colony while John White was away, had died yesterday. He had done as well as he could, but Ananias had been ailing for the past six months and a sick man could not carry out his own orders. Now that he was gone, and no authority reigned, there was bound to be bickering. All most of the colonists could think of was getting back to England, and the fool ideas they had for getting there. . . .

Tom rose to throw his bolo again, and added three more ducks to his catch. He could stay here all day, and all tomorrow, and the colony could still eat all the ducks he was able to catch. But somebody had to hunt, and they depended on him because he was better equipped than any other to get along in this new land. He had been self-supporting since he was eight, when his father had been cast into debtor's prison. Some of the methods he had employed in order to eat had proved useful, if not lawful. He had poached many a rabbit and grouse from manor estates and taken many a trout from the gentry's streams. He'd been tinker, pedlar, and vagabond, by turn. But fortunately he had become a cobbler's apprentice in London when John White stopped in to be fitted for a new pair of boots. Tom had listened, wide-eyed and open-mouthed, while White spoke of the second Virginia colony that Sir Walter Raleigh was organizing. Offered an opportunity to join, Tom had signed on two minutes later.

And, somehow, the land was all John White had said it was and very much more. Where, in England, could you stop at a slough and kill as many ducks as you wished? Where in England, outside your own guild and social circle, could you consider yourself equal to any other man? Where could you walk any-where at all, and be warned away by no keeper or bailiff? This Virginia had something England never would have. An unclothed man here, with no posses-sions other than those to be found at hand, was better off than—well, at least better than a cobbler's ap-prentice in London. Tom grinned wryly. He had been on the verge of thinking himself better off than an English lord, but he had no basis of comparison for that. Anyhow, under no conditions, was he going back. He must have been born to live a life like this. Maybe he was half savage.

But the savages got along all right. Only the wealthiest Englishmen ate as sumptuously as they did, and no Englishman was more free. The savages had the right idea. They worked when they felt like it, and loafed when they didn't. And nobody was more stealthy in a forest or more quiet in a thicket. They killed their deer, caught their fish, and even tilled their fields after a fashion. But certainly no savage would work in a London cobbler's shop from the first light of day until the last of night. That sort of life was fit only for those who liked it; probably al-most any man on Roanoke would choose it in pref-erence to what he had. But not Tom Weston.

He threw his bolo again, and retrieved the ducks entangled in it. Snatches of a hymn drifted to his

ears. The colonists should be finished with the burial
by this time, and Ananias Dare resting in his forest
grave.

He, the hunter, would probably be branded a
heretic and a hopeless savage for not attending the
funeral. But he was a heretic anyway for counselling
that the colonists get busy and help themselves. And
it was far more important to help those living than to
attend the funeral of even a man like Ananias Dare.
Tom knelt, and slipped the heads of the teal through
loops on a buckskin thong. Two of the fattest he
separated from the pile, and tucked inside his leather
jerkin.

He started toward the settlement.

HE BROKE OUT of the forest into a small natural
clearing that swept to the sea. The huge, unwieldy
skeleton of a quarter-finished sloop, made of adze-
hewn timbers, was as prominent as a beacon fire on
the east side of the island. Tom regarded it caustically.
Simon Fernando, the pilot who had brought them
over, was supervising the building of that sloop. Most
of the men in the colony, who looked upon it as a
means of going somewhere else—preferably back to
England, but anywhere so long as they didn't have to
remain here—worked on it from time to time. Tom
sniffed audibly. Simon Fernando was a Spaniard and

a Papist, and the fact that Englishmen would listen to his plans at all was an indication of the low estate to which the colony had fallen.

Smoke from a lackadaisical fire drifted up through a wooden rack and curled lazily around three huge fish that somebody had caught. Beside them was a great pile of wild grapes, drying in the sun. Still desperately hoping that a ship from England would come, at least some of the colonists were awakening to the probability that it would not, and were starting out to gather a reserve of food.

They should have started in the spring. But better late than never. And nobody was going to starve anyway. Fish were easy to catch, there would be geese and some species of ducks all winter, and they still had three guns with which to bring down deer and bear. There were only half a dozen charges for each gun, but they could fashion bows and arrows when that was gone. The Indians killed big game with such tackle, and anything an Indian could do a white man could do better.

Tom dropped his string of ducks in the center of the square formed by the bark-thatched huts. A fresh-faced young woman wearing clothes that she had patiently fashioned from deer skins looked up from her cooking fire and smiled at him.

"Fresh barley bread and greens for a brace of those fowl, young huntsman," she called. "Is it a trade?"

"It is that, Molly." Tom's white teeth flashed in a smile. "Here's two of the best for you and your John."

Clutching the two teal, Molly Gibbes disappeared into her hut. Other colonists gathered around. Old Granny Desmond, who at seventy-one still hadn't been too old to try something new, hobbled over and held up a pewter mug in her stained hands.

"Tom Weston, you've been gone since afore dawn!" she scolded. "Huntin' for idle folk too lazy to work! Here's summat to drink. The juice o' wild grapes won't touch a pint of English ale, but 'twill serve, if a body's thirsty. I've been pressin' it out all day."

"Thank'ee, Granny. And here's a duck for you. A fat one, too."

"Give it to those in need of it," Granny Desmond sniffed disdainfully.

"I'll give them where I please, you toothless old dame," Tom answered with a grin. "Don't worry, Granny; it will eat as tender as any sucking pig."

Molly Gibbes had come out of her hut and was staring at the sea. She took a tentative step toward the sloop, then walked up to touch Tom's elbow.

"There's trouble afoot, Tom, and I fear my John's temper. Look yonder."

Tom swung on his heel to stare at the little knot of men clustered about the sloop. John Gibbes, a square-jawed farmer who was one of Tom's few friends in the colony, was backed against the skeleton of the

43

ship. Simon Fernando, his head belligerently lowered and his expressive Latin hands gesturing, stood directly in front of him.

Dropping the ducks, Tom strode hurriedly down to the sloop. At a softly spoken word from one of the men behind him, Fernando turned away from John Gibbes. The slow-thinking, slow-talking farmer's face was red with anger, and his thick forefinger trembled as he pointed it at the Spaniard.

"I am a freeman here, and till my land at no man's order. No Spanish sailor will provision his ship with *my* grain, governor or no!

"And why not?" Simon Fernando purred. "Was I not chosen your new leader this very day? Will not my ship provide passage for all who have—how you say—cooperated?"

"No," Tom interrupted. "Firstly, if by chance this ship is finished, I doubt it will float. Secondly, it would hold but a score of souls. You delude the rest with false promises. You know full well our labor were better spent in making needful preparations against the winter."

Practical and true as they were, his words only angered the little group behind Simon Fernando. All of them wanted to go back to England, and they'd have been loyal to anything that promised even a faint hope of getting there. They believed in Fernando because they wished to. Even though only a

44

dozen people might go in his sloop, those nearest Simon would be among them. But here were two who would not.

Side by side, they walked back to the village, the ex-poacher who had found a free hunter's paradise, and the former leaseholder whose only landlord now was nature. John Gibbes was a stolid, unimaginative farmer, whose only loves had been his wife and the soil that his ancestors had tilled for countless generations. But he had found a new soil with neither rents nor restrictions, poor and unproductive though it was, and the harvest he had coaxed from it with patient skill he regarded as his rightful possession.

"So you would cling to your rocky fields, John?" Tom asked. "I could make you a hunter, if you would but try."

"Farming is in my blood," the older man replied. "'Tis all I know. Poor as this soil is, I would not change my lot."

Tom stopped suddenly. "This little island will soon become too small for Fernando's unruly crew and us. I have a plan. Meet me tonight at the little bay on the west shore. It's the bay with the three big sycamores in a line. Tell Molly I have asked you to hunt with me tomorrow."

Before the mystified Gibbes could answer, Tom turned on his heel and left him.

He walked to the last building, knocked softly, and

when a feminine voice answered, he rolled the skin door aside and entered. Light streamed through the unglassed windows to reveal in soft outline the neat interior. There were joint-stools and a carved chest from England, and English pots and kettles hung from hooks set in the stone fireplace. Fresh rushes had been strewn on the smooth earthen floor. There were traces of tears in the eyes of the young woman who knelt before the hearth. She rose to her feet.

"Oh, it's you, Mr. Weston."

"Yes, Mrs. Dare. I—I just stopped by."

"You are always welcome."

"I'm sorry about Ananias," Tom mumbled. "It was not right that he had to be taken."

"It was God's will," Eleanor Dare said softly. "How are the rest accepting it?"

Tom hesitated, then said bluntly, "They have chosen Simon Fernando in your husband's place."

Eleanor Dare nodded. " 'Tis no surprise. Is there anything I can do for you, Mr. Weston?"

"Could I—er—see the baby?"

"Mr. Weston! You, the woods-runner, to take an interest in my babe! How long has this affair of the heart been in progress?"

"Since she was born."

"Virginia should be flattered!" Eleanor Dare laughed. "How many English girls, think you, have an admirer when they're scarce a twelvemonth old?"

She went to the rear of the room, bent over a crude, homemade trundle bed, and lifted a golden-haired chubby-cheeked child from its feather mattress. Tom shrank away.

"What! Afraid to touch her?" Eleanor Dare smiled She held out the baby toward him.

"Uh—oh, no," Tom said lamely. "I just wanted to look at her. And to give her—you, that is—these birds." He pulled the two teal from his jerkin and laid them on the hearth. "And if there's aught I can do, if you need help. . . ."

"I won't forget," Eleanor Dare said soberly. "And thank you, Mr. Weston."

A ROUND, yellow-orange moon rose to shine through the tall trees. The quavering whicker of a raccoon floated softly as the call of a ghost through the darkness. From somewhere out in the forest came a shrill scream. Tom walked on, unheeding and unafraid. The night woods were no more dangerous than those of the day, and when a grouse clucked sleepily in a tree he paused with one hand on the hilt of his knife. Slowly he walked two steps backward, his head bent. But he had to dodge and twist about, stepping from place to place, before he saw the grouse that had clucked and seven others silhouetted against the moon on the limb of a gum tree.

Cautiously he withdrew the knife from its belt sheath, and poised, grasping its tip with thumb and forefinger.

But he slid the knife back into its sheath. He had no other, and there was too much danger of loss involved in throwing it at night. Very slowly, making no noise, he withdrew the bolo. He threw that, and when it dropped to earth there was a sodden thud and a frantic beating of wings as a grouse dropped with it.

Tom picked up his game. Grouse were fine eating, much better than teal, and for a moment he thought of Eleanor Dare and her baby. But it was too late to return to the settlement now. He hadn't spent a night there in six months, anyway, because he liked the forest better. It was good to be away from people who seemed always at cross purposes and never satisfied.

Suddenly he stepped out of the trees onto a beach. The shining moon danced on the water, painting it with rich gold that little waves were trying to wash away. A raft of ducks—not teal but bigger, ocean-faring ducks—cast a shadow as they drifted across a patch of moonlight.

Tom walked to the base of a huge tree whose low-sweeping branches almost touched the water, and stooped to lift long streamers of moss from a canoe. Moss was a much better covering than almost any-

48

thing else because it stayed green. Withered foliage was a certain give-away to anyone who knew what should and should not be. Carefully he laid the moss at the side of his canoe, noting each piece so that it could be replaced, and examined the little craft that had taken so many painful days of labor.

Sixteen feet long, the canoe was fashioned from a single tree trunk, the ends of which had been shaped with adze and knife. The inside of the log had been burned out, and then scraped clean with the adze, to form a heavy but serviceable craft. An outrigger, a piece of buoyant dead log supported on green sticks, prevented the canoe's tipping even in rough water. A paddle lay under it.

Satisfied, Tom re-covered the canoe, then gathered a pile of tinder and struck a spark into it with his flint and steel. The tinder glowed, sparkled, and climbed into leaping flame. Tom added more wood. When the fire was blazing he dressed his grouse, rolled the unplucked bird in wet mud, plastered more mud about it with his fingers, and buried it in the fire to cook. When it was done the feathers would come away with the mud pack.

For half an hour he fed the fire, then suddenly stiffened in the act of adding more wood. Somebody was coming. Silently he stepped away from the fire and slunk behind the bole of a tree. His fingers curled about the hilt of his knife.

But it was John Gibbes who, a moment later, broke out of the trees and stood peering about in the light of the fire. His russet doublet, leather breeches, and coarse kersey stockings looked oddly out of place in such wild surroundings. Tom grinned in the darkness.

"It's a poor hunter you'd make, John, with those great boots of yours. You sound like a west-country ox."

The farmer started, then smiled his slow smile. "That's as may be. But I've brought a loaf of my goodwife's bread, and a bit of souse. You'd hunt a long time in your plagued woods to find the like."

"Molly's bread is more than welcome, but here's something better than pickled fish."

Tom raked the grouse from the fire, cracked the mud packing from it, and broke the steaming bird in half. He laid both halves on the projecting root of a tree, and when they had cooled gave one to John Gibbes. They ate in silence, and after they had finished Tom sat staring over the moon-dappled sea at the dark, mysterious mainland. There was a great swamp just across the water over which he gazed. But what was beyond the swamp? Well, he was ready to find out at last.

"John," he asked suddenly. "What does England have that you miss here?"

"Well," John Gibbes said ponderously, "well, kindred souls, you might say, for one. A mug of ale at the ordinary, now, and friends to drink it with! There's farmers enough on this island, but the land is poor, and that Spaniard fellow has made 'em shiftless. There's not a real husbandman left in the lot."

"But suppose there were a thousand farmers here?"

"They could never live on this godforsaken land," the practical Gibbes replied.

"But there's more land beyond."

"Aye, a wilderness."

"It may be," Tom admitted. "And if it were, I would not care. But you are a tiller of the soil, and want your neighbor to be, likewise. Suppose your neighbors had red skins?"

"What do you mean?"

"I mean that these savages on the mainland cannot live wholly by hunting. I know not where they get their crops. But they must have some."

"Do you mean there may be farmers yonder?" John

Gibbes asked, and for the first time there was a note of enthusiasm in his voice.

"I warrant there are. At least, I have fashioned a canoe, and mean to find out. Will you go with me?"

THE SUN BROKE over the trees, poured itself down on the water, and broke into a thousand little shimmering jewels as a breeze danced across the river in front of them. With John Gibbes, an apprehensive but stalwart passenger, Tom had paddled his dugout canoe over the water separating Roanoke from the swamp land and turned north along the swamp's borders. It had still been dark when he entered the mouth of what he had known was either a lagoon or river. Now, when he scooped up water in his hand and tasted it, he knew they had come into a river.

He drove the crude craft toward the bank, where they could be ready to disembark and run into the shelter of the trees if anything happened which made such a course necessary. But it was a peaceful river, a wild and primitive place which, judging by outward appearances, had not been disturbed since the beginning of time. Trees crowded to its very edge, and trailing vines interlaced them to dangle their ends in the water. A pair of cranes, snow-white save for a smooth red crest, lumbered awkwardly out of the water and flapped slowly away.

"Tom, look you there! What is that ugly thing?"

There was a note of amazement and incredulity in John Gibbes' voice, but no fear. Tom looked at the fourteen-foot, greenish-black creature that floated on top of the river. It submerged until only its little balls of eyes showed above the water. Involuntarily Tom reached for his knife, then let the puny weapon slide back into the sheath. John White, who had sailed along the borders of this land—Croatan, he had called it—had said that many strange things inhabited it. He had spoken truly!

Tom drove the dugout forward, cleaving the water with long, clean strokes of his paddle, and watching the dark, tree-fringed shore on either side. Ahead of them a little sand spit jutted into the river, and on it a herd of deer stood gazing curiously at the dugout. Their heads outthrust and their long ears alert, they stamped their feet as though in cadence to the rippling wake that curled from the stern of the canoe. A million birds seemed to call among the trees, and an unconcerned black bear watched the dugout slide past. This was a forgotten land of unimaginable plenty, a place where a man might find anything, and live forever without need, fear, or restraint.

"Tom, do you note the blackness of the soil, and how lush the vegetation? 'Tis the richness of the river silt, I reckon."

With a jerk Tom's thoughts were dragged out of

the clouds and back to the passenger in his dugout. He saw unfettered opportunity, John Gibbes saw fertile land. But that was the way it should be. This land had everything to offer. It was a challenge to the man who had never known contentment elsewhere, and a promise to him who wished only to till its soil. Neither Roanoke nor England itself had that.

The river narrowed, and Tom edged the canoe away from the bank. Nothing had appeared to dispute their way. It was almost inconceivable that, in so wealthy a land, there should be no one to enjoy it. He drove the canoe around a bend in the river, and almost before he was aware of it the trees to his left gave way to a big clearing.

In the center of the clearing was a small village of bark-thatched huts, surrounded by fields of standing corn. Pumpkins yellowed on the vine among the cornstalks. Nearer the huts were other fields that bore, Tom guessed, the new world crop which Ananias Dare had described as potatoes.

Not until then did he notice the half-dozen men who had been sitting indolently on the bank of the river. Almost imperceptibly, dipping his paddle as lightly as possible, Tom edged the canoe toward the center of the river. Attired only in breechcloths, moccasins, and necklaces or armbands, the savages had risen to stare curiously. One turned to gesture toward the village. More men and boys, even women with babies tied to their backs, streamed down to the river's edge.

"Let us land," said John Gibbes in sudden excitement. "They do not appear unfriendly."

Tom swung the canoe around cautiously. You never could tell about new people. There was always the possibility of a trick, and he had no wish to step into a trap. But none of the Indians were armed, and who gained anything without venturing? Tom hesitated another second, and then drove the canoe toward shore with long, deep strokes of his paddle.

The dugout grated softly on the river bank. John Gibbes stepped out, and without hesitation started toward a group of squaws who had stopped work in the cornfield to stare at the strange visitors. Tom followed, and the remainder of the village's population trooped amicably by his side.

Gibbes turned to him, held out a handful of the rich, black earth, and crumbled it between his fingers.

"There's naught like this in all England," he said reverently.

Tom turned to look at the forests that hemmed in the little clearing, and his own excitement leaped higher. This, assuredly, was the place for a man. He could go as far as his own strength and courage would take him, the only obstacle his own indolence. This was an unbelievable land. Probably not even Governor White had known of its existence. If the Roanoke colonists had only been brought here, instead of being settled on a tiny island shut in by salt water!

Gibbes had been kneeling in the dirt, his stolid face red from excitement and the unaccustomed effort of trying to express himself by signs. Suddenly he leaped to his feet, the mouldy remnants of a fish skeleton in his hands.

"Tom," he exclaimed, "I do believe these benighted heathens are real farmers. Look! They must fertilize with dead fish; there's a skeleton in every hill of this turkey-wheat."

Tom laughed. "As I live, the savages think you're hungry! See, they wish us to go to their huts."

John Gibbes was still looking back over his shoulder as the Indians led them away. Bearskin mats were spread before the largest hut, and as they sat down, an old squaw brought bark slabs on which lay sizzling hot venison steaks. Smaller dishes contained fish, potatoes, a mixture of beans and corn, and fresh berries. The white men, sitting cross-legged like their hosts, gorged themselves until they could eat no more.

"Well, friend Gibbes," said Tom at last, "what think you of this land of Croatan?"

"If I could but find a way, I'd move here tomorrow."

"Would Molly come?"

"She goes where I go, and gladly, too."

"Yes," said Tom thoughtfully, "and Granny Desmond would come. If Mistress Dare would listen to us, mayhap some of the fools who now think of naught but England could be persuaded, too. . . ."

IT WAS MID-AFTERNOON when they again reached Roanoke Island. It had been a hard crossing, for even on the inland side of the island there had been a nasty little cross-chop to the waves, and an uneasy swell on the normally placid water. As they beached the dugout and pulled it up to its hiding place, Tom noted a thin, thread-like V-line of geese winging its way southward. The coming of the geese meant that storm or cold, or both, were on the way.

As they approached the settlement, a man's voice, frantic with excitement, carried to them.

"A ship! A ship! At last a ship!"

Tom stopped, felt John Gibbes stop behind him, and for a brief space stood perfectly still. The rattling hammer of a woodpecker seemed unnaturally loud. Then, again, came a joyous shout.

"She's heaving to! She's heaving to!"

On the dead run, they broke into the clearing, to see a knot of colonists gathered on the beach, staring out to sea. Sure enough, there was a ship out there, a great, war-rigged ship with furling sails. The sun winked from the brass culverins on her main deck, and the polished rail on the poop. But the flag restlessly snapping in the rising wind was the red and yellow banner of Spain!

TOM KNOCKED SOFTLY on the door of the hut.

"Who is there?"

"Tom Weston."

"Come in."

Tom stooped to enter, and dropped the deerskin covering in place behind him. Eleanor Dare was sitting before the fire, with the baby on her lap. The child stretched its arms toward Tom, and gurgled. There was a muffled shouting from those gathered on the beach. Eleanor Dare spoke almost gaily.

"Well, Mr. Weston, which shall it be now: more colonists to hunt for, or a return to England?"

"Neither, I think," Tom said bluntly. "That ship flies the Spanish flag."

Eleanor Dare looked searchingly at him, and then glanced down at her baby. For a moment she was silent.

"I can only suspect what that means," she said at last. "But I think a Spanish ship would not dare approach an English colony unless something were amiss."

"I'll not be a prisoner of Spain, Mistress," Tom said hotly.

"No more will I," was the cool reply. "But what can we do? This little settlement is helpless."

"John Gibbes and I have just returned from a land across the water—the place that your father called Croatan. There is safety there for us. If I send Granny Desmond and Molly Gibbes here to you, will you take all the guns and whatever else you can carry, and meet John Gibbes at the north path? He knows where my canoe is. Hold it in readiness. If the Spaniards mean trouble, John will take you to the place we found yesterday, where friendly savages will give you shelter. Will you trust us?"

"I trust you," Eleanor Dare said. "But what of yourself?"

"I propose to talk with the others; perchance I can persuade them to hide on the island until the Spaniards go."

Tom stepped from the hut and walked slowly down to the beach. Granny Desmond hobbled to his side and spoke soberly in his ear.

"What d'ye make of it, Tom?"

"Little enough, Granny. Take Molly Gibbes and go to Mistress Dare's. She will tell you what's to be done."

The waves were crashing up on the beach now, showing their white teeth and falling back again like angry dogs. Tom walked up to Simon Fernando. The big, bearded man looked at him with malice.

"So," he said, "the Adam of our little island paradise! I regret you have no Eve to stay with you, Master Weston. Naturally, one who loves this place so much will not choose to leave it, eh?"

"Fernando, listen to me."

"Listen to you! For more than a twelvemonth we have heard you sing the praises of this Roanoke. Sing them to yourself henceforth, and be damned to you!"

Tom mastered his temper with difficulty. "That's a Spanish ship," he said loudly, for all to hear. "Who knows whether it comes in peace or war? Better to hide until we are sure, than be prisoners of the Papist Dons."

Simon Fernando lashed out with his fist and caught Tom a tremendous blow on the cheek. Tom staggered backward, and tasted the blood that oozed from a cut lip. He looked toward the sea, and saw small boats putting out from the ship.

Without a backward glance he walked toward the forest. At the beginning of the north path he met Eleanor Dare, who carried a gun in her hands.

"You should not be here," he cried fiercely.

"I am not accustomed to being ordered about, Mr. Weston," she said with composure. "And, if need be, two can fight better than one. Granny Desmond and Molly are watching my babe, and I have been watching you. Your venture met with ill success, I fear."

The ship's boats touched land, and the murmur of

many voices came from the beach. A voice spoke loudly and authoritatively in Spanish.

"He called them English pigs and commanded them to silence," Eleanor Dare translated in a whisper. Her eyes flashed. "Spain and England are at war, and he says their great armada has already destroyed the English fleet. He lies, the rogue! Hawkins and Drake and Raleigh defeated by those lisping lapdogs? Never!"

They slipped back into the forest as a detachment of Spanish marines marched up toward the settlement and began to attack the huts with the colonists' own mattocks and adzes. There came the sound of rending bark and falling timbers. A man yelled. Another voice—a strangely familiar one—spoke in Spanish. There was a reply in the same tongue.

"That was Simon Fernando!" Eleanor Dare said contemptuously. "He said others remained on the island, and was told they could starve here. The ship must get off ere the storm strikes."

AN HOUR LATER, when they dared come out of their hiding place, they found the huts in ruins and the beach deserted. The Spanish ship was already a spread of white sails putting out to sea. As they watched, a powerful gust of wind swept across her, and she heeled dangerously.

61

"There goes my lord Raleigh's second venture," said Eleanor Dare sadly. "Would you still have us go, too?"

"We must wait for the storm to pass," Tom replied, "and gather whate'er we can from these ruins. Next time, the Spaniards will not find us so easily."

"True, Mr. Weston." Eleanor Dare's eyes were clouded. "But could an English ship find us, either? God send there may be one, some day."

Tom looked to the westward, the unbounded land where there were none but them to carry Raleigh's dream.

"I can promise only this," he said gently. "There will be some to follow us, and we can point the way."

He stepped to a tree and with the point of his knife carved one word:

CROATAN

THE

MEDICINE BAG

1615 The beginning of the Seventeenth Century saw the French firmly established on the St. Lawrence. Shrewd Breton and Norman merchants had realized that if New World fish furnished a livelihood for their grandfathers, New World furs would provide a fortune for themselves, under the guiding hand of the great Champlain. In 1611 they built an advance trading post where Montreal now stands, for it was here that the Ottawa River emptied its waters into the mighty St. Lawrence. The Ottawa was the highway of the fur-trading Hurons, who lived on the shores of the great inland seas of Georgian Bay and Lake Huron.

If furs could come down the river, faith could go up. France not only wanted furs, but she was eager to give Christianity as well as trade goods for them. So the Ottawa became as familiar to missionaries as to merchants. In fact, the first white man to make the arduous and dangerous trip to Lake Huron was neither a trader nor a soldier, but a humble priest whose zeal lighted a path for more famous men to follow—Father Joseph LeCaron.

FATHER LeCARON rose from his knees and stood looking down at the covered form of the dead Huron. He had saved his first soul from pagan savagery and committed it to God's mercy. In this strange, wild country of New France, it was a comfort to know that in his last extremity, deserted by all his fellows, one simple savage had listened to and believed the Truth. The priest uttered a final prayer over the body of the Huron, then gathered his gray robe about him to walk through the long lodge—a building so cunningly joined and covered with bark that neither wind nor rain nor snow could penetrate it.

The other Indians in the lodge looked respectfully at him as he walked by. But Joseph LeCaron's mind and thoughts were still occupied with the dead warrior whom he had comforted throughout the night. Yesterday morning the warrior had been borne down the river to the village by six of his fellows, and left in the priest's care. Father LeCaron tried to tell himself that they had done so because they loved and respected the word of God. But in his heart he knew that none had wanted to bother with the wounded man, who, as anyone could see, was as good as dead.

The savages had been much more interested in the two Iroquois scalps which the war party had also brought. In a most heathenish and unseemly manner they had exulted over their grisly trophies. Indeed, the whole Indian village had joined the wild party that celebrated both the killing of the Iroquois and the arrival of Samuel de Champlain, who was going to help them fight their mortal enemies. The savages' was an un-Christian faith, so far removed from the True Belief that, in moments of extreme discouragement, Father LeCaron had wondered if they would ever be converted. His heart sat heavily within him. His task seemed too great.

But, when he walked out the door of the lodge, and lifted his eyes to the sun on Mont Royal, his doubt departed. Could one see for himself that the Supreme Being had seen fit to lift the sun on another day and, witnessing that miracle, still doubt? Father LeCaron smiled. He had known, when he left the Récollet convent at Brouage to answer Champlain's plea for friars to work among the savages of the New World, that his would not be a simple nor an easy lot. Arriving at Quebec with three brother friars at the end of May, 1615, Father LeCaron had been assigned to work among the Hurons, and he had hurried up the great river to the Indian village here at Place Royale, where Champlain had set up a trading post four years before.

Father LeCaron walked through the village, his thick wooden sandals making a strange "clop-clop" on the ground where, for the most part, only moccasined or bare feet had trod. He watched two Indians with necklaces of bear claws about their necks hurry toward the council lodge. Later in the morning, in order to plan the war party that he would lead against the Iroquois, the Hurons would have a meeting with Champlain. There would be endless talk, and much argument about preparations: who was to go and where the war party would strike. They would need to go up the Ottawa River, to recruit warriors from the Huron tribes who lived on the unknown inland sea. That much even the unworldly priest knew, for it was obvious that this trading settlement was far too small to make a large-scale raid on the bloodthirsty Iroquois of the Five Nations.

Father LeCaron paused a moment, as two Indian curs started to snarl over a bone at his feet. More curs appeared, seeming to slink from nowhere, and within seconds had become a snarling, yelping tangle. A ring of Indian children gathered, and excitedly screeched encouragement to the dogs. An old squaw with a stick in her hand appeared, went methodically among the seething pack, and struck right and left until they had slunk away.

Father LeCaron watched without seeing, because it seemed that suddenly he had received the revelation for which he had been praying. Since he had known in his heart that his true mission in life lay among the savages of the New World he had been eager to arrive among them. Coming to Quebec, he had been restless until he had been able to push on to this outpost at the mouth of the Ottawa. But even here the turbulence within himself had not abated. These savages were unenlightened souls who needed guidance. But other priests were coming to them, and what of the savages farther back in the wilderness, on the inland sea of the Hurons? No light had entered their heathen world, and certainly light would glow most brightly in the darkest places.

His mind made up, Father LeCaron walked happily away from the bark lodges that made up the Indian village, and through the stockade gate toward Champlain's tent.

"Has the Sieur de Champlain arisen yet?" he asked the soldier who stood guard.

"Yes, Father, he is at breakfast," the soldier replied.

The priest entered the tent to come face to face with Samuel de Champlain, who was breakfasting on venison, wild strawberries, and good French bread. Of medium stature, he had about him a dynamic quality that had nothing to do with dimensions, a forceful, indefinable aura that made him a man apart. The hand of destiny, brushing its careless way among men, had paused to leave its imprint here. He rose.

"This is indeed an honor," he said graciously. "Will you breakfast with me, Father?"

"No, thank you," the priest answered. "My hunger

is only of the spirit. I have come to request a favor."

"Yes?"

"I have not found my true mission here. I wish to go deeper into the wilderness."

"Most certainly. I am going there myself to lead an expedition against the Iroquois. If these warlike tribes to the south are not kept in check, there will be no peace for your work or mine. As soon as I have gone to Quebec, and returned with more supplies, you shall go with me."

Father LeCaron said gently, "It is not seemly for a man in the service of the Prince of Peace to travel with a party serving the god of war. I wish to go now."

Champlain looked down at his plate, and lost himself in thought. When he raised his head, his face was grave.

"I would advise against your going," he said. "The country of the Hurons is many days' journey up the Ottawa. I myself have explored this river only part way, but I can assure you that it is not the broad St. Lawrence. It is swift and dangerous, with many rapids and portages. Moreover, the Iroquois make constant raids on the friendly savages who travel it to trade with us. Even the Nipissings, who, I am told, inhabit a lake along the upper reaches, are thieving and hostile."

"Mine is the Greatest Protector of all," replied the priest firmly. "I am not afraid. And what are privations and hardships to him whose life is devoted to poverty?"

Samuel de Champlain sighed. "Must you go now?"

"Yes. I would mingle with the Indians, study their customs, and try to teach them the Word of God, before you arrive and turn their hearts to war."

"You will not be dissuaded?"

"I cannot be," Father LeCaron said simply.

"Well, if you must go . . ." He rose and called out, "Find Francois Grellon and send him in here." Champlain sat down, his eyes still grave. "I insist on sending my best canoeman with you. My conscience will permit no less."

Father LeCaron smiled. "I shall concede that much."

A moment later the tent flaps rustled and a stocky little French-Canadian entered. He stood silently while Champlain addressed him.

"Francois, you are to select the proper equipment, crew, and guides, and conduct Father LeCaron up the river as far as the Huron country on the inland sea. I will follow as soon as may be."

"But Sire!" Francois Grellon's liquid black eyes were filled with doubt and misgiving.

"You have your orders."

"*Oui, M'sieu.*"

Grellon left the tent. But the disapproval still lingered in his eyes.

THE MEDICINE BAG

ELEVEN DAYS OUT, as he washed his face this morning, Father LeCaron hummed a gay *voyageur's* tune. His washing finished, he bent over the river's edge and gravely regarded the image that stared up at him. His thin face was already showing the effects of insects and briers and scanty food. Curly black hair tumbled halfway to his shoulders, and water dripped from it. But his eyes best expressed him as he was. They were clear and black, with depths of wisdom and understanding far beyond his twenty-seven years. Some of that understanding had come very recently.

The priest grimaced at himself, and rose to his knees. Vanity was a sin, and it was just as well that none of the *voyageurs* should see him staring at his own image. But he had only wanted to see if some of the wonderful happiness that filled him showed in his eyes. Father LeCaron turned his face toward the sky and uttered a prayer of thanksgiving. He was on his way to do his work for the Cross and the good God would watch over them, as He had done thus far.

At a barely perceptible motion from up-river, Father LeCaron looked in that direction. The Cat, one of the two Huron guides accompanying them, broke out of the forest and walked on silent feet down to where the rest of the party was gathered in the overnight camping place. The Cat, Father LeCaron supposed, had been out on a scouting trip. He stooped

to talk with Francois Grellon, and Father LeCaron
rose to his feet.

He picked up the bag that had lain beside him
while he washed. It was a commodious leather bag,
worked especially for him by some of the skilled
leather craftsmen among the Récollet friars at
Brouage, and the one bit of luggage which Father
LeCaron retained at all times in his personal possession. Not that he had so very much luggage: only his
books and some simple utensils. A man who would
keep a pure spirit had little time for seeking luxuries
of the body.

He slung the bag across his shoulder and walked
up the river to where they had encamped. Anchored
with slender sticks tied to the gunwales and to the
bank, the two canoes in which they were travelling
rode easily on the river's surface. The paddlers, Henri
and Honore Armand, Pierre Latour, Baptiste Le
Grand, Denis Fourmand, and Simon and Georges
Lordez, were squatting around the fire, waiting for
their breakfast of mush to cook. The Cat left Francois Grellon's side when the priest approached, and
padded silently over to join the other Huron guide,
the hulking, amiable man known only as The Little.
Father LeCaron threw himself down beside Grellon.

"It is obvious that your scout doesn't trust me,"
he said in quiet amusement.

Francois Grellon shrugged. "That Cat, he trusts

nobody but himself, and not himself half the time."

"What does he seek?"

"Iroquois."

"But I thought we had reached the country of the friendly Ottawa savages."

Francois Grellon took his knife from its sheath and a small, smooth stone from his pouch. Methodically, with a rolling motion of his fingers, he began to work the stone up and down the blade of the knife. The plaintive little "weet, weet, weet" of the honing stone sang out on the morning air and seemed, Father Le Caron thought, curiously like the song of a small but sinister bird. The woodsman tried the edge of the blade on his thumb, and grunted.

"Iroquois don't care whose country it is. If they want to come, they come. They sneak through Huron country if they're a small party, fight through if they're big. The Nipissings are too poor to bother with, and the Ottawas are just old women to Iroquois."

"But surely we French have nothing to fear from these tribal disputes."

"No?" Grellon looked pityingly at the priest. "I will tell you. Six years ago twelve Frenchmen and many Hurons raided the Iroquois. I, Francois Grellon, was one, and the great Champlain himself led us. Why? I do not know. I myself say it was a bad mistake. By boat and canoe, we travelled many leagues south of Mont Royal, to the Lake of the Iroquois, and killed some of them. Not many. But Iroquois do not forget." He ran his knife around an imaginary scalp-lock, and grinned mirthlessly.

Father LeCaron sighed. He was only a simple priest, and it was not his place to question the deeds of Samuel de Champlain, founder of Quebec and leader of New France. No man was without sin, and surely Champlain's good deeds overbalanced his evil ones, if evil they were. Had he not seen the need of missionaries to go among the Indians? Was not he himself, because of Champlain, the first priest to journey up this wild, spruce-lined waterway to the inland sea?

Denis Fourmand, stirring the kettle, took a bit on the end of his finger, tasted it, and pronounced it done. The hungry *voyageurs* filled their tin plates, dipped their fingers into the steaming brew, and licked them off. Gathering his gray robe about him, Father LeCaron joined the group and ladled his own share of the pounded corn boiled in water from the common kettle.

Scooping up the last morsel with his horn spoon— it was really amazing how such fare could give one strength—the priest looked up to see the canoemen still squatting in a circle, their eyes fixed on his leathern bag. He smiled inwardly. Since the start of the journey that bag had been the subject of intense

74

curiosity which he would have liked to gratify. But what the bag contained was, and must remain, his secret. If, at the proper time, it proved of any value, of course he would tell them. But until he had proven its worth or worthlessness, the contents of the bag must be disclosed to no one, lest his holy calling be exposed to ridicule through fault wholly his own.

Again sure, as they had been every morning, that he would not open the bag, the *voyageurs* packed their canoes. All stood on the river bank while Father LeCaron asked a blessing on this day's journey. It was exactly like any other embarkation—except that each man kept his musket within instant reach.

DURING HIS REST PERIOD from the paddling, Father LeCaron was sitting comfortably in the center of the canoe piloted by Francois Grellon, writing a letter to Father Monet, back at Brouage. It might be a year or more before it reached the convent, but impressions of this vast new country must be put down while they were fresh, so that those who came after would know exactly what to expect. The priest held the strip of white birch-bark steady on his knees, and traced the letters carefully:

It would be hard to tell you how tired I am with paddling all day, with all my strength; wading the rivers a hundred times and more, through the mud and over the sharp rocks that cut my feet; carrying the canoes and luggage through the woods to avoid the rapids and frightful cataracts; and hungry at all times, for our only food is sagamite, a sort of porridge made of pounded corn and water, of which we have a small allowance every night and morning. But I find abundant consolation under all my troubles; for when one sees so many infidels needing nothing but a drop of water to make them children of God, one feels an inexpressible ardor to labor for their conversion. . . .

"Iroquois!"

Francois Grellon's musket banged over his head, and the startled priest just had time to glimpse a strange canoe full of painted figures when the foremost Indian toppled into the water, overturning the frail craft. Their own canoes shot forward, propelled by the redoubled efforts of their paddlers. Looking back, Father LeCaron could see a few dark heads on the water, heading for the overturned canoe. There were two more shots, this time at the canoe itself. Gaping holes appeared in the bark hull as the heavy shot ripped clean through.

The Huron guide known as The Cat deserted that night.

FIVE DAYS LATER, they were well past Allumette Island, the farthest spot reached by Champlain, and in the upper reaches, watching for the outlet of the river that would lead them to the Lake of the Nipissings. They had seen no more Iroquois, and the few Ottawa villages they had visited had shown only a friendly interest in the bearded white men and the gray-robed priest. If the Nipissings did not prove hostile, they should have no further obstacles than the ever-present dangers of travel on a wild and unknown river.

Father LeCaron had had much time for meditation these last few days. He had achieved a cleared and truer picture of this untamed, endless wilderness into which he had come. He wasted no speculation on his own place in it, because that had been decided even before he had left France. But even the most complete accounts that he had read conveyed only a very sketchy idea of the immensity of the New World. Only personal contact with it revealed the truth, and then not all the truth. Probably years would not bring that. But one who saw it knew that it was an incredibly wealthy world, remote and uncivilized though it was.

He looked at the smoothly straining backs and rhythmically swinging arms of the men ahead of him. Profound indeed were the ways of God. Without their even suspecting it, He had chosen such men to be

77

His instruments in penetrating this world and in doing His will there. And, as always, He had chosen wisely. Francois Grellon knew a waterway as well as he did the palm of his own hand. He had an instinctive feel for lakes and rivers, and could handle himself on unknown water as easily as he could on lakes and rivers that he had travelled a hundred times.

Up in the prow of the canoe, Grellon was shading his eyes with his hands and staring at the river. Father LeCaron followed his gaze. Up ahead, about three hundred yards away, white water shot through a dim, high-walled canyon. But Grellon would know whether to portage, or whether to try to pole up through the rapids. He made his decision.

"Land by the leaning spruce," he called back. "We portage."

The canoe hove to. Father LeCaron stepped carefully out of it and waded ashore. His face expressionless, the Huron known as The Little cast up and down the bank, a short gun in his hands. Father LeCaron watched with interest. Suddenly The Little grunted with satisfaction, and pulled aside a low-hanging branch of spruce, to reveal a plainly marked portage trail. It was amazing, reflected the priest, this instinct woodsmen and savages had for water and wilderness ways. Certainly Grellon had never been this way before. Just the same, when he had looked up the white water—in outward appearance like many rapids they had poled up—he had known that they must portage around it.

The paddlers stepped from the canoe, waded ashore, and made packs of their food and cooking utensils. Boastfully Georges Lordez hoisted an enormous load, at least two hundred pounds, to his shoulders. The rest divided what remained, and murmured among themselves in imitation-woman voices while they looked at Lordez in feigned amazement. Father LeCaron turned his head to hide his smile. Canoemen were little more than children, and took a child's pride in outdoing each other. At the last portage Honore Armand had seized most of the load and walked fastest with it.

Two men took each canoe, overturned it, and balanced it on their heads and shoulders while they walked up the portage trail. But each man kept one free hand on his musket. Simon Lordez padded ahead, alert and watchful, while Grellon brought up the rear, in order that none of their precious equipment might be dropped or thrown away by a tired canoeman. Cautiously as a lynx, The Little beat back and forth on either side of the trail. He came to the rim of the canyon wall, looked carefully up and down the river, then disappeared in the undergrowth. Father LeCaron shouldered his heavy bag, and began to trudge up the steep, rocky path.

Suddenly there was the twang of a bowstring, and

Simon Lordez dropped his rifle, to clutch at the shaft of an arrow that had gone clear through his neck. He staggered backward and plunged into the river. Looking down where he had fallen, the priest had one fleeting glimpse of the body as the rapids sucked it under and whirled it away.

Father LeCaron felt himself seized by the legs. Thrown off balance, he landed heavily on the stone-studded ground, to be pulled unceremoniously behind a canoe. He looked around at the face of Francois Grellon.

"I do not like to lay rough hands upon you," Grellon apologized dryly. "But can one name the place from which the next arrow may come?"

"Do you think there will be more?"

"Of a certainty. One savage, alone, would not attack eleven men."

"I see no more."

"You do not see them. You are aware of their presence only when their arrows fly. Stay behind the canoe."

"Are they Iroquois?"

"Nipissings, I think, but I do not know."

Father LeCaron marvelled. Of all the foes that one might battle, certainly the savages were the strangest. They were invisible as the wind, and as deadly silent as night itself. But the canoemen had shown themselves to be as adept at battling savages as they were

at handling their canoes. The four men carrying the frail craft had thrown them down on the bare ground, prows touching and keels to the forest, and all crouched behind them. Out in the forest another bowstring twanged, and an arrow sang from the trees to thud into a canoe and through it to the ground. It was a chopping, harsh music, Father LeCaron thought. It sang of death and things that should not be.

Francois Grellon raised over the canoe to fire his musket, and Father LeCaron closed his eyes. But he recovered himself swiftly. This was what he had expected when he entered the wilderness. If brotherhood of man existed in this place there would be neither need of nor work for him. But the thud of an arrow and the report of a gun, fired in anger at other men, were the most terrible sounds he had ever heard. However, he must face it and there would be no more moments of weakness.

At one end of the canoe Georges Lordez, brother of the slain Simon, was lying on his back working with his gun. He emptied the powder from it, and carefully re-charged it. Then he drew his long knife from its sheath, and clasped it between his teeth. His face was set and furious, his black eyes smouldered.

He rose to his feet and called insultingly, "Here I am, *Messieurs les sauvages*. Shoot *me!*"

A tree wriggled slightly. As though the gun were merely an extension of his own arm, Georges raised it and shot. There was the sickening sound of a bullet striking flesh, and the tree that had wriggled shook convulsively. With the knife in his hand, Georges sprang over the canoe. A long shrill yell pealed from his throat. The twang of a bowstring seemed to punctuate it, and, an arrow flew out of the trees to bury itself to the feathers in his chest. As though the arrow were not there, Georges ran straight into the spruces. There was another yell, a rattling groan, and he ran out again, red blood dripping from his knife. Almost at once he ran back into the spruces. There was another yell, which ended in a choking gurgle.

Then all was silent. Father LeCaron crossed himself, breathing a prayer for the soul of Georges Lordez and one for the savages who might have died under his knife or gun.

"Simon can rest in peace now," said Grellon's voice in his ear. "Georges got one for him, and at least one for himself."

As though the words were a signal, a very rain of arrows soared out of the spruces to chop through the canoes. Father LeCaron looked unflinchingly up, then crawled the length of the canoes to where Honore Armand lay with his head on his arms. Father LeCaron looked at the arrow that had gone through the dying man's side, and lifted the rosary from about his own neck. He pressed it into Honore's hand, and the stricken canoeman smiled wanly at him. Father

LeCaron bent very close to Honore's lips, but no words came forth. The canoeman sprawled on the ground, clutching the crucifix as though all his fading strength had been transferred to his hand, and he could not let go. The priest smiled through the tears that clouded his eyes. No man was without sin. But so long as all in extremity turned to the Cross with reverence and faith, humanity was not lost. As he administered the last rites, Honore collapsed, and even in death it seemed that his slowly unfolding hand was reluctant to let the crucifix go. Leaving Honore where he lay, Father LeCaron crawled back to Francois Grellon.

"Is he mortally hurt?" Francois asked, without taking his eyes from the forest.

"Honore is dead."

Grellon shook his head. "The rest of us soon will be. There's too many devils and the sons of devils out there. I'm sorry you had to be caught in this."

"This is my place," Father LeCaron said softly.

Francois Grellon looked curiously at him, and the priest returned his gaze, steadily.

"What do you mean?" the canoeman asked.

"Because I have consecrated my life to preparing men for death. And it is inspiring to see how well they die. I am ever more certain that death is not the end."

"I'm just a canoeman," Francois Grellon said. "I haven't thought much about such things."

84

His glance fell to the leather bag still slung from Father LeCaron's shoulder. The priest's thin face flushed at the unspoken question. He turned to unbuckle the leather straps that closed his bag. But just then something struck him beside the head and the world went black.

When Father LeCaron regained consciousness, he did so slowly and reluctantly, aware of a great pain in his limbs and an uncomfortable chill throughout his body. He raised his aching head, but promptly lowered it because it seemed that the world upon which he gazed was an entirely unreal place, one that he had never seen before and in which he should not be. With a prodigious effort he again drew his head up and kept it there. He fought to bring clarity of thought to his numbed brain, and at length the distorted vision before his eyes assumed shape and form.

The sun had not yet risen in the early morning sky. But a gray dawn revealed an Indian village, a collection of fourteen bark-thatched huts. Slender poles were erected before all of them, and a varying number of scalps fluttered from the poles. To one side was a cleared space where fields begged mutely for the crops that should have enriched them. The butchered carcass of a dog hung before one of the huts but, strangely, no dogs barked or growled. A small child emerged from a hut to stare curiously at the priest.

Except for a breechcloth that encircled the child's

middle, he was naked. Black hair strayed in a snarled tangle down the sides of his head and into his eyes. The child reached stolidly up to brush it away. Father LeCaron stared back at the youngster, and it seemed to him that at once his own sufferings were less.

His robe was torn, and stained with his own blood. One arm was numb. But, by some miracle, the leather bag was still suspended from his shoulder. He attempted to move his hands, and discovered that they were bound to a post set upright in the earth. His feet were likewise bound, so tightly that the thongs cut deeply into the flesh. He turned his head.

Francois Grellon was there, similarly bound to a post inserted in the earth. His head slumped forward, and even while Father LeCaron watched he made a feeble effort to raise it. Beyond were three more posts, and even though Father LeCaron could not turn his head far enough for a clear view, he thought that Henri Armand, Baptiste LeGrand, and Pierre Latour, were tied to them. There were, then, five remaining out of what had been twelve.

"They came from the river bank," mumbled the voice of Francois Grellon suddenly. "There must be a ledge there and they knew how to walk on it. We fought them. But they got us."

"What will they do?"

"Turn us over to their women—the heathen devils! Taunt them into killing you if you can."

"Do not despair," replied the priest. "They can hurt only our bodies."

A great sadness swept through him. Men were sinners, and must do penance for their sins. But, perhaps, when the final ends and reasons were understood none sinned willingly. If only there were some way to get word back to his brother friars!

Father LeCaron looked again at the thin, nearly naked little boy, and then out over the fallow fields. Just at that moment two women emerged from the nearest lodge and came toward him. Their stringy black hair was plastered to their heads with the grease of some forest beast. They carried short knives in their hands. Hate was the most ignoble of passions, and even now he could not find it within him to hate these fellow-humans who shortly were to cut his living body to pieces. But prayer might help. Father LeCaron closed his eyes.

"Forgive them, Father," he murmured. "They know not what they do."

He opened his eyes to see the women very near him now. The venom that had taken possession of their souls showed in their snapping black eyes. One of them spat squarely in his face. Father LeCaron smiled at her.

Even now hope lived within him. It was not hope for his own flesh, because that meant nothing in God's work. But he had come to bring salvation to these people, and there was still hope that he might do that. The priest inclined his head toward the leather bag at his shoulder and said, "It is for you."

The women drew back. Hate still flared in their eyes, now deepened by suspicion. Father LeCaron waited patiently. He did not know why the bag remained on his shoulder. Perhaps, when they had carried him here, the Nipissings had been in too much of

a hurry to remove it, and, last night, in the darkness, it had remained unnoticed. But now the women saw it. One stepped forward, cut the strap with her knife, and sliced the top from the bag. She looked within. The other woman looked, and they clucked together.

At a swift little trot they went back into the village.

When they again emerged, they were followed by nearly a hundred Indians. Save for the women, who still carried their knives, they were weaponless. One of the squaws walked to the back of Father LeCaron's post, slashed the thongs which bound him to it, and eased him gently to the ground. One by one the rest of the prisoners were cut free from their bonds. Francois Grellon shook a bewildered head, and stared fixedly at Father LeCaron. A warrior spoke in his own dialect, and the *voyageur* stared at the Indian in amazement.

"He says they will take care of us, and when we are all able to travel they will send us back down the river," Grellon translated. "I don't understand it."

"Look about you," Father LeCaron said. "Perhaps then you will understand. And I am not going back down the river. My work is in the wilderness."

Realizing that one of the white men could understand him a little, the warrior spoke again, illustrating his words with sign language.

"What does he say?" the priest asked eagerly.

"He says they had a very harsh winter," Grellon went on. "They had to eat whatever there was, even their dogs. They thought that in this coming winter they would all starve. But now, thanks to the magic of your medicine bag, they will not. They're sorry they killed some of us. But they had bad hearts because starvation faced them. Father LeCaron, what did you have in that bag?"

The priest looked again at the brown fields, that even now should have been green with growing corn. But the season was early, there was still time to plant. And God had abided both by himself and by this tribe of woodland dwellers who had shown need of His care. Father LeCaron smiled happily, certain now that a great and infallible hand was guiding him.

"I am a man of God," he said simply, "but I have also been trained in husbandry. The bag was filled to the brim with seeds."

SAVAGE
TREK

1661 In the years following Father Le-Caron's voyage, Jesuit priests set up mission after mission in the Huron country lying east of Lake Huron and north of Lake Ontario, and with amazing perseverance converted the entire nation. But the great Champlain had made one irreparable mistake—alienating the Iroquois of the Five Nations. Not only did these fierce warriors keep the French from expanding south of the St. Lawrence, and thus give the English colonies time to establish themselves, they also, in 1649, exterminated the Hurons in a bloody war, and wiped out the missions. Thereafter, the Ottawa River was a dangerous highway. Only the bravest Frenchmen dared travel it in quest of furs from the western tribes. These hardy souls were known as coureurs de bois, "runners of the woods," and they became as crafty, ruthless, and woods-wise as the Indians themselves.

Two of the bravest, and certainly the most important, were Pierre Esprit Radisson and his brother-in-law, Medard Chouart, Sieur des Groseilliers. Their "savage trek" was one of the most thrilling and far-reaching exploits in American history.

GOVERNOR D'AVAUGOUR, newly appointed ruler of New France in the name of his majesty King Louis XIV, looked up with curiosity as his two visitors were ushered in. Even during his short term at Quebec, he had heard of this strange pair who had only the year before returned from the wilderness with a small fortune in furs. The Governor indolently flicked back the lace from the sleeves of his velvet robe, and touched the tips of plump, white fingers together. But there was nothing indolent about the eyes or the features that he turned toward the two.

"I presume you are Medard Chouart, Sieur des Groseilliers, and captain of militia at Three Rivers," he said, glancing at the older man's uniform. "And this wild man dressed in skins—would he be the celebrated Radisson?"

The lean features of the man in buckskin darkened, but before he could reply his companion spoke for him.

"Pierre Esprit Radisson is my brother-in-law, Sire," Chouart replied stiffly. "He is a man who has lived much in the wilderness, and now wishes to return in a further search for furs. He has asked me to accompany him, and for that reason we have requested this audience with you."

"So." The Governor eyed them speculatively. "I have already authorized an expedition up the Saguenay, to Lake St. John. Perhaps, upon its return——"

"The Saguenay!" Radisson interrupted contemptuously. "The best furs were trapped out of there in Champlain's day. We propose to go a thousand miles to the west, to the country of the Chippewas, which no white man except me, Pierre Radisson, has seen."

"It is quite true, Your Excellency," added Medard Chouart eagerly. "As a lay brother at the Jesuit missions, I myself heard of these lands, and also of a great sea to the north of them."

Governor D'Avaugour tapped his fingertips gently together. "Possibly it could be arranged," he said thoughtfully, "provided that you go as my agents, and that I have adequate assurance that half the furs will be turned over to me."

Radisson's hard face showed no expression, because his own decision had been made before he had ever seen the Governor. But Chouart could not repress a gasp of dismay.

"But, Sire," he protested, "surely the value of our explorations and our contact with the Indians should be of sufficient value——"

"This is 1661," said the Governor sharply, "and high time you *coureurs de bois* learned that this is royal domain, ruled by the King's representative. If you wish to trade for furs, it will be on my terms. Furthermore, two of my men are to accompany you."

"To watch us," Radisson added pleasantly, but with a glitter in his eye. Suddenly he was aware of the pressure of Medard's foot on his moccasin, and sub-sided, to stare woodenly at the Governor's tapping fingers. Unconsciously, he rubbed his own calloused forefinger against his scarred thumb. As a prisoner of the Iroquois, he had once had a red-hot coal pressed against the ball of his thumb, until the nail on the other side was as red as the coal. How would this laced and scented courtier have liked that? The Governor was no fool, of a certainty, but Quebec was a long way from Paris, and he had many things to learn about this New France. By virtue of his royal appointment he claimed and ruled for the King vast territories that neither he nor his soldiers had ever seen or ever would see. This fat pig, Radisson reflected angrily, who didn't know a beaver from a rabbit, but thought he could put his greedy fingers into more piles of money if other men brought in enough pelts, had forbidden them to go trading unless they went in his service! It was an outrage, and under no circumstances was it to be endured.

". . . . final decision," the Governor was saying. "If my instructions are disobeyed, your furs will be confiscated. You are dismissed."

THE TWO WALKED through the streets of Quebec in silence, Chouart sunk in gloomy despondency, Radisson grim and stony faced.

95

"It is intolerable, Pierre," Chouart broke out at last. "Half the furs, and two spies to watch us!"

"The spies will not watch us," replied Radisson calmly, "because they are not going. Besides," he added slyly, "if they did go, they could not last a month. You would not have their deaths on your conscience?"

"I don't know," answered Groseilliers doubtfully. "It seems unwise to defy the Governor's orders. Suppose our furs are confiscated on our return? To go into the wilderness for two or three years, then to risk losing everything—it's not good business."

"That is the chance we take. But consider, Medard. That fat fool of a Governor may not last until we return. If he does, he should have learned not to steal the goods of better men than he. Nor would he dare, when our reports are made known." Radisson's eyes lighted up. "There are rivers and lakes back there in which no white man has dipped a paddle. There are forests so vast that one can never come to their end. There are Indian tribes whose presence no one suspects. Think of it! We shall be the first to go into that unknown land, where we may live like men, and return like kings." He glanced sideways at Chouart. "Sieur des Groseilliers! You would not be Lord of the Gooseberries the rest of your life? Think of what an estate three hundred canoe loads of furs would buy!"

"Three hundred canoe loads! You are mad! No such fortune has ever come down the river."

"You have been in the wilderness with me. You have seen creeks choked with beaver lodges, you have seen countless otter, fox, sable, ermine. You have seen dogs in Indian villages sleeping on furs the like of which King Louis himself does not possess. The last time we had only one canoe loaded with trade goods. This time we'll have eight, and Chippewas for paddlers and guides."

"What Chippewas?" demanded Groseilliers suspiciously.

Radisson grinned. "Did I not tell you, Medard? Seven canoes have come all the way from Sault Ste. Marie, to beg us to return with them. They are waiting for us now, above Three Rivers, at Lake St. Peter."

The older man's lips twitched in a faint smile "An amazing coincidence, is it not? Well, there will be no trouble from the authorities at Three Rivers, for I am still captain of militia. But trade goods and supplies must be loaded at once, and secretly."

"It has already been done," Radisson replied calmly. "I took the goods to the chief, Clacte, last week, and they should be ready to start. We can leave tomorrow."

Chouart snapped his fingers, as if to dispel his last doubts. "So be it; it is a good omen. Let the Gover-

97

nor D'Avaugour sit on his fat rump in Quebec and wait for us. Radisson and Groseilliers will play for all or none!"

AS *THEIR CANOE* glided up the St. Lawrence through darkness that gathered like a slow-falling black mist, they glanced back once toward the dim lights of Three Rivers. Groseilliers had been right; his sentries had bade them Godspeed, then turned their backs so they could truthfully report that they had seen no one leave.

Pierre Radisson flexed his muscles and dug his paddle deeper. It was good to be leaving the cramped and confining life of the village. Around Three Rivers a man could scarcely stretch his arms without bumping into a peasant, or a lumbering ox, or a grunting pig. Once more to hear the drumming of a partridge, and not the crow of a cock! To listen to the snort of a stag, and not the neigh of a horse! To know that one could sleep where one pleased, and go where one pleased, and not be subject to constant bickering and petty restrictions! The wilderness was where he belonged. A warm house, a wife, and a sufficient supply of food were all very well, but what donkey, in its own way, did not possess as much? Men, if they were men, needed more, and what pleasure could equal that of launching your canoe on some untravelled lake or river, and wondering what your eyes would encounter within the next mile, or ten, or a hundred?

And no man could ask for a better companion in adventure than his brother-in-law. Although ten years older, and a cautious trader at heart, Groseilliers was woods-wise and tireless, with a bold and fearless spirit. Once committed to an enterprise, he would recognize no obstacles.

There was the soft swirl of a paddle beside them, and a low-pitched voice spoke out of the darkness.

Radisson's hand stole down to his gun. He lifted it softly, and held his thumb on the hammer.

"Clacte?" he asked guardedly.

The voice spoke a few words in Chippewa, and Radisson answered in the same tongue.

"Fall in behind us. We paddle all night, and meet at dawn at the foot of the long carry, above Montreal."

THEY WERE FAR UP the Ottawa when Chouart sat stiffly up in the bow of their canoe. Radisson snatched up his rifle, and the seven canoes of the Chippewas drew in beside them. The smell of smoke drifted to their nostrils.

"Paddle toward the north bank," Radisson whispered.

They slipped in behind a small island, and Radisson made his way up its green length to the head of it. He peered from behind a sheltering clump of willows, and saw ten war canoes drawn up on the opposite bank. Half a hundred Indians sat or sprawled on the sloping bank. Fish were broiling on a wooden rack over a few small fires, and an Indian with a long green stick in his hand lackadaisically turned them. Radisson crawled back through the brush.

"A war party of Iroquois," he announced. "We'll have to get past them somehow." For a moment he lost himself in thought, then spoke rapidly. "Medard, listen carefully. Take two canoes and go to the head of the island, where they can see you. Go around the island and down the other side. As soon as you get back here, build a line of fires clear across the foot of the island."

"Do we outnumber them?"

"They're triple our strength, but we can make them believe they're outnumbered. Clacte, as soon as the canoes round the head of the island, take the rest and follow them. Then, Medard, you take a different number of canoes, with a varying number of men, and go around again. Do this three or four times, and make it fast. Better hold off with your fires until the last group of canoes has started around. Then, as soon as they've come to the foot, make a lot of noise. Yell, as though more canoes are coming and you're telling them to land because the Iroquois are ahead."

Chouart chuckled at the ingenuity of the scheme. "And you?"

"I'll be watching the Iroquois."

Radisson slunk back through the brush, and lay behind the same willow clump, watching Medard and his paddlers come around the island. The Iroquois set up a yell, and rushed to their canoes. But they were just launching them when Clacte and his five canoes appeared. The Iroquois on the far bank hesitated. Presently Chouart appeared again, with one canoe and six men. Chouart fired a wild shot across the river, and the Iroquois hastily began to cut trees and gather rocks. Radisson grinned. They were going to build a fort.

Four more canoes came, then two. Down at the far end of the island smoke arose, and Clacte could be heard shouting in Chippewa.

"Land here! Land here! There is room for twenty more canoes. Make ready to attack the Iroquois!"

With the first shades of evening Radisson stole

back to the foot of the island. Their canoes were in the water, ready for instant flight should that be necessary. The fires were burning merrily. Chouart stood with his rifle ready.

"What now?" he asked. "The Iroquois are no fools. As soon as it gets a little darker they'll send scouts."

"True," Radisson admitted, "but I have an idea that should delay them."

He waded out to the moored canoes and from one took a small cask of powder. He poured a pewter cup three-quarters full of the black grains, then broke a candle and thrust the extracted wick into the cup. The remainder of the cup he filled with dry, crumpled birch bark, packing it as tightly as he could. Finally he rolled his improvised bomb in bark, and tied a buckskin thong around it.

"We must gain time," he explained as he worked. "Even otter do not slip unnoticed past the Iroquois. I'm going to swim the river and toss this into their fort. Medard, when you hear the horned owl cry three times, start up the river with all the canoes. I'll be on the south bank, four hundred yards above the Iroquois camp."

"It's a dangerous scheme, Pierre."

"But a good one. I can carry it off."

Radisson removed his leather shirt and trousers. Retaining only his moccasins and pouch, and holding the bomb in his teeth, he waded into the Ottawa and swam across. An inch at a time, he slunk toward the fort. If he should be caught, he knew that the best he could hope for was instant death. But the trick lay in not being caught. Ten yards from the fort he put his hand over his mouth and three times imitated the cry of the great horned owl. Then he lit the fuse on his bomb, threw it, and began to run.

Ten seconds later there was a blinding flash, and the exploding bomb flared in the night. Radisson ran upstream, and waded up to his neck in the cool water. A single canoe cut from the flotilla of eight that was paddling upriver, and Radisson climbed aboard.

Ten minutes later, down at the embattled Iroquois camp, a lone figure stole silently away, launched a small canoe, and began to paddle upriver.

THEY LEFT THE OTTAWA by the familiar portage to Lake Nipissing, and thence through French River to Georgian Bay. Once on the lake, there was little danger of being overtaken by the Iroquois war party they had outwitted. Nevertheless, Radisson continued to drive his Indians steadily on. Following the island-studded northern shore of Lake Huron, they became lean as wolves and lithe as panthers while they wielded their paddles ceaselessly. Although every day brought them nearer home, the easy-going Chippewas began to grumble.

"What's driving you, Pierre?" Chouart asked one morning. "You go on like a crazy man. No war party could catch us in this maze of islands, anyway."

Radisson grunted and shifted his paddle, while he peered through the overcast that had settled on what had been a bright day. A sudden blast of wind struck, and one of a line of waves smashed against the side of the canoe. It rocked dangerously, and settled into the following trough. Almost as one the rest of the paddlers turned their craft, and the little fleet made for the distant shore. The wind was howling now, screaming its rage at the water it had battled for centuries. The first trailing sheets of rain swept over the lake. Radisson guided the thin-skinned canoe around a headland, and into a tiny bay which was stirred only by echoing ripples of the holocaust that raged across the lake. After they had beached their canoes, Clacte and his Indians spread a deer-skin shelter, whittled away the outer parts of a dead stick, shaved tinder from the dry inner part, and started a fire.

Meantime, Radisson sat at the lake's edge, oblivious to the pouring rain, and stared out at the storm-lashed water. He turned his gaze to the west and north, in response to the mysterious magnet that seemed set beyond the horizon there. Suddenly Chouart squatted beside him and gripped his arm.

Radisson peered through the seething sheets of rain, pouring so thickly now that it was as though the surface of the lake had erupted in a fine mist of lashing water. Monstrous waves tossed and tumbled, crowding eagerly on the heels of each other. But there was something else out there, a tiny speck in the lashing inferno of a Great Lakes storm.

"It's a canoe!" Chouart exclaimed in amazement. "A little canoe with one man in it!"

The tiny craft bore on, sometimes lost in the troughs of the great waves or obscured by the sheets of rain, but always bobbing up again. Radisson watched it idly, interested in the progress of the little craft only because it was still afloat. It was a foregone conclusion that it would capsize and its paddler drown. The largest and finest of birch-bark craft could not live in that storm.

But still the little canoe fought on, meeting each wave in precisely the right fashion and slowly drawing nearer. Radisson craned his neck, fascinated now by the superb lakemanship of the paddler. Obviously he knew everything there was to know, both about big water and about handling a canoe. There was a grunt beside Radisson, and he turned to see Clacte with a tomahawk in his hand. In these waters a stranger was someone to kill as speedily as possible. There were no friends; anyone was an enemy.

"Let him land," Radisson ordered.

Anger flashed in Clacte's eyes, but he sheathed his tomahawk. The stranger turned his canoe to meet a huge wave, and rode in on its crest. He was paddling furiously now, driving his little craft with swift and sure strokes toward the haven offered by shallow water. He reached it, leaped out, and began to drag his canoe ashore.

Radisson strode forward, and they met at that point where the water lapped the land. The stranger was a short man, stockier than any Indian Radisson had seen, and his black hair was not cut in the scalp lock. His right thumb was gone, and a terrible, recent scar disfigured his cheek. Radisson spoke to him in the Iroquois dialect.

"Why did you follow us here?"

"Not follow," the Indian answered haltingly, but with quiet dignity. "Storm come; I land."

"Where are you going?"

"Home." The Indian gestured north and west.

"Where did you come from?"

"Iroquois capture me. Make me slave. Big noise and fire at night. I get away."

Radisson frowned. If one Indian from the Iroquois camp had overtaken them, so might the others. And from his own experience, he knew how relentless they were in pursuing escaped prisoners.

"Is your tribe at war with the Iroquois?"

The Indian said simply, "Crees do not make war."

Radisson looked at the canoe again. It was an absurdly small thing in which to brave the waters of

Lake Huron, even when there were no storms. But there were more lakes to the west, and no doubt this Cree's tribe lived along one of them. Obviously he was a past master of big water.

"Where did you learn canoeing?" Radisson asked.

The Cree gestured vaguely north, and a puzzled frown creased Radisson's brow. There were rumors of vast inland lakes to the north and west, but not in the direction indicated by the Cree.

"Is it a lake?" he asked.

"It is a sea," the Indian said proudly. "It is mightier than any lake. Long ago, when my grandfather was young, ships with white sails entered it."

Chouart leaned forward, his intake of breath sharply audible. "Ships with white sails? Sailing on a sea to the north? Are you sure?"

The Indian nodded.

"Pierre, did you hear?" Chouart cried. "Up there to the north is an inland sea, one ships may enter! If we can find it, we can tap an entire new land. What an opportunty for trading!"

"Don't fall into the lake, Medard," Radisson admonished. "Are there furs about this sea?"

"Hunt two days—skins for whole winter."

"Pierre," the frantic Chouart said, "we must go!"

"We'll go," Radisson promised. "What's your name, Cree?"

"Stemaw."

"Can you take us to this mighty sea, Stemaw?"

"If you come in peace."

"We not only come in peace, but"—Radisson indicated his gun—"we have these to protect you."

"Then I take you."

Clacte stepped up to the little group, and stood glaring at the Cree. He turned sullenly to Radisson.

"You said you would trade in our village if we came to help you."

Radisson faced him coldly. "Have you ever known me to break a promise?"

"No."

"Do you think me a woman, one who cannot make up his own mind? We will trade in your village. We will also visit this inland sea, if there is one."

The Chippewa looked at the ground, and shuffled his feet uneasily. He turned to glance at his warriors, who stood in stony silence, then faced Radisson.

"I believe you," he said. "But I do not like this stranger from the north who does not fear the Storm God. It is a bad omen."

THE NINE CANOES wound their way through the narrow Sault Ste. Marie, paddling where they could, portaging where the angry water lashed its boiling self over rapids and falls, until they finally reached the mightiest of all the mighty inland lakes—Lake

Superior. Along its southern shore they pursued their steady westward course toward the Chippewa villages. They marvelled at the grotesque shapes and colors of the Pictured Rocks. They found great chunks of almost pure copper glistening in the sun. It was a wild and entrancing land, and they were tempted to stop and investigate its wonders. But the lodestar still gleamed in the north and west. Somewhere up there was a great inland sea, pounding its waves against a land where Cree hunters had to seek only two days for enough pelts to last a whole village through the long, cruel winter.

As they travelled, they lived richly. Great lumbering moose stood in the shallow bays and inlets, and raised their ponderous heads to watch the canoes pass. Deer were never out of sight, and black bears were common. To drop a hook any place was to catch fish, some of which were savage, saw-toothed pike with bodies almost as long as a man's.

Then, one morning, white frost glittered on all the leaves and brush, and with that a subtle change crept over the whole land. There had always been an abundance of waterfowl paddling about and attending to their usually serene business. Now their serenity had departed. A flight of green-winged teal, thousands upon thousands of the little birds, skittered out of the sky to alight on the water in front of them. Almost immediately, with a flutter of wings and a mighty splashing, they rose to speed swiftly southward. Mallards, redheads, canvasbacks, all were coming down from the north. High in the air, an immense flock of whistling swans serenaded themselves on their long journey to the south. Flying lower, but just as swiftly, a flock of trumpeter swans set the heavens ringing with their harsh, unmusical notes. The squirrels in the forest were bustling about, laying up their winter stores of fruit, seeds, and nuts, and the black bears were adding layers of fat to that which already cloaked their bodies, so they would be prepared for their long winter's sleep. Cold weather was coming, and the forest creatures knew it. The wind blew almost constantly from the north, and made the lake pitch restlessly.

Guided by the Chippewas, they came at last to a long point of land jutting out into the lake. But instead of starting around it, the Indians landed and prepared to portage, explaining that a series of trails and streams cut across the base of the peninsula. This was welcome news to the Frenchmen, for already shell ice was beginning to form in the lake shallows, and they had no desire to cache their trade goods so far from the Chippewa villages.

When they had reached the end of the portage and were again launching their canoes in the lake, Stemaw beckoned to Radisson, and pointed north.

"Big island there," the Indian announced.

Shading his eyes, Radisson gazed intently over the sparkling water, but could see nothing.

"Is that the way to the inland sea?" he asked.

The Cree nodded. "For me, but not for you, with loaded canoe."

"Then how can we get there?"

The Indian pointed to the Chippewas, then swung his arm in a half circle, first west, then north. "Go with them. Beyond their country, lake shore turns north. Follow shore to river opposite big island. My people winter there. I go now. When snow melts and ice goes, you come to river. I meet you there. Take you to inland sea."

Without another word, or a backward glance, the Cree launched his tiny canoe and started paddling straight out into the lake. Radisson and Groseilliers looked on, frankly admiring the audacity of a man who would set out for land they could not even see.

Clacte joined them, nodding his head in satisfaction. "Now I believe you. The man from the north has gone without trade goods. Now we go to my village."

THEY PADDLED ON, and snow appeared in the air for a few minutes at noon. Nor was there any clearing of the sky when the snow stopped. A belated flock of five geese beat hasty wings southward, and a limp kingfisher on a dead tree stared forlornly at them as they passed. The snow started again that night, and toward the end of the next day three inches of it lay on the ground. Radisson, handling the stern paddle in their own canoe, looked at the forested shore and worried. Winter struck with varying degrees of suddenness and harshness in this north country, and obviously this season it was going to come early and stay late. He voiced his thoughts to Chouart.

"I don't think we'll get to the Chippewa villages with anything except a small part of our goods."

"I agree, Pierre. Snow's going to stop us. We'll have to cache them."

"How about that southern bay Clacte spoke of, where we have to leave our canoes? But I want a secret cache. These Chippewas might never disturb it, but I haven't seen these goods come all the way from Three Rivers just to have them stolen."

"You'll have to explain that to Clacte."

"I'll explain it. I'll just tell him that we're going to cache some of the goods, and why. We can carry some, and I'll tell him that you and I will be back to trade the rest after we've visited this northern sea. That'll serve a good purpose. If they know what awaits them, the Chippewas will be anxious to get out and trap furs. But how to send them away while we make our cache . . . ?"

"Tell them to go out and hunt."

"It might work," Radisson said thoughtfully. "On the other hand, they might hide and watch to see what we're doing. I think it's better to play on their superstitions. I'll go through some kind of ceremony, and when the Indians want to know what I'm doing, you say that I'm calling down a spirit to watch our goods. Say it will blind anybody who looks at it unless they know the right magic."

Snow fell sporadically, hissing into the water and piling up on the land. By the time they reached the southern end of Chequamegon Bay there was a foot or more on the exposed beach, and the spruce branches were heavily laden. This was the end of their water route, and they had reached it none too soon.

Winking at Groseilliers, Radisson stepped out of the canoe and walked solemnly up on the beach. Uncorking his powder horn, he sprinkled a few of the black grains on the snow, then lay flat on his back, and began to whisper into the horn. The Chippewas watched this strange performance with awe. Holding them back with outspread arms, Chouart spoke to the Indians, and the Chippewas looked at each other uneasily. Then they ran hastily toward the sheltering trees, and disappeared from sight.

Chouart walked over and looked down on the grinning Radisson. "Get up, you fool, or you'll scare them away for good," the older man smiled. "I told them nobody would be safe around here for many hours, but that the spirit would be gone by twilight, and it would be safe to camp then. Pierre, had you thought that these goods will be handy in the spring, just in case we want to take some among the Crees?"

"I'd thought of that. But we can't take all this stuff to the Crees, and we're going to need these Chippewas, and anybody else we can get, to help us carry furs back to Quebec. Let's get to work."

They cut spruce branches, and in a sheltered spot well up from the beach swept the snow away. Fortunately, its protecting blanket had kept the ground from freezing. They dug a deep hole with an iron mattock, and dumped the loose dirt into the bay. When the hole was deep enough, they lined it with spruce boughs and withered grasses that thrust above the snow. Then they piled in most of the trade goods, covering them with more grass and branches and finally with dirt. When they were finished Radisson wiped his face on his sleeve.

"I hope it snows," he said. "If a winter's snow lies on this place, not even an Indian could tell there's anything buried here."

As though answering his wish, a light wind swept across the lake and drove a flurry of big flakes before it. While Chouart built a fire, Radisson went into the spruces with his gun. But there was little game, and it was only after hunting for an hour that he shot a small doe. He dragged it back to the beach, and was skinning it when the Chippewas began to straggle timidly into camp.

That night the wind screamed across the lake, and the heavy clouds that tumbled in the sky belched heavy loads of snow. It was still snowing when, guided by the Chippewas, each carrying a small load of trade goods, they struck south, up the course of a small creek. In the middle of the next day they came to Clacte's village, a collection of forty lodges huddled close together beside the frozen lake in which the stream had its source. The chief left them, and went forward to speak to an old man who stood on the bank. After a moment Clacte returned, his face thunderously dark.

"Remember that we helped you, white man!" he said. "While we were gone, a war party from the Tribe of the West came here. Lacking enough warriors to beat them back, my village had no choice but to surrender all the food in its possession."

Radisson walked slowly forward. "We could not stop this thing, Clacte. But it is done. Wailing or anger will not get you more food. Let your warriors hunt, and we will hunt with them."

The two Frenchmen took their rifles and entered the surrounding forest. There was not much game. But there had to be some. They walked cautiously on, probing the deepest thickets and heaviest stands of trees. Game did not like to move on winter days such as this. Finally a deer stirred, got up from its bed, and walked a little way, to stand looking back over its shoulder. Radisson shot, and the deer fell, to lie for a moment kicking its legs. It was all they could find. They looped a buckskin thong over the buck's antlers, and dragged the whole carcass back to the village. It was going to be a hard winter for them all, and even those portions of animals which were ordinarily thrown away had now better be saved.

That night more snow fell, and the wind that howled out of the north brought cruel frost with it. With morning Radisson and Groseilliers threw off the robes that covered them and again started out to hunt, accompanied by a few half-hearted braves. In a good many ways, Indians were like children. When there was plenty of game, and it could be easily had, whatever spirit watched over them was benign and smiling. When there was no game, or a time of crisis arose, the spirit was angry, and an Indian felt there was no use in combatting the will of the spirit. That day Radisson shot two wolves, and came back to camp to find Chouart with a small doe. The Indians killed a fox and a few rabbits. But it was all food.

Every day, and all day, wearing crude snowshoes which they had fashioned themselves, the two white men went into the forest with their rifles. There were days at a time when the village had no meat at all, and one orgy of feasting when the two hunters found five moose in a yard they had trampled, and shot them all. Radisson and Chouart grew lean as weeds, and hunger gnawed constantly at their bellies. But, in the entire village, only two old people died.

Then one day a shivering robin perched on the wind-swung branch of a tree, and the wind blew from the south instead of the north. Almost magically, the breeze seemed to bring the game back out of its retreats. Soft grass shoots began to show in sheltered places. Where there had been one deer, herds of them now frolicked over the flat land. The lean-waking she bear led her cubs out of the den where they had passed the winter, and took them down to water. Grouse sported in the thickets, rabbits played in the grassy openings. The village grew fat.

On a bright day in early April, sixteen tall warriors filed out of the forest, over the remnants of dirty snow. Armed with strung bows, tomahawks, and knives, the hawks' wings in their hair swaying arrogantly, they stalked into the village.

"Who are they?" Radisson asked Clacte.

"They are Sioux, from the Tribe of the West," the Indian scowled. "They have heard that we have men with white skins, and hair on their faces, here in the village. They are mighty warriors, but with your help we could defeat them."

"There will be no fighting," said Radisson sharply.

"We have trade goods for many tribes, but only those who live in peace. Ask them where they come from."

Clacte reluctantly interpreted the Frenchman's words. The Sioux warriors listened impassively, then their chief replied in a strange tongue.

"He says," Clacte translated, "that their hunting grounds extend from the land of a thousand lakes to the great water——"

"What great water?" interrupted Chouart. "Is it a lake or a sea?"

"It is a river—a mighty river that flows to the south. He also says that their country has many furs, but I do not believe him."

Radisson ignored the Chippewa's belittling words. "Tell him," he commanded, "that we would see this country of his, but we will do so only if he leaves your tribe in peace." He tapped the stock of his rifle. "Tell him we have powerful magic to enforce peace. Tell him this magic kept your village from starving during the winter. Tell him to go back and make his people collect furs against the time of our visit. Tell him we will give him knives, axes, beads, cloth, for these furs. But there must be no war."

Deliberately turning their backs on Sioux and Chippewa alike, the two Frenchmen stalked regally away and entered the lodge where they had lived throughout the winter. As soon as they were inside, safe from prying eyes, Radisson turned to Chouart.

"Well, Medard, an inland sea to the north, a thousand lakes to the west, and a great river to the south —which shall it be?"

"And a greedy governor back in Quebec," added Groseilliers dryly. "Perhaps we should go back and ask him."

"Of a certainty, we must visit this Tribe of the West," said Radisson thoughtfully. "But the Cree promised to wait for us. If we do not find him this spring. . . ."

Just at that moment a line of Canada geese flew over the village, gabbling and honking to each other as they made their steady way northward. Radisson and Groseilliers looked at each other in silence, and there rose within both a vision of a great inland sea, and the long way they had come toward it. Each knew what was in the other's mind. The geese were an omen. North it would be.

A week later, having bartered what goods they had, and having exchanged solemn promises with the Chippewas for their return, they left the Indian village and returned to the lake shore where they had cached their canoe and trade goods. New bark was cut for the frame, laced on with the long, flexible roots of the spruce tree, and sealed with spruce gum. The Frenchmen loaded the canoe with as many trade goods as it would comfortably hold, and struck out along the lake shore toward the river to which Stemaw had directed them. On the afternoon of the fourth day they reached it, to find a small village of bark huts on the farther bank. But there was no smoke from cooking fires, no barking dogs, no canoes.

"Deserted!" exclaimed Radisson bitterly.

"No," said Chouart. "That lodge under the big pine. See the smoke?"

At their shout, a lone figure came out and advanced to the river's edge. It was Stemaw.

"My people go," said the Cree simply. "I wait."

THEY ABANDONED their canoe toward the headwaters of a little stream that flowed into a big lake, and made packs of their trade goods. There were so many beaver dams above that point that it was hardly possible to paddle twenty feet without portaging. The Cree, guiding himself with the sure instinct of any half-wild thing, took them steadily overland.

Now that they were at last travelling toward the fabulous inland sea, the Frenchmen's unrestrained eagerness began to be tempered by anxiety. They were by turns moody and ecstatic. The fur was here, all the Cree had promised and more. They crossed swamps, lakes, and creeks in countless numbers, each fairly alive with beaver, mink, muskrat, and otter. The flat, wooded plains were thick with game and valuable fur-bearing animals—ermine, marten, red, white, and black foxes. It was a trapper's paradise. But down in Quebec a governor of absolute power still sat in his state house, and furs were of no value until they reached Quebec. What would be the outcome? Would D'Avaugour have been replaced, or would he still be there, waiting to carry out his threat of confiscation?

At last, they came to the banks of a sizeable river, and the Cree turned to them.

"This flows to the great sea," he announced.

Their packs lightened by excitement, they followed the banks of the sluggish river for three days. On the fourth, they saw motion downstream, and five warriors with drawn bows appeared, to stand watching them silently. Stemaw shouted happily. Running down the river bank, he embraced one of the warriors. The five braves were with him when Stemaw came back. He indicated the one he had embraced.

"My father," the Cree said proudly. "He is chief. He says you are welcome."

The chief was looking curiously at the rifles. Carefully, he touched the barrel, stock, and trigger of Radisson's gun.

"Stemaw must have told him about our guns," said Chouart. "Fire it and show them our magic."

Radisson raised the gun and fired at the dead trunk of a big hemlock. The heavy ball smashed into the smooth surface. From the Crees' lack of astonishment, the Frenchmen concluded that Stemaw had described their weapons well. The Indians examined the mark, huddling together so that all could see. When they returned there was childish pleasure on Stemaw's face.

"My father says it is good medicine," he explained. "Same mark as on old spirit house."

Radisson and Groseilliers looked at each other, puzzled. Old house? Bullet marks? Could they mean there were, or had been, white men living here?

"Where is this old house?" Radisson asked. "Will you take us there?"

Stemaw nodded. "But all dead, many years. Only spirit live there now."

Three days later they stood on the shores of the inland sea, and gazed out on its storm-tossed expanse. There was no sign of a far shore, so they had no way of telling how large it might be. On an impulse, Radisson scooped up a little water and tasted it. Salt! Before he could speak, Chouart cried out in sudden excitement.

"Look! Over there, on the point!"

On a bleak and treeless little promontory stood the ruins of a small building built of hewn timbers which no Cree would possess the tools for working. On a dead run the two Frenchmen raced out to the point. The door had long since fallen off, but the stout walls and part of the roof still stood. Awed, but consumed with curiosity, they stepped into the dimly lighted interior. There was nothing there save a crude table, a bed, a crumbling fireplace. But, roughly cut into the timbers on the far side, over the bed, was an inscription: 'Hendryck Hudson, 1611.'

Chouart placed a trembling hand on Radisson's shoulder. "Hudson's Bay!" he breathed. "It is not a new discovery, only a lost one! There *is* an outlet to the Atlantic!"

"So . . . ?" Radisson left the question in the air, and turned his restless eyes to the west. In memory he retraced their long, arduous journey: through forest and swamp, across frozen ponds and along the shores of vast, storm-tossed lakes, down spruce-lined rivers and around leaping cataracts—two thousand miles back to Governor D'Avaugour's state house in Quebec. D'Avaugour! Would the spiteful, greedy little man dare to carry out his threat now?

The lean, hard face turned toward Groseilliers. "Medard, it will be a year, maybe two, before we can get our furs back to Quebec. But I tell you this, now: we have found a fortune and an empire. If D'Avaugour steals one, we will sell the other to the English!"

THE
OPENING GATE

1753 Radisson and Groseilliers returned to Montreal with a fortune in furs, only to have most of it confiscated by the Governor. True to their threat, they did go to the English, with the far-reaching result that the Hudson Bay Company was chartered in 1670. Although a private company, it was English to the core, and became the top half of a pincers that was to squeeze France out of America.

The other half of the pincers—westward expansion of the English seaboard colonies—was slower in forming. Almost too slow, for the French, operating on the interior line of the St. Lawrence, gained control of the Mississippi. The link connecting the two was the Ohio River, and by the middle of the Eighteenth Century the French were ready to weld that link into a chain that would hold the English on the eastern seaboard. It was a tense moment in American history, although few knew it.

One who did was Christopher Gist, a strangely forgotten frontiersman who explored Ohio and Kentucky a generation before Daniel Boone. Through his reports he influenced Virginia to send young George Washington in 1753 on his first mission of importance, guided by the veteran Gist. This is the true story of that mission, which led directly to the French and Indian wars.

BARNEY CURRAN and William MacGuire left Stony Run just before nightfall, padded silently through the short stretch of forest to Wills Creek, and waded across the Potomac. Ahead was a high bank, above which they could just see the blockhouses surmounting the stockade of the Ohio Company's fort. This fortified trading post on the upper Potomac was the westernmost outpost of English civilization.

Holding his long Pennsylvania rifle in one hand, Barney Curran stooped to squeeze the water out of his leather leggings.

"Well, here we are," he said. "Wonder what Christopher's up to?"

MacGuire, who was already climbing the bank, made no answer. Suddenly he stopped. He turned around, a broad grin splitting his leathery face, and beckoned silently. Curran joined him, cautiously thrusting his head over the top of the bank.

Directly before them were three log warehouses, with short connecting wings running from the walls of the outer two to the west blockhouses on either end of the main stockade. The tops of the other two blockhouses showed above the nine-foot walls, as did the roofs of the scattered buildings within the stockade.

But the two woodsmen were not looking at the fort. Their eyes were fixed on a lackadaisical, pimply faced youth who stood an indifferent guard by the stockade gate. MacGuire nudged his companion, and gestured with his free hand. Curran winked and nodded.

Separating, the woodsmen crawled quietly over the lip of the bank and wriggled forward without a sound. Curran made his way into a low-hanging clump of laurel, waited until MacGuire had completed a longer circuit to get behind the sentry, then whistled softly.

The sentry came to with a start, and peered sharply in the direction of the noise. As he did so, MacGuire rose soundlessly to his feet behind him, and twitched the sentry's gun from his terrified fingers.

"Tsk! Tsk!" the hunter said plaintively. "Imagine fallin' fer an old trick like that! It's a good thing the Injuns are friendly, ain't it, Barney?"

Guffawing, Curran crawled out of the laurels. "Jest a little free eddication, sonny, fer your own good. Where's Christopher Gist?"

"In his cabin, natur'lly." The pimply youth sullenly jerked his thumb toward the stockade gate.

As Curran and MacGuire entered the Company agent's cabin, a tall, lean man whose black hair was tinged with grey at the temples arose from the table where he had been writing. A smile of pleasure wrinkled the corners of his piercing black eyes.

"I see Tampaloosa found you!" he exclaimed.

"Yup," the loquacious Curran asserted, "and jest

in time, too. Bill and me was headin' back into the Ohio. What's up, Christopher?"

"I want you to go with me."

"Sure. Where we goin'?"

For a moment Christopher Gist stared thoughtfully at the opposite wall, where a map of his own making was fastened. When he spoke, he chose his words carefully.

"You know I explored the Ohio country two years ago, and reported to Governor Dinwiddie that unless Virginia got busy, the French would beat us into the valley?"

"Sure do," said Curran. "And the Injuns told us last month that the Frenchies had grabbed Frazier's cabin and were goin' to make it into a fort. What about it?"

"Just this. There is a Major Washington being sent here by Governor Dinwiddie. I'm to guide him to the French forts, and I want you two and Stewart and Jenkins to go along——"

"Good!" Barney Curran exclaimed. "So we're goin' up and run them Frenchies clean back into Canada! I'll need an extry horse jest to carry my bullets and powder, Christopher! When we——"

"Wait a minute, Barney. France and England aren't at war. This is a diplomatic mission. Major Washington's merely going to tell the French that they'll have to abandon their forts and get out of the upper Allegheny, because it's English territory."

"Well of all the fool ideas! He's goin' to tell the Frenchies to run, is he, and he expects they'll do it! I—uh—I ain't so sure I kin go, Christopher. I got a little business to do on my own hook, and—uh—you know how it is. Mebbe France and England ain't at war, but the Frenchies and me are!"

"I understand," Christopher Gist said with a smile, "and I'm sorry I sent an Indian runner to fetch you in, Barney. Of course, this expedition may have many sides. I, too, do not believe that the French will pack up and go when we give them Dinwiddie's order. But we can't tell what's going to happen. Suppose Washington's the right sort? Suppose he sees the necessity of action in this Ohio country, and takes that news back with him? What I'd really hoped to have, Barney, was a few men who could judge the strength of the French, see how much influence they're having over the Indians, and sort of look around and see how big an army we'll need to throw 'em out."

"Wal, that's more like it!" Barney chortled. "Whyn't you say that in the fust place?"

Gist eyed the taciturn MacGuire. "Will you go too, Bill?"

"If you say so."

"All right. Find yourselves a place to sleep, and draw what supplies you need. Major Washington should be here any day now."

After the two had gone, Christopher Gist sat down at the table, and prepared to resume work on his accounts. But he could not. Staring at his map on the wall opposite, he seemed to see a picture of the lush, wonderful wilderness over the mountains. He had been there two years ago, in 1751, on a surveying and exploring trip for the Ohio Land Company, which hoped to settle the region with emigrants from Virginia. As a reward for his services, he had been made the Company's agent at this trading post on Wills Creek. But he had little liking for it, and felt himself constantly pulled by the rich, unspoiled land to the west. No other Englishman knew the upper Ohio valley as he did, nor the importance of its settlement before the French should push down from the St. Lawrence and the Great Lakes. The English *had* to have it, unless they were to be forever closed in on a narrow strip of land between the Appalachian Mountains and the sea. But how to explain to the English authorities the importance of taking that land at any cost . . . ? He shook his head. Action was needed. Much depended on this expedition he was to guide, and on what kind of report Governor Dinwiddie's emissary took back with him. It was nearly midnight when he finally blew out his candle.

The morning mists that rose from Wills Creek still hung over the fort when Gist was awakened by a loud pounding on the door. A true woodsman, he was instantly awake, with no interval of half-consciousness between deep sleep and full wakefulness.

"What do you want?" he called.

"Mr. Gist," came the answer, "this is the sentry, Willis. Two men have just come who say they've got to see you."

Slipping on his clothes, he went out into the cold dawn of a November day, to find two travel-stained men mounted on tired, steaming horses. His heart sank. The two men were obviously no frontiersmen. The older one, who looked like a merchant, reeled with fatigue. The other, dressed in the uniform of a major of Colonial militia, could not be more than twenty or twenty-one years old.

"Mr. Gist?" asked the younger man. "Forgive our awakening you, but we have ridden all night to get here. This is Mr. Jacob Vanbraam, our French interpreter. My name is George Washington."

"Come in," Christopher Gist directed. "I've been expecting you, Major."

He followed the two into his own quarters. Jacob Vanbraam gave a tired smile and tried to stifle a yawn. But his young companion, seemingly unaffected by the night's ride and its difficulties, removed his cloak and looked about the room with interest.

"You'll find a bed in the next room," Gist suggested. "Would you like to use it?"

"I would indeed," Vanbraam said decidedly. "Anyone who tries to keep pace with this sprig has a right to be weary."

As he disappeared through the door, the young officer looked indulgently after him.

"I should not have pushed him so hard," he explained. "But I considered it necessary to get here as soon as possible. Do you understand my mission, Mr. Gist?"

"Yes, and I think it's a futile one."

"Why do you say that? Are the French not trespassing on English territory?"

"We say it is English because of treaties with the Indians; the French claim it on the basis of LaSalle's and Bienville's explorations. But let me remind you, young sir, that the wilderness is not Williamsburg, with robed and wigged judges haggling over a point of law. The Ohio country will belong to those who can take and hold it."

"You are a realist, Mr. Gist. But, for the present, my mission is purely a diplomatic one, and time is getting short. This is the fourteenth of November. When do we start?"

Christopher Gist looked at him in surprise. True, this George Washington was a young man. But even so, he had not expected a militia officer, after riding all night, to be ready to start on such an expedition without resting.

"It is for you to say," the frontiersman answered

quietly. "The men and horses are all ready now."

"Then, suppose we allow Jacob four hours of sleep? In the meantime, if you'll be so kind, I'd like to have you instruct me in some of the details of this Ohio country into which we are going. There are many things I must learn, and Governor Dinwiddie told me that there's no better teacher than yourself."

CHRISTOPHER GIST had long ago learned that he who spoke little had the best chance of hearing a great deal. And often what a man heard, if correctly pieced together, would open the door to important knowledge. But, though he had listened carefully to every word spoken by George Washington, Gist was still not able to figure out just how much responsibility had been placed by Governor Dinwiddie in this Virginia gentleman who held the rank of Major in the Colonial militia. He had watched the young man all the way from Wills Creek to Gist's own wilderness cabin on the Youghiogheny, from there to Frazier's, on the Monongahela, and he was still watching him this morning, as they neared the junction of the Monongahela and Allegheny that marked the beginning of the Ohio River proper. Despite the rain, wind, cold, and snow they had encountered, none of the journey so far could have been called uncommonly hard. But it had been hard enough to prove that the

Major was not a tenderfoot playing soldier. Every night he was the last to seek his blankets and every morning he was the first to leave them. He seemed to be impelled by a great restlessness and an insatiable curiosity. Not a stream, a valley, or a pass through the hills escaped his notice. But was it the interest of a responsible official, or only youthful curiosity?

They rode out of the forest in a thin flurry of snow-flakes, and saw ahead of them the wooded point where the two rivers met. A sudden gust from the northeast momentarily lifted the flakes, and the low ridges at the intersection of the rivers came into sharp focus. Gist noted with satisfaction that Stewart and Jenkins were camped on the point with Frazier's canoe and their extra baggage. Without hesitation he rode his horse into the icy water and swam him across. When the rest of the party had grouped themselves around the fire by the canoe, Christopher Gist drew Washington aside.

"This is it, Major. This is the proper, and the only proper place for a fort."

George Washington frowned. "I had understood that the Ohio Company was to build its fort below here, at Shurtee's Creek."

"That was the plan," the older man replied, "but its location was chosen by somebody who had never been over the mountains. Let me show you."

He broke a twig from a tree, scuffed the snow away

with the heel of his moccasin, and with the stick traced a map on the bare ground.

"This gives you the idea," he explained, pointing with the stick. "Here is the Monongahela, down which we have come. You see that it flows north, from the English settlements. It's a navigable stream, and the natural English waterway into the Ohio. Here, where we are now, it is joined by the Allegheny, to form the Ohio. The Allegheny flows south, from the French settlements, and this northwest branch, French Creek, reaches nearly to Lake Erie. Do you see my point?"

"I do!" Washington's eyes were alight with excitement. "You have made it very plain, Mr. Gist. Who controls these forks controls all the Ohio country!"

"Exactly! That's it exactly! And we *must* have the Ohio country! It's fine, rich, level land, with all the resources an indulgent God ever bestowed upon earth. There is nothing, absolutely nothing, in Virginia that excels it! But we're going to lose everything to the French unless we can stop this wrangling and get busy. Petty politics in both Pennsylvania and Virginia is robbing us of an empire."

Washington nodded thoughtfully. "Unfortunately, both provinces claim this Ohio country. Neither wishes to appropriate money for its settlement and fortification so long as the claim is in dispute."

"Yes," Christopher Gist scoffed, "and while addlepated legislators wrangle over a few thousand pounds, and wonder if a neighboring province might possibly get a few acres they have developed, the French are taking it all!" He jabbed the stick viciously into the ground. "Look here! The French have fortified Presqu'Isle, on Lake Erie. From there they have built a road to their second fort, on French Creek. According to the best information I have received, they have descended from there to the junction of French Creek and the Allegheny, and have there fortified an English trading post which they have illegally seized. What does that mean to you, Major?"

"It means," George Washington said with quiet decision, "that the French are following their natural route of expansion. They're coming down the Allegheny to the Ohio, and up from the Mississippi. A chain of forts across the country will cut it in two."

"And do you think they're going to give up those plans and go back to Canada because you order it?"

"Mr. Gist," said Washington quietly, "aren't you forgetting that my rank is that of Major? A Major takes orders, too. Were I the Governor, and knew what you have just made so clear, rather than go one step farther I'd return and try to recruit an army to fortify and hold this spot. But I am not the Governor; I am a young officer on my first mission of importance. Shall we be on our way, Mr. Gist?"

A slow, satisfied smile spread across the frontiersman's face as he rose and scuffed out the map. To outward appearances he again became the matter-of-fact guide.

"From here we go to the Indian villages at Logstown to see Tanacharison, the Half-King. He has already warned the French to come no deeper into Indian country, and has promised to fight them if they do come. He'll give us guides to the French forts, and possibly come along himself."

LEGARDEUR DE SAINT-PIERRE, commandant at Fort Le Boeuf, was sitting down at supper with his staff. The cold December wind, screeching out of the north across Lake Erie, down into the forests about French Creek, whistled through the cracks of the blockhouses, reddened the faces of the sentry detail, and chilled the unheated barracks of the soldiers. But a great fire roared in the fireplace of the commandant's dining room, and its companionable glow was reflected in the faces of the men about the table. Saint-Pierre sat at the head, flanked by his staff officers in order of rank.

The table itself was fashioned of the materials to be found in the forest. But it was covered with a fine damask cloth, and carved silver candelabra held real wax tapers. A haunch of roasted venison and one of black bear occupied silver platters. A heaping mountain of roasted grouse was on another platter, and there were steaming dishes of Indian corn and pumpkin. Bottles and decanters of wines and brandies represented France's finest cellars.

Saint-Pierre raised his glass. "Gentlemen, to the English! May they continue to slumber and bicker, until we have secured New France from Montreal to New Orleans!"

"To the English!" came the chorus. "The bovine English, who've eaten so much beef they've got it between the ears!"

They drank, and fell to the feast, while serving orderlies moved unobtrusively about.

"I cannot but admit that I am disappointed," said a rapier-slim captain of infantry, as he helped himself to a great slice of venison and two grouse. "I had hoped we'd have at least one good battle with the English before winter set in."

"Listen to Croecoeur," a major jibed. "Have you forgotten so soon last summer's trip to the Wyandotte village? Who was it climbed a tree, and ripped the seat out of his best military breeches, when the Wyandottes' dogs came barking at us?"

A laugh went around the table, and for a few moments all devoted themselves to eating. Then a young lieutenant at the end of the table, a newcomer to the Canadian service, cleared his throat.

"If I may speak, sirs," he said, "I think it reflects a great deal of credit upon the military men who planned this venture, when their accomplishments are considered. To move fifteen hundred men across Lake Erie, build two forts and begin a third, and cut a road twenty miles through the forests, is, to me, a miraculous achievement."

"You are right, Lieutenant Manot," Captain Croe- coeur agreed. "Much has been accomplished in one short season, even though the fortified trading post at Venango can scarcely be called a fort. And we cannot regard our achievements as being exclusively confined to building forts. The Miamis and the Wyandottes have been definitely weaned away from the English, and both tribes are good fighters."

"Even the Iroquois and Shawnees are beginning to see that the English cannot prevail against us," Major du Chesne pointed out. "Wait until our two hundred canoes arrive at the junction of the Alle- gheny and Monongahela rivers next spring. Do you not think, Colonel Guideau, that such a fleet will im- press every tribe on the upper Ohio?"

"I think that you underestimate the English," the scholarly looking Colonel said quietly. "Very much has been done, but it is merely a start. And you gentle- men seem to forget that, owing to scurvy and fever, we have only a fifth of our original complement on this side of the lake. Should the English attack in force, we will almost certainly be badly defeated."

"Will you tell me, sir," Saint-Pierre inquired, "how the English can attack at this juncture? France and England are at peace. Furthermore, winter is our ally. Their last outpost of any strength is at Wills Creek. How, think you, can they send a sizeable force four hundred miles through winter-bound woods?"

"I did not say that they would," Colonel Guideau pointed out. "But I still think that the English will fight for the Ohio country."

There was a knock at the door, and one of the orderlies moved to open it. A red-faced lieutenant, bulky in his greatcoat, entered and saluted.

"Lieutenant De Pere reporting, sir. I was detailed by Captain Joncaire, senior officer at Fort Venango, to escort a party of seven Englishmen and four savages to you."

"Who are they, Lieutenant?" demanded the commandant.

"Two gentlemen, a Major George Washington, of Virginia, and a Monsieur Christopher Gist. There is an interpreter, Jacob Vanbraam, and four woodsmen. Of the savages, one is the Half-King."

"The Half-King! What's the matter with you fellows at Venango? Couldn't you detain him there, and win him over to our side?"

"We tried, sir. But the Half-King refused to accept our gifts."

"Show the gentlemen, their interpreter, and the Half-King in, Lieutenant," Saint-Pierre said quickly. "Lieutenant Manot, will you ask the Sergeant of the Guard to see that the beasts are cared for, and that the servants get the best possible food and quarters? Make the savages with the Half-King your own special charges, and spare no effort to please and impress them."

"Yes, sir."

Major Washington, Christopher Gist, Jacob Vanbraam, and the Half-King entered the room. The assembled officers rose and bowed.

"Welcome, gentlemen, welcome!" cried Saint-Pierre. "You must be cold, hungry, and tired. So shall we, for the time being, forget the business that brought you here? Come, refresh yourselves!"

TO CHRISTOPHER GIST, walking with Washington around the parade ground at Fort Le Boeuf, had come a great confidence. On the long, thirty-four day journey up here he had come to feel a warm regard for the young Virginian, and that had ripened into the deepest friendship. The young officer was only twenty-one years old, but within him was a perception and a maturity of judgment that would befit a man twice his age. Also, he had a quality that Gist found it hard to define. It was not something that appeared on the surface, or was evident at first sight, but a deep-hidden intensity that at times seemed to glow like a light. George Washington had met the polished, urbane Saint-Pierre with equal suavity— and firmness. He had presented Dinwiddie's letter without being either tricked or forced into revealing anything that he did not want to reveal.

Captain Croecoeur passed them, and saluted.

"I wonder if the French really think that we're walking out here for exercise alone?" Gist observed with a smile.

"It is very doubtful, Mr. Gist," Washington smiled back. "They are no fools. Evidently they think we'd never be able to send an army this far, and they don't care whether or not we see the fort. Are you carrying a good image of it in your mind?"

"I could map every log, every cannon, and every loophole."

"Excellent! The map we shall make may be very helpful some day."

"You are, then, agreed that——"

"Answer that with your own good opinion, Mr. Gist. But you know the answer. You knew it before I saw this country. And I might say that I have concurred with every one of your ideas. More than that, I have been much influenced by your judgment. You have been a most valuable guide in every sense of the word."

"Thank you, Major. When is Saint-Pierre going to give his answer?"

"He has promised it as soon as he has deliberated sufficiently. But there can be only one answer. Saint-Pierre is a soldier who was ordered to erect this fort and then hold it. As a soldier he must continue to do so until he receives contrary orders."

"Then this delay is for only one purpose. Saint-Pierre wants time to lure the Half-King over to the French!"

"I have protested his attempt to do so," George Washington said angrily, "and I was received with the customary evasion."

The older man stopped and laid his hand on his companion's arm. "Give Saint-Pierre the delay he wants, Major. The Half-King has always been loyal to the English. The time may come when we shall have to stake everything on that loyalty. If the French can win him away, now is the time to find it out."

Washington considered. "I think you are right, as usual, and I bow to your knowledge of the Indians. Very well, we shall wait and see how the wind blows."

Gist looked out toward the forest, through the swirling snowflakes. "A lot of wind is going to blow, too. The snow will be deep by the time Saint-Pierre gets through deliberating. What would you think of sending the woodsmen back to Venango with the horses?"

"An excellent suggestion. They will be rested when we arrive, and we can set out on our return journey at once."

Jacob Vanbraam approached, and said that Saint-Pierre wished to see them. Evidently he had his answer ready. The three Englishmen entered the commandant's quarters, took seats, and waited expectantly. Saint-Pierre cleared his throat and spoke slowly, giving Vanbraam time to translate at the end of each sentence.

"Gentlemen, to review the contents of the letter from your Governor Dinwiddie: he asserts that the lands of the Ohio belong to the crown of Great Britain, he expresses surprise that the French have trespassed, demands to know by whose authority an armed force has crossed the lakes, and urges a speedy and peaceful departure. I deeply appreciate that he has sent a diplomatic mission instead of force, but I regret that his mission was not sent directly to the Marquis Duquesne, the Governor of Canada. Your letter will have to be forwarded to him for consideration. I have consulted with the commandant at Presqu'Isle, and he agrees with me that we cannot comply with the summons to withdraw, without authorization from the Marquis."

As Vanbraam finished translating, George Washington bowed gravely. "Tell him," he instructed the interpreter, "that I will so inform Governor Dinwiddie. We appreciate his courtesy, and now, with his permission, we shall start our return journey."

"There is no need for haste," Saint-Pierre smiled. "Remain as my guests for a few days more. I shall be happy to furnish you with canoes for the trip to Venango."

"You are very kind. In that case, we shall send our horses on ahead, and accept your most hospitable offer."

On the morning of the third day, the Half-King stalked into their quarters and contemptuously threw a string of wampum on the floor.

"Twice I offered it back to the Frenchmen to show that I wished no friendship with them," he said darkly. "And twice they refused it, offering to send presents and trade to our villages." He ground the wampum belt into bits with the heel of his moccasin. "The canoes are ready. Brothers, let us go."

SIX DAYS LATER, after following the hundred and thirty winding miles of French Creek, they arrived at Venango. By Saint-Pierre's order, the canoes had been stocked with the finest foods and liquors Fort Le Boeuf could provide. But winter had descended with snarling force. Snow lay deep in the forest, and a dozen times, while coming down the creek, those in the canoes had been forced to get out and wade through icy shallows. There had been one exhausting portage, where the ice was too thick to break, and when they disembarked at Venango Christopher Gist looked with concern at Washington's drawn, weary face.

"Perhaps," he suggested, "we should rest for a few days here at Venango. Captain Joncaire will afford quarters for us. The least you can say about the French is that they're courteous."

George Washington shook his head. "No. Saint-Pierre's answer must be in Governor Dinwiddie's hands at the earliest possible moment."

The Half-King and his warriors stepped out of their canoe, caught up their packs, and waded ashore. The Half-King turned, raised his hand in salute, and without looking back, he and his little band marched silently into the forest. That part of their mission, at least, had been successful.

Barney Curran came running to the landing. "Wallopin' leprechauns!" he exclaimed. "You finally got here! We was jest about to come up and shoot the pants off them Frenchies so's we could git you out."

"How are the horses, Barney?" Gist asked.

The hunter shook his head. "Poorly, Christopher, poorly. Only a couple of 'em kin carry a man, and most kin carry only half packs."

Curran was right. They were scarcely out of sight of Venango when the horses began to falter in the deep snow. For three days they fought their way southward, battling the drifts that blocked their path, and, at night, huddling close to the fires for the warmth they offered. Small creeks were frozen hard, and tortured trees snapped and crackled under the intense cold that crept into their seams. Almost by the hour, the horses, which found little forage, grew more feeble.

On the evening of the third day George Washington sat for a long time staring into the fire. He looked up.

"Mr. Gist, I must have a swifter mode of travel."

"There is none."

"But there is. Suppose we leave Mr. Vanbraam and the woodsmen in charge of the horses, with instructions to come on as best they can. You and I will carry packs and proceed on foot."

"You are not used to foot travel in the wilderness, Major," Gist said bluntly. "It is both difficult and dangerous in the winter."

Washington spoke with quiet authority. "Mr. Gist, you realize as well as I the importance of the Ohio country. You know the necessity of moving quickly. I propose to put the knowledge I have in Governor Dinwiddie's hands as soon as may be. A week, even a day, might make a great difference."

Gist reluctantly consented, and they started at dawn the next morning, each carrying a small pack in which was necessary food and important papers, and their rifles. They swung away from the Indian trace they had been following, cutting through the woods toward the Allegheny. Although the frontiersmen purposely shortened his customary, mile-eating stride, they made eighteen miles before dusk forced them to camp in the lee of a little grove of trees. After they had eaten, George Washington sought his blankets and immediately sank into deep sleep. Before stretching himself out by the fire, Gist sat staring moodily at the drawn face of the sleeping man. He shook his head uneasily. . . .

The next morning they went on, breaking through the snowdrifts that opposed them, and moving steadily toward the Allegheny. They had reached Beaver Creek, near the Indian summer settlement of Murdering Town, and were breaking through the ice for drinking water, when Gist suddenly snatched up his rifle. An Indian was approaching.

In the deep recesses of the frontiersman's brain half-forgotten memories began to awaken. It paid to remember faces; where had he seen this one before? Logstown? Fort Venango? He shook his head irritably. He couldn't remember.

"Why are you on foot?" the Indian asked in the Algonquin tongue.

"We choose to travel that way," Gist said shortly.

"But you had horses?"

"We had them." So the Indian knew the party had split, did he? That probably meant he was one of the French Delawares from Venango.

"When will they arrive here?"

"Soon," Gist evaded. "They are following us."

"Ask him," the impatient Washington interrupted, "if he knows the nearest way to the forks of the Ohio."

The frontiersman put the question, and the Indian replied, "Yes, I know an easy way. I will show you." He nodded his head at Washington. "That man is very tired. I will take his pack."

They started out, under a lowering, leaden sky and interminable flurries of snow. Although relieved of his pack, Washington was plodding now, shuffling his military boots wearily forward through the snow. His foot came down on a snow-hidden log, and he winced sharply. The Indian turned to Gist.

"He is very tired," he said. "Let me carry his gun, too."

"We'll carry our own guns," Gist said sharply. "But we'll camp soon."

The Indian shook his head. "There are Ottawas in these woods. They will kill you. I have a cabin only a little way farther. It is safe there."

Gist nodded, and squinted at the sky. There was nothing to give a sense of direction, but his woodsman's intuition told him something was wrong. He dropped back, surreptitiously slipped from his pocket the surveyor's compass that he always carried, and took a bearing. He looked to the priming of his rifle, and shifted it from his left hand to his right.

"We will camp at the next water, if we do not reach your cabin by then." As he spoke, he quickened his pace.

They came to a natural open meadow, and the Indian suddenly whirled about. Gist snapped his rifle up, and pulled back the hammer with his thumb. He saw the Indian start, shoot wildly toward them, then dodge behind a huge oak. Gist ran forward, raising his cocked rifle. As he passed Washington, the young Virginian touched his arm.

"No."

"He tried to kill us, Major."

"We cannot afford to antagonize any Indians. Do not shoot, Mr. Gist. It is an order."

The frontiersman reluctantly lowered his rifle, and did some quick thinking. Then he called to the Indian, still hidden behind the tree.

"Did you shoot to let the people in your cabin know you were coming?"

"Yes," said the Indian sullenly, cautiously coming into sight.

"My friend is too tired to go there tonight. You leave his pack here and go on. In the morning, when we have rested, we will follow your tracks to your cabin."

The mystified Indian lost no time in disappearing into the gathering dusk. Telling his companion to rest there, the frontiersman silently followed their treacherous guide, calling into play all the Indian lore that years spent among them had taught. When he was satisfied that the Indian had really gone, Gist returned to the exhausted young man who sat with his back to the great oak.

"I was suspicious when I found he was taking us too much north and east," the woodsman said grimly. "And I think that Saint-Pierre or Joncaire, who don't like to have us know too much about their forts, could explain why he tried to kill us. I'm sorry, Major Washington, but we'll have to travel all night. Those Delawares will be on our track as soon as they can see it. If you're able to travel we should reach the Allegheny before they can catch us, and cross it on the ice. I doubt if they will pursue us farther."

"I can travel," said Washington gamely. "Lead on, Mr. Gist."

In the morning they were at the head of Piney Creek, down whose frozen length they travelled all day, without one word of complaint from the indomitable Washington. But at dusk the next night, when they finally reached the Allegheny, they looked out to see ice formed for only a few feet along either bank, and a ragged mass of great ice cakes floating down the swift center.

BUCKSKIN BRIGADE

THE NIGHT SHADOWS LENGTHENED, crawling one into the other like sinuously undulating scraps of gauze which had neither a beginning nor an end. Christopher Gist sat on the banks of the Allegheny, staring across the black river and hearing the mighty cakes of ice grind their cold teeth. But his ears were attuned to anything that might come out of the darkness. His rifle, knife, and tomahawk were ready. Near him, stretched on the bank and covered with all the blankets, George Washington slept the sleep of utter exhaustion. Back in the forest a feeding deer rustled the brush; the watcher relaxed a little. There was good forage for deer in there, and this one would feed for some time. If an enemy approached, the deer would run and he'd hear it.

A melancholy rain, that changed to a harsh mixture of sleet and snow, rattled through the trees. Christopher Gist shivered, and huddled a little nearer the small fire they had built in the lee of the bank. The endless night crawled on, until at last the first streak of mournful gray showed very faintly in the storm-ridden sky, and George Washington sat up.

"You have stood sentry duty all night!" he exclaimed indignantly. "Why didn't you waken me?"

"Because we'll need you rested." The woodsman yawned and stretched. "Well, are you ready?"

"By all means. What do we do?"

"Make a raft, and try a crossing on it."

THE OPENING GATE

After a quick breakfast of cold hoecake and cured venison, they fell to work with Gist's tomahawk, cutting dead trees into ten-foot lengths. Lacking an axe, it was slow, wearing work, and it made more noise than Gist liked. Fortunately, it had snowed all the previous day, and he was sure that the Delawares had lost their trail. But there might be other Indians about. Noon came and went. At last they had a dozen lengths, and while Washington dragged them down to the river's edge, Gist walked up the creek bank, and searched the trees on either side. When he saw the vine he wanted, he cut it down with his knife and worked it through his hands until it was pliable. Returning to the logs, he bound them firmly to the cross pieces of the raft. It was late afternoon before the craft was ready for launching.

They cut two ten-foot setting poles, and stood for a moment watching the ice cakes move downstream —white, tumbling blocks in the black water. Then, without looking again at the river, Gist put the end of his setting pole under the raft and used it as a lever. The bindings on the raft strained, and one piece in the center buckled. It settled back again. Washington, beside him, slid his setting pole in, and between them they moved the raft out to the very edge of the formed ice, where it tilted precariously.

Thrusting their rifles under the lashings, Gist walked to the edge of the ice, mounted the raft, and with a heave of his pole pushed it into the river. Quickly sliding his pole over the raft to the bottom of the river, he held the clumsy craft in place while Washington stepped on the back end. They started across.

A cake of ice heaved itself like a seal over a corner of the raft and was gone again. The current gnashed white teeth at them, and a little cascade of water surged around their feet. But they were almost halfway across, approaching a small, treeless island that from shore had appeared to be a large ice floe. Then, upriver, a great mass of ice blocks separated and swept down on them. They both strove frantically to steady the raft with their setting poles. But the ice heaved all about them now, gnawing at the logs and ripping the bark away. Out of the corner of his eye,

Gist saw the younger man's pole, caught in the ice's inexorable jaws, snap straight up. There was a lurch to the raft, a splash, and Washington was in the river. He disappeared from sight.

But almost instantly he was up again, gasping with cold, clinging desperately with all his strength to the raft. The next cake would crush him. Gist clambered frantically over the ice that had slid up on the raft, reached down, and pulled him aboard. But the raft was dangerously tilted now, with ice below and under it. Footing was precarious, and any sudden movement would throw them both into the water.

For a moment, clear black water showed between them and the island. Gist's decision was instantaneous. With one arm around Washington's shoulders, he slid from the end of the raft into four feet of ice water, and began to push his numb companion toward the island. The water shoaled beneath their feet, and they climbed up on the barren, treeless island. Washington slumped forward, then caught himself and struggled to his feet.

"Keep moving," Gist said sharply. "Stamp your feet. Run around. Keep warm."

"I am warm," Washington mumbled drowsily. "Only tired."

"Listen to me!" Gist said harshly. "Keep moving, or you'll freeze to death. Keep moving, I say!"

"I'll try," said a voice that seemed to come from

very far off, from some warm haven that only the speaker knew. "I'll try."

With his own numb hands, Gist beat Washington's already freezing clothing. He pounded the young man's chest, his back, his arms—and kept him walking. His own hands, striking the icy clothing, soon lost all feeling, and he knew his fingers were frozen. But within him rose a fear that dwarfed frozen fingers. Providing they survived the night, could they reach the other side of the river when morning came? To try to swim was death. But, if no other avenue of escape opened, they must try to swim. As if to mock him, the ice cakes, on their way downstream, gritted their frigid, monotonous tune as they scraped past the island.

All night they walked, with only short periods of rest. And to keep them both awake, Christopher Gist talked as he had never talked before. As they kept their lonely vigil with the cold, the hardy frontiersman told of his early years in Virginia and Maryland, of his life on Wills Creek, of his wilderness cabin on Chestnut Ridge, of experiences with the Indians— how they lived and hunted and fought. He described his trip down the Ohio to the mouth of the Scioto, his visit to Pickawillany on the upper waters of the Miami, his return through Kaintuck, over the mountains to the Kanawha, and hence to Roanoke with his report.

"You should know this Ohio country, Major," he said insistently. "There has never been a fairer land. When I was there I saw the marvels it contains. Would you believe that there are innumerable natural open meadows where the settler need not even clear the land for farming? It is rich and level, well-watered with small streams and well-timbered with walnut, ash, and sugar trees. In the meadows, wild rye, blue grass, and clover. There are turkeys, deer, elk in profusion, and I have even seen the great, shaggy oxen they call buffalo, thirty or forty in a single herd."

He felt the young man beside him stir, as though magic new life had been injected into him.

"Tell me more," he said weakly.

"I shall need the night just to begin. To know what manner of beasts, or men, inhabited that land before the Indians were there opens a whole mysterious realm. There are salt licks where prehistoric beasts have died. I found rib bones eleven feet long, skulls six feet wide. One tooth, which I brought back with me, weighed four pounds.

"And the wild pigeons are there in such numbers," he continued, "that their flights darken the sky . . ."

Christopher Gist was no longer marooned on an island in the Allegheny River. He had gone back into the Ohio country with George Washington, a young man whose eager intelligence and sharp mind had to drink in every drop of knowledge. He was showing this tidewater Virginian the buffalo and elk that roamed the Kentucky meadows, the lumbering bears that prowled through the endless forests.

"There is ample room there for thousands, yes, for hundreds of thousands of people. There they may live in peace, without crowding, and enjoy plenty such as people have never before known on the face of this earth."

A sharp little blast of wind cut across the river, and the walkers turned their heads in surprise. It did not seem that they had walked so very long, or talked so very much. But dawn had come. As they stood, side by side, the east reddened as the sun prepared to shine on the first fair day in many. And at their feet, frozen from bank to bank, lay the dark river, a highway that stretched away to the forks of the Ohio—the Gateway to the West.

WILDERNESS
ROAD

1780   *The British attempt to seize the Forks of the Ohio—known to history as Braddock's defeat—was the beginning of the French and Indian Wars, which resulted in the French hold on North America being forever broken. By the treaty of peace in 1763, England gained possession of Canada, Florida, and all the territory from the Atlantic to the Mississippi. Louisiana went to Spain. New France had ceased to exist.*

But the English did not enjoy this vast colonial empire long. The struggle that began at Lexington and ended at Yorktown created a new owner of the middle kingdom—the United States of America.

Through both wars the original inhabitants—the Indians—waged a bitter, bloody, hopeless struggle to preserve their ancient hunting grounds. In western New York, Pennsylvania, and Virginia, and particularly in Kentucky, they fought their losing fight with a craft, stealth, and cruelty matched only by that of the white settlers who pushed them ever westward. They taught their wilderness skills to the white man, and by so doing hastened their own doom.

CRAWLING CAT stood beside a huge live oak, his long rifle leaning against the tree. The Indian looked down at the quiet stream whose dark waters purled near the base of the great oak, and was satisfied with the warrior's image that stared back at him. Turning his head, he looked toward the village, where thirteen of his finest young braves were whirling in the wild gyrations of the war dance. It was time for him to join them.

There was a shade of melancholy in Crawling Cat's eyes as he watched the scene. Those lithe, hard young men, the proudest warriors left in this Shawnee village, thought war was a game, a delightful adventure wherein one crawled through the forest, made a proper ambush, killed his enemy, and forever afterward basked in endless glory. But the entire war experience of most of those young braves had consisted of an occasional brush with the Iroquois, and they were not going to fight Iroquois on this war path. They would fight warriors whose cunning and courage were fully a match for the Shawnees' own, and whose equipment was far better. Some of those bold dancers would never see their village again. Still, war was a warrior's business. When the time came that a brave must be struck down, it was well to be conquered by a worthy foe.

There was a light tread beside him, and Crawling Cat turned to face the slender young woman who

1 6 3

had approached from the village. Her raven-black hair was bound with a leather thong, her soft doeskin clothing fell gracefully about her. Crawling Cat turned away, a frown on his face.

"Why does a woman bother a warrior on the hour of his departure for battle?" he demanded.

The creek's black water dimpled as a fish rose from the depths to pluck a floating fly from the surface. The widening circle of ripples crawled across to the opposite shore. The young woman, Crawling Cat's wife of one year, slipped her arm through his and laid her small face against his shoulder.

"I do not wish you to go," she whispered.

"I am a warrior, a chief of warriors."

"You are also a husband and a father," she answered softly.

Crawling Cat glanced toward the dancers and the villagers watching them. All were absorbed in the dance. He turned to face his wife, looking silently into the dark, worried eyes.

"That is why I am going," he said at length.

She seized eagerly on the opening he had left. "You do not have to go. You could go with me to the west, my husband. We may return, with our son, to that village from which you brought me here."

Crawling Cat thrust her from him, ashamed of his moment of weakness.

"Yes," he said scornfully. "We could go. But this is

the country of the Shawnees. The Shawnees will defend it."

"My father, the Chief, would welcome us," she pleaded desperately.

"Your father, the Chief, would also know that Crawling Cat is a coward, who dared not join Blackfish and help drive the white men out of Kentucky."

"Is not our country big enough for both white man and Indian?"

"No," he said bluntly. "You are a woman; these things are not for you. But since I may not come back, I will tell you. Twenty-five years ago, when I was a boy of ten, the first white men came to Kentucky. My father, who had gone there on a hunting party, met them. They were harmless. Then came other white men, until finally hunters led by the one they call Boone brought their horses to Kentucky, and killed more deer in one season than this village would use in ten. Now they have built their forts. Soon they will be so strong that they will drive us out."

"Are these white men good warriors?"

"The best. They have fine rifles and much powder, and they laugh when they fight. But the white men now fight with their brothers across the sea, and it is a good time to drive them out."

"Must you take all our young men to fight, also?"

"I have accepted the war belt from Blackfish. Would you have a chief not keep his promise?"

"No," she said dully. "Go, Crawling Cat! And you shall not have the memory of a woman's tears to weaken you in battle. Go, warrior! Fight for your wife and son!"

She turned, hiding her face, and ran from him. For a moment Crawling Cat looked after her. Then he picked up his gun, strode over to the wildly leaping dancers, and joined the circle. The sure, solid rhythm of the war drums fired his martial spirit.

Twenty minutes later, as though by a prearranged signal, the fourteen warriors seized their weapons and disappeared into the dark, brooding forest.

THERE WAS A PATH, a beaten, well-marked path floored with brown earth and strangely out of place among the nodding trees and thick brush that lined it on either side. Yet the path was older than most of the trees that hemmed it in. For a thousand years before the *Pinta,* the *Nina,* and the *Santa Maria* had ever set sail from Spain, warriors who pitched their lodges or built their bark huts beside the Ohio had trod down it to hunt in the fabled land of Kentucky. It was the tribal wonderland, an age-old hunting paradise, with so much history that the mind of one man, or one generation, could not begin to know all the things that had taken place in it. Now, though nominally controlled by the Iroquois, it was a great larder for all the tribes who lived on or near its borders. Settled by no Indians, it was used by all who came along its ancient paths to replenish their food stocks from the countless buffalo, deer, bear, and elk that roamed its forest glades.

Crawling Cat led his warriors single file down the path, while he listened to and interpreted the voices of the forest. That blasting whistle was the snort of a white-tailed buck, disturbed at its browsing and resentful of those who had broken its peace. The shrieking in the trees ahead was a flock of parakeets, crying their jealousy of each other while they fed on wild grapes that had crawled up the highest trees to find a place in the sun. That sudden alarmed chatter was a squirrel which, surprised at its daily affairs, scampered to safety and spat invective at those who dared disturb it.

Crawling Cat recognized all, but stopped to investigate none. This was a war party, not a hunting trip, and only a portion of dried corn filled the pouch slung at each warrior's side. Corn was not as succulent as the meat of any of the animals sheltered by this great forest through which they travelled, but warriors going out to fight must travel light. There was strength in dried corn, and endurance. Corn gave to those who ate it part of the hot sun and rich earth from which its own nourishment was drawn. It had within it cooling rain, and soft, heavy dew. No man who carried corn needed to stop and hunt.

That was well, for to the north and to the south, on every little faintly marked path that fed this winding warrior's trace, more braves were on the march. Blackfish, the great chief of the Shawnees, had sent his bloody wampum belt to every village. All knew what it meant. Where the warrior's trace led past the great sycamore, so old and gnarled that it was venerated by all passing Indians, there was a natural clearing in the woods. Blackfish would be waiting there with his private council, and there the warriors who had run down their narrow, gloomy little paths would assemble in a mighty show of strength.

The little party led by Crawling Cat travelled far into the night, and only the eerie crying of the screech owls in the branches overhead could be heard when they finally turned aside to hide themselves in the forest and sleep. For a long while Crawling Cat re-

mained awake, listening to the screech owls' senseless clamor, and thinking about the wife and son he
had left back on the Ohio. Now he was possessed by
a great hatred, a mighty yearning to come to grips
with the white men who would take the Indians'
hunting grounds. Dawn had not yet spread its pale
fingers across the sky when he roused his band and
went on. The third day after leaving the Ohio they
came to the great assembly of Shawnees.

The clearing, one of those natural open spaces
which exist in the thickest of forests, was two hundred
and twenty steps beyond the old sycamore. Crawling
Cat hesitated, taking a step, a half step, as he approached. The thirteen warriors who followed imitated him, perfect images of the leader who must go
first and encounter any danger that might present
itself. Crawling Cat stopped, peering through the sun
streaks that stole down through the leaves. Then, un-
hesitatingly, he went forward.

He saw the warriors arrayed before him, and a
proud light shone in his eyes. Usually, when either
hunting or war parties went down into Kentucky,
there were not more than a dozen men at the most.
Here there were almost two hundred. They lined
both sides and the center of the clearing, lurked in
the forest, sat wherever there was room. Perhaps half
of them had guns. The rest were armed with bows
and arrows. All carried tomahawks and knives, and

every one of the warriors was a man in the physical prime of life.

Crawling Cat's little band dispersed among the braves already there, while their chief stalked regally forward to meet the man who sat in a leafy bower at the head of the clearing. His mantle was the finest of doeskin. A spotless rifle leaned beside him, powder horn and bullet pouch dangled from his belt. The knife and tomahawk he bore were of iron, the equal of the finest boasted by any white man. Deep, intelligent eyes glowed fiercely in the dark face beneath the scalp lock. There were bitter lines around his mouth, and hatred in the grim set of his jaw.

Crawling Cat faced him eye to eye, as befitted a proven chief.

"We have come, Blackfish," he announced.

"I see you, Crawling Cat. What strength have you brought from your village?"

"Fourteen braves, including myself."

"It is well." Blackfish nodded his satisfaction. He swept his hand around the clearing. "You know why we have gathered?"

"I know."

Blackfish turned toward the forest, as though the wind-rustled leaves could tell him something that he did not know. But he was the leader, the chief of all the Shawnees, and it was up to him to carry out the plans that had been made in council.

"Tonight, when the moon is high," he said, "depart with those warriors who came with you. We go from here in small parties, to burn scattered cabins and kill all those who dwell in them. In six days we meet at the fort the white men call Boonesborough. We shall burn the fort and kill all its defenders—all!"

FAR OFF IN THE NIGHT WOODS a wolf howled. Another answered it, and the fear-maddened stag, on whose hot trail the wolves were closing, plunged through the moon-sprayed Kentucky forest. Crawling Cat, swinging down the warrior's trace with his thirteen men, gave himself over to thinking about the chase.

The wolves were not howling now. They were racing through the forest side by side, while the reeking scent of the buck they pursued floated up from the earth to tantalize their nostrils. The stag would make a mighty leap from some little hillock. Scarcely breaking stride, the wolves would gather themselves and leap after him. Then would come the final wild, fierce struggle in the night. The stag would turn, try desperately to defend himself with sweeps and thrusts of his craggy antlers, and strike with his front hooves. The wolves would dart and slash, panting in their eagerness to bring down the exhausted quarry. Finally they would do it.

Crawling Cat tore his thoughts away from the wolf chase and forced them back to the business at hand. It was a simple business. There were no complex problems to be solved; Blackfish himself had said that. They would all meet at the gates of Boonesborough, and reduce that white man's settlement to ashes. The white men themselves would burn in the flames that consumed their fortress. Then, after Harrodsburg and Saint Asaph had also been burned and their defenders killed, the Shawnees could go home to live in peace again. That was the way Blackfish had planned it.

As he walked through the night, he became lost in admiration for the plan the chief of the Shawnees had conceived. A lesser chief would have kept all the warriors together, and if they were attacked they would all be surprised. But Blackfish had broken his band into small groups. If the leading party should be attacked, those coming behind could always surprise the attackers. More reinforcements would be steadily arriving. Also, small, scattered war parties could destroy more isolated cabins than one large one.

Dawn was already in the sky when Crawling Cat led his warriors off the trace they had followed, and into the woods. Now he was possessed by a great eagerness to push on faster. He knew this country, through which he had often hunted, as well as he did the beaten earth before the door of his own lodge.

Just ahead should be a small creek whose snake-like course wound southeast. By following that, and then heading east where it made a sharp U bend, they should come out almost at the very doors of Boonesborough. Furthermore, they would be the first ones there. It would not, of course, be wise for fourteen men to attack the fort, nor even give away the presence of such a large war party. They would lie in the trees and brush, and ambush anyone who came out. To them, and their village, would go the honor of first blood. They slept, ate of their parched corn, and started down the winding creek. Forty-eight hours later they broke over a ridge and saw the cabin.

IT WAS A SMALL CABIN, made of the usual logs chinked with clay, and it was built almost in the center of a ragged clearing from which the owner had laboriously removed the trees. The remains of their trunks and branches lay, a heap of blackened ashes, on one side of the clearing. A black cow with a white face was tied to one of the stumps that rose like broken hafts of lances. Crawling Cat nodded to two of his warriors, who slipped away from the band. They wriggled like snakes through the forest, slipping from tree to tree and working their way around the clearing toward the cow. Five minutes later, as though she had been struck by some invisible force, the cow's legs buckled and she went down in a twitching heap. Crawling Cat nodded in satisfaction. He himself, watching closely, had barely seen a warrior rise and swing his tomahawk.

Exactly at that second the sharp crack of a long rifle blasted the stillness in the clearing, and almost at once another followed it. One of the warriors by the cow leaped crazily into the air, and came down to roll spasmodically about. The other took a few staggering steps toward the forest, then collapsed in an inert heap.

Crawling Cat turned his eyes toward the cabin, hatred for all white men plain in his face. His tongue licked out over dry lips, and his hard black eyes took flame from that hatred. At the same time, he did nothing rash, for he recognized a well-planned and finely executed maneuver. The white men in the cabin should not have known that enemies were about. They had known it, and had held their fire until they were sure of killing. They would be difficult to deal with.

But they could be dealt with. There were twelve warriors and two, or at the most, three white men. The odds were all against the cabin's defenders, although the Indians had only five guns among them. They would soon have more.

Crawling Cat spoke softly over his shoulder, and four of the warriors slipped back down the ridge.

They would go around to the trees at the rear of the cabin, and cut off retreat. Then, if the white men could not safely be approached and killed by day, they might easily be had under the protecting cloak of night. The warrior lying beside Crawling Cat grunted and raised his gun. He was too late.

A white man, a lanky, bearded white man carrying a long rifle and wearing buckskin clothing, had dashed out of the cabin door and run around to the rear. The warrior beside Crawling Cat grunted again, and raised his head out of the grass, waiting for the man to reappear. From the cabin door another rifle cracked, and the bullet plowed a bloody furrow along the warrior's head. He clapped his hand to his temple, and dropped back into the grass.

Crawling Cat gritted his teeth, but kept his eyes on the cabin door. At least one white man remained within, and one had gone out. They must join each other if they were going to make any effective defense. Crawling Cat trained his rifle on the door, and when he pulled the trigger a moment later he saw the white man who had run almost straight into his line of fire flinch and stagger. But he kept running, while two badly aimed arrows from other warriors thudded into the wall beside him. The white man disappeared behind the cabin.

Crawling Cat waited, watching to see if any more riflemen should appear, while shame enveloped him in a surging flood. Thirteen warriors, led by himself, had attacked two lone white men. Two of his young braves lay dead and a third was wounded. The best they'd been able to do was wound one of the cabin's defenders. That insult must be wiped out.

The white men could not stay in the clearing or behind the cabin, for they now knew that there were enough Indians to encircle it. They must run into the forest, and forest fighting was made for the Shawnees.

Retreating below the rim of the hill, Crawling Cat ran halfway around the clearing. He looked behind him, and nodded in satisfaction when he saw that three of his warriors had followed. That was right. Four here, three back where he had left them, and four who should by now be in the rear of the clearing. They would know what to do.

From far off in the forest, behind the clearing, came a quick shot and a high-pitched scream. Crawling Cat started toward the noise, slipping from tree trunk to tree trunk and travelling as softly as the shadows that flitted beside him. He came to the place where the trees grew sparsely, and squatted down to watch.

Just ahead, a huge tree trunk sheltered one of his own warriors. The man was carefully poised, all his eager attention straining toward a bit of brush and something he saw there. Crawling Cat followed his eyes, and saw the brown shape that belonged to no animal or bird. It was only a small patch, perhaps two inches square, but it certainly belonged to one of the two white men. He had thought to hide there. The warrior behind the tree trunk drew his knife, and hurled it straight to the mark. Just then, from a wholly different quarter of the forest, a rifle cracked like a whiplash and the warrior slumped to the ground. Still looking at the brush, Crawling Cat saw the piece of leather hunting shirt fall away. The white man had placed it there as a decoy, to make one of the Shawnees betray himself. And he had done so.

Crawling Cat had definitely located the source of the shot now, and he wriggled toward it, his eyes glittering. An inch at a time, he slunk around the trees and through the brush that hemmed them in. He was Crawling Cat, the warrior who could approach and kill an enemy before that enemy was aware of danger. He saw the white man. Stretched out full length behind a log, he was reloading his rifle. Sticky wet blood made a great stain on the back of his shirt. Three times he tried to ram home the patch on top of his bullet, and three times the ramrod fell from his trembling hand. Crawling Cat levelled his rifle and pressed the trigger. There was a hollow click. The gun had missed fire.

The white man heard it, and turned on his side, trying once more to ram the patch down his gun. Failing, he cast the useless weapon from him and fought to stand. He clawed against the log, drew himself over to a sapling, and pulled himself erect. Snarling laughter came from his drawn lips as he drew a knife and awaited the Indian's coming. Crawling Cat felt the blade bite deeply into his thigh, as the white man stumbled and fell even as he was struck. Crawling Cat had swung his tomahawk only once.

He stood over the body of his enemy, looking down upon it, then knelt and sliced off the scalp with one deft motion of his knife. A warrior appeared, and another, and another, until eight were beside him. Crawling Cat looked up inquiringly.

"The other has gone," a warrior said. "We cannot find him."

"He fought well," Crawling Cat said savagely. "He fought better than we did. They were two against fourteen. They killed four of us and wounded one. Then, at the last, this wounded man stayed to fight so his companion might escape."

"White men are devils," said a young warrior.

Crawling Cat did not answer. Silently he picked up the white man's rifle and led his braves toward Boonesborough.

THE GREAT, CRAGGY-HORNED BUCK that stood beside the warrior's trace and pulled at the tender branches of a maple sapling could understand only the forest things about him. Nothing could tell

178

him that white men and red had fought great battles at Boonesborough, at Harrodsburg, and at Saint Asaph, or that, inside their stockades, the white men had beaten back every attack the red ones made. All the buck saw of that mighty test of strength were the five braves who walked back up the warrior's trace.

Crawling Cat, bearing a fresh bullet wound in his shoulder and a scarcely healed knife wound in his thigh, led the way. Behind came two more warriors, and between them they supported a third who could no longer walk by himself. The fifth brave trailed far behind, and sat down to rest frequently.

Crawling Cat remained ahead of his warriors as they came to the Ohio, as they approached the village from which fourteen able-bodied men had departed. The five beaten warriors reached the last little creek between themselves and their clearing, and forded it. Crawling Cat's walk became a little more sprightly. He had left his village as a chief. As a chief who had won honor in battle—the scalp of a white man dangled from his belt—he was coming back. He arranged his weapons as befitted a chief, and gave the cry that announced his return with a scalp. Suddenly the sound was throttled in his throat.

On lazy wings, two sinister black objects were purposefully floating high over the clearing. At the same moment the stench of stale ashes became evident. Crawling Cat held up a warning hand. The two warriors who supported a third took him to the side of the trail, eased him down in a thicket, and themselves sought places of concealment. The one who had lagged behind found a fallen log and sank down on it, grateful for anything that would offer him rest. Crawling Cat went forward alone; if he led no men at all, it was still a chief's business to know what lay ahead.

Cautiously entering the clearing, he looked about. For a moment he turned his eyes away. Then he looked again.

The scorched leaves of the trees around the clearing bore mute testimony to the fire that had raged there. The lodges lay in cold ashes from which all flame had long since departed. Fire had spread through the fields of standing corn, and scorched the pumpkins that had once colored the ground. A black vulture with a naked head and neck sat on a fire-killed tree and surveyed the ruins of which he alone was now monarch. He flapped away on lazy wings when Crawling Cat walked slowly into the clearing. The chief's face was expressionless, but his head drooped.

He jerked himself erect as he saw a woman with a child in her arms timidly emerge from the unburned forest on the other side of the clearing. She came slowly, leaving her moccasin tracks clearly imprinted in the black ruin that had been a thriving village. She stopped before Crawling Cat.

"I am glad that you have returned, my husband. There was no minute you were away that my thoughts were not with you."

Crawling Cat asked stonily, "Who did this?"

"The white men," his wife said. "They came in the early morning, with blazing guns and swinging hatchets. I had risen before dawn, and taken our son to pluck the mushrooms that must be gathered before the sun is upon them. We alone escaped. We waited for you."

Crawling Cat turned his head toward the east, where the undermanned forts of the white men were still standing, after the fiercest attacks of the Shawnees. His wife followed his gaze.

"Do not go back!" she pleaded. "We cannot fight white men! Let us take our son, let us go west, to the village where my father is still chief. He cannot call you coward now."

Crawling Cat's gaze swept around the clearing, lingered on the forest that rolled away over the ancient hunting ground of Kentucky. In his mind's eye he saw its endless acres, broken only by the warrior's trace of the red man and the cabin clearings of the white. He spoke sadly, half to himself, half to the woman who stood there.

"My fathers' fathers lived and hunted in this green land, and it was good to them. But now it is a dark and bloody ground. Yes, we will go to the west."

CAP GITCHIE'S

ROOSTER

1791

There was to be no rest for the Indians. The trickle of pioneers that was crossing the mountains at the beginning of the Revolution reached full flood after peace assured a new nation. From New England settlers poured into the region north of the Ohio and east of the Mississippi—the Northwest Territory. Likewise, the region south of the Ohio rapidly became a promised land for homesteaders. By 1790 Kentucky and Tennessee —not yet states—boasted a hundred thousand new inhabitants.

Their highway was the Ohio River, their trade outlet the Mississippi and its Gulf port of New Orleans. But New Orleans, and all the land west of the Mississippi, was Spanish, and Spain levied a high duty on all goods passing through its great port. But not for long. The traders and keelboatmen who ran the river traffic were a rugged, fiercely independent lot. In loud voices and explosive action they called attention to their plight, and by so doing paved the way for the Louisiana Purchase.

The characters in this story are a fictional synthesis of the breed.

CAP GITCHIE came out of the Kentucky woods three miles ahead of the posse that was chasing him. As he approached the huts, cabins, and houses that sheltered the inhabitants of Louisville, he slowed down to a leisurely walk, and strolled down to take a look at the river. The sun had not yet climbed over the eastern horizon, and a fine mist hovered over the famous falls, where the Ohio River dropped twenty-two feet in two miles. But, at this flood season, no white water boiled and thundered over the cataract. Disappointed, Cap walked down to Bear Grass Creek, where the keel and flatboats were tied. From the bow of the biggest flatboat—fourteen feet wide by fifty long—a black and white dog rose from the coil of rope where it had been sleeping, and growled at him. The dog's ruff bristled, and it began to bark in a loud and irritating voice.

Cap Gitchie drew back his right foot, the one that had kicked many a clamoring dog from his path, and experimentally snapped it forward. A wide grin split his mouth, and raised the ends of his straggling mustache. He had travelled something over a hundred miles in two days, and there had not been much time for sleeping or resting. But there was enough power left in his foot to take care of any flatboat cur. Cap shifted the long rifle, a bare ten inches shorter than his own six feet three, from his right hand to his left. The movement woke up the rooster on his shoulder.

It was a small rooster that could not have weighed more than four or four and a half pounds. But its sweeping length, that started in a slim, snake-like, combless head, and ended in a long, gracefully curved sickle of tail feathers, lent an impression of much greater size. The rooster's legs were long and trim, and his spurs were sharp. But it was his fierce, intelligent eyes that set him apart from the ordinary rooster found prowling about the barns and manure piles of the settlers along the Ohio. They were the eyes of a thoroughbred game cock.

When the rooster came awake it flapped its wings. Standing erect on its owner's shoulder, it sent its challenging crow echoing over the river. From one of the moored flatboats another rooster answered. The red cock preened itself, turning its head from side to side and blinking in the half-light of early morning, while it sought the exact source from which its invitation to battle had been accepted. It clucked throatily, and made ready to crow again. Cap Gitchie reached up with his right hand, and twined his fingers softly about the red rooster's throat.

"Suppose," he suggested, "that you shut up. Ain't you got me in enough trouble already?" And as though suddenly remembering, he glanced back at the dark forest out of which he had come.

It was just about a year and a half ago that he had landed in America, at Baltimore. His arrival had not been wholly orthodox. But, on the other hand, it hadn't been exactly jumping ship, either, because to go back on the *St. John* would only have meant to be clapped in irons while the vessel sailed back to England. Captain Marritt, of the *St. John*, was a hard driver of men. But it had been a mistake when he chose, after the anchorage in Chesapeake Bay, to use his lash on Cap Gitchie. After the fight started, Captain Marritt had even used a belaying pin. But he hadn't used it well enough, and he had been lying on the deck in an undetermined state of disrepair when Cap Gitchie took a hasty departure.

Ashore, Cap had seen the red rooster scratching about a refuse heap on the water front. A man had to eat, and chicken was mighty tasty. Snatching up the rooster, Cap had resumed his journey. Ten miles out of Baltimore, with every intention of wringing its neck, he had taken the red rooster from his shirt and had had his hand soundly pecked. A man just couldn't eat a spunky rooster like that, especially after it climbed to his shoulder and seemed entirely content to ride there. He was in a strange land, where a man needed a good friend, and the rooster had amply proven his friendship in Pittsburgh, where, in less than a minute, he had whipped to a standstill the gray rooster that a Pittsburgh merchant brought against him. So doing, he had also enriched Cap's purse by two pounds five shillings. But, after he had defeated the town's champion, it was impossible to get any more fights in Pittsburgh—for the rooster.

By slow stages, sleeping where night overtook him if he happened to be in wild country, and sleeping between blankets when he came across an inn, Cap and his rooster had fought their way down the Ohio. Two of a kind, they had accepted and defeated all comers. But it was not until they had reached Limestone, a raw Ohio River frontier town, that they had met with real trouble. Cap had wagered all the money he had picked up since Baltimore—twenty-five pounds—that his red rooster was better than Limestone's best blue cock. And it had been.

But how was he, Cap Gitchie, to know that Limestoners were hard losers, or that, without settling their bets, they'd threaten him with a long rifle and order him to leave town? And how was he to know that, after he'd taken the rifle away from the man who held it, and collected his winnings, he'd have to race into the southern forest with a posse of Limestoners on his heels? A man couldn't guess such things in advance. All he could do was run—fast.

The rooster crowed again, flapped his wings, and a second time sent his ringing crow rolling over the assembled keel and flatboats. There was a sudden motion on a keelboat anchored to some willows a bare twenty feet from where Cap was standing. A brisk little man dressed in a suit of almost-white woolen underwear emerged from the cabin and blinked his eyes sleepily. A fringe of gray hair clung precariously to the sides of his otherwise bald head, and his chin was adorned with a matted beard that resembled nothing so much as a handful of gray-colored straw.

"Now who might ye be?" he demanded snappishly.

Cap Gitchie folded his long arms, cradling the rifle in the crook of his right elbow.

"Might be George Washington, or the King of France. But I ain't."

"Where ye from?"

"From every place but here, and I'll soon be from here."

The little man stamped to the bow of his keelboat, and surveyed Cap from top to toe.

"How old are ye, mister?"

"Old enough"—Cap was twenty-four—"to mind my own business."

The little man suddenly smiled. "Ye talk like a boat-man. Moreover, ye talk like a keelboatman. Ever been to New Orleans?"

"Now what would I be doin' in New Orleans?"

"Talkative cuss, ain't ye?" the bearded man snapped. "How should I know what ye'd be doin' there? All I want to know is do ye want to go? If ye do, I can use another boatman—fifteen dollars and found for the trip. If so be ye can ever make up yer mind, come and see me—Abijah Ezekiel Primpton Crabbe, owner and cap'n of the *River Belle*, cargoes to and from New Orleans, and tradin' done to order."

Cap Gitchie wandered back into Louisville, and the rooster flew from his shoulder to scratch about in a patch of green grass. He industriously swallowed bugs and worms, while Cap stood gazing at an inn, thinking of his own breakfast. It was too early for the inn to open, but he was hungry. A kick on the door might awaken the proprietor, and Cap was ready to deliver that kick when motion back at the edge of the forest caught his eye. Eight tall buckskinned men broke out of the woods, and with long rifles held ready marched grimly into town.

Cap snatched up the rooster and raced toward the river. He paused momentarily before the *River Belle*, then leaped from the bank and landed on the deck. Almost instantly he was confronted by Abijah Crabbe and a big flintlock pistol. Cap smiled pleasantly.

"I decided to take your offer," he said, "if my rooster gets passage and found too."

"That'll cost ye a dollar," Abijah Crabbe said.

"And we'll have to get off right away."

The little man glanced toward the shore. He'd had previous experience with men who suddenly made up their minds to go keelboating in a hurry.

"That'll be four dollars extry," he snapped.

Cap sighed dolefully. "A third of my wages gone, and we ain't even started yet. Let's move."

CAP GITCHIE took his place at one of the two starboard oars and timed his stroke to that of the blithe and carefree Irishman ahead of him. Directly across, on the other side of the same seat, sat a lanky Kentuckian with a solemn face and brown eyes as sad and mournful as a spaniel's. The fourth oarsman was a lithe Creole who moved like a cat, and even purred like one when he talked. Cap'n Abijah Crabbe stood on top of the cabin with the handle of the long steering sweep in his hands. From this post of vantage he could keep one eye on the oarsmen and the other alert for obstructions in the water ahead. Navigating the clumsy, forty-foot craft among the other boats in the narrow creek was a job that called for a sure hand.

As they moved steadily down the creek and out into the Ohio, Cap suddenly ducked his head. The eight armed Limestoners had appeared at the river's edge and were closely scanning the boat. Without seeming to notice them, Abijah touched the steering sweep and swung the boat so the starboard oarsmen were hidden by the cabin.

"They must be lookin' fer somebody," he said.

"Could be," Cap agreed. "There's a lot of scoundrels back in the woods."

"Not near as many as there is on this here river," the Kentuckian said. "And the Spanish is the biggest scoundr'ls of 'em all."

"How do you make that out?"

"I don't make it out. It jest is. The Ohio's crowded with all the settlers as has been comin' sinst the war ended. And what kin they use fer a road? The old Mrs. Sippi, in course. And what is their market? N'Yurlens, in course. And who owns N'Yurlens? The Spanish, in course. And what do the Spanish do? Charge a high duty fer everything goin' through. They make this law, and they make that law, and a boat can't sell its cargo without it's at their prices. Or they keep it waitin' so long that the owner's profits is all eat up."

Cap Gitchie had been hired to help take a boat down the river, not to worry about what happened to its cargo after it got there. But talking with the pessimistic Kentuckian helped pass the time.

"Well," he said, "if there's so many settlers along these rivers, whyn't they march down to New Orleans, and tell the Spanish where to head in?"

"Heh, heh," the Kentuckian laughed dryly. "The Spanish is scairt lest we're goin' to try jest that. That's why they let Wilkinson's boats by with light duty."

"Who's Wilkinson?"

"Prob'bly the worst of the scoundr'ls. He went down to N'Yurlens four years ago, in '87, with a ladin' of terbaccy. The Spanish confiscated it, and Wilkinson dared 'em to keep it. Said he was a gen'ral in the American army, and he'd like 'em to keep his boat and cargo on account that would give him an excuse fer gettin' his army and cleanin' up every greasy Spaniard. Anyhow, he scairt 'em and they says, 'Well, Wilkinson, we got each other where the hair's short. S'pose we talk turkey? You do what you kin fer us, and we'll do what we kin fer you. You swear allegiance to Spain, and go back up the river. Tell everybody who wants to bring a boat down, that if they swear allegiance to Spain, they kin get by fer fifteen per cent duty 'stead of twenty-five. Tell anybody as wants to settle on Spanish land that they kin do it.' Lemme tell you, them Spanish is scairt. They're scairt we're goin' to come down and kick 'em out."

"And did Wilkinson swear allegiance to Spain?"

"Sure. Most people as goes down the river does."

"What about the United States?"

The Kentuckian shrugged. "That's a long haul away from N'Yurlens. Besides, you don't have to stay Spanish. If'n you take a flatboat down the river, nacher'lly you can't row it back up on account flatboats don't row up-current. So you sell or give the boat away after you've sold the cargo, and walk up the Natchez Trace, back into the States. If'n you go down in a keelboat, you row back up. You kin allus unswear after you're out of Spanish country."

Cap Gitchie chuckled. The situation was not too full of either ideals or ethics, but it did have its practical side.

Abijah Crabbe scowled. "It's no laughin' matter,

mister. This country has got to have a free and open river, clear to the Gulf!"

"Well, I sure hope you get it," said Cap amiably. He turned to the Kentuckian again. "Are there any fightin' roosters down the river?"

"Sometimes you'd think there wasn't nothin' but," replied the Kentuckian dolefully. "All them Spanish got 'em, and most of the settlers. Kin your rooster fight?"

"Can he fight! He's the red-roarin'est, peel-haulin'est, scrappin'est, maddest, fastest, fightin'est thing that ever grew feathers! He can lick his weight in hound dogs, wild cats, and Spaniards."

"We'll have fun," the Kentuckian said, as though that were a very dismal prospect.

The red rooster walked nonchalantly around the deck, peered into the cabin, and experimentally pecked at the Irishman's moccasins. Then he flew up to the cabin roof, cocked a bright eye at Abijah Crabbe, and flew down to cuddle up beside his owner. The feline Creole followed his every move, his eyes reflecting the love of a good fighting cock that had been born in his heart. He turned to smile at Cap Gitchie.

"That ees fine bird," he purred. "I, Baptiste Amante, say so."

The Irishman nodded. "Me old man told me when I left Dublin, 'Mike, never bet on cock fights; they'll ruin ye.' Up to now, he's been right. But I have a feelin' that red bird will bring us luck."

"Bad luck," the Kentuckian said gloomily.

The Irishman laughed, and struck up a song:

> The boatman is a lucky man,
> No one can do as the boatman can,
> The boatmen dance and the boatmen sing,
> The boatman is up to everything.

> Hi-ho, away we go,
> Floating down the O-hi-o.

They anchored that night to some willows below an outjutting headland. They rowed the boat up to the trees, made it fast, then paid off line until they floated free in the current, far enough out so a sudden fall of water would not leave them stranded. While the Creole cooked a savory gumbo over an open fire in a sand-filled box, the Irishman sang songs of the old country. The night was warm, and they slept on deck, under the stars, while the river gurgled and rolled steadily past them.

THEY ROWED ON day after day, passing more cumbersome flatboats and barges on the way, and waving to the settlers who had built their rough-hewn homes on both sides of the river. There was scarcely a day when they did not see some kind of settlement, and often plowed fields gleamed richly black among the stumps of trees. Still the settlers came, having started from as far away as Olean, New York, guiding their craft down the Allegheny to enter the Ohio at Pittsburgh. Men, women, children, horses, cattle, hogs, chickens, and farm implements occupied these floating arks impartially, and all used the river to arrive in this promised land to which they were journeying. But the *River Belle* was a fast boat, bound for New Orleans with a cargo of furs, and could not tarry long for visits.

They were many days out of Louisville, and well below the settlements, gliding between high stone cliffs that bordered both sides of the river, when Abijah Crabbe left his place at the steering sweep to place an extra horn of powder and pouch of bullets beside each man.

"What's comin'?" Cap Gitchie asked curiously.

"Cave-in-Rock," the gloomy Kentuckian asserted, as though that in itself was sufficient explanation.

Abijah climbed back to the top of the cabin, and guided the *River Belle* out to the center of the river. The mystified Cap continued to pull on his oar, until from the western bank floated an agonized appeal.

"Help! For God's sake, help!"

Cap turned his head, to see a white man running frantically along the river bank. His buckskin clothing hung in ragged shreds from his gaunt frame. A breechcloth was draped about his thighs, and his beard fluttered as he ran along the bank, parallel to the keelboat. Again the agonized, heart-wringing cry floated out over the water.

"Help! Help me! Take me on board! I've just escaped from the Indians."

Without flicking an eyelid or changing his melancholy expression, the Kentuckian let his oar rest in its lock, picked up the rifle that lay beside him, took careful aim over the rail, and squeezed the trigger. The pleading man on the bank took two more running steps, then two slow ones. His knees buckled, and he pitched forward, to lie motionless on the shore. Cap rose in his seat, hot anger inflaming his face.

"Why, you——"

"Sit down!" came Abijah Crabbe's commanding voice from over his head.

There was a wild yell from the bank. A long canoe with twelve Indians in it put out from the cove where it had been hidden, and bore down on the *River Belle*. Sitting calmly on top of the cabin, for he could not desert the steering sweep, Abijah Crabbe picked up a musket and shot. The foremost Indian dropped his paddle to slump backward against the next man. A rattle of rifle fire came from the canoe, but the bullets thudded against the stout hull of the *River Belle* or splashed in the water nearby. No longer in doubt, Cap knelt beside the rail, sighted on another Indian, and saw him drop. He was aware of other rifles cracking beside him. The canoe hesitated, then put back toward shore. Just at that moment, the red rooster, excited by the noise and confusion, flapped his wings and crowed.

"You!" Abijah Crabbe called imperiously. "You, rooster man! Come on up here!"

Cap rose, and climbed the ladder leading to the cabin roof. The little captain's beard worked up and down in indignation. His mild blue eyes glowed.

"Is this yer first trip down the river?" he demanded.

"Yup."

"I thought so!" Abijah Crabbe sputtered. "Let me tell ye something, mister——"

"Could you sort of gentle yourself down before you tell it? I never did like being hollered at."

The captain calmed down. "It wa'nt yer fault. Ye didn't know any better. But that white man was a renegade. He wanted to toll us into the bank so's those Indians could climb our hump for us. They try the same thing every time we pass Cave-in-Rock, and other places, too. Don't ever pick up anybody who hollers at ye from this river bank, and don't stop a man who knows what he's doin' better'n ye do."

"I won't," Cap said mildly. "But it don't do any harm to give a man a little warnin'. What's Cave-in-Rock?"

"It's a big natural cave where river pirates—renegades and Cherokees, mostly—meet and store the plunder they've taken from simple folks who believe all they hear. Ye got to go down river a couple of times before ye get on to all the dodges—like tollin' boats in to the bank. They get lots of 'em, too."

"I reckon so," Cap said, abashed.

He returned to his seat to find the red rooster standing on its edge, clucking to himself. The panther-like Creole was gazing at him in frank admiration.

"It ees lucky rooster," he said softly. "Nev-aire before have I pass Cave-in-Rock without somebody killed or wounded."

Cap Gitchie swept his oar back, while a happy little grin lighted his face. He seldom had much of an idea where he was going next, or what he was going to do after he got there. But this river life was not a bad one, at all. A man didn't have to wear the scat of his pants out on some office stool, or wonder too much about where his next excitement was coming from.

"What else is on the river?" he asked the Kentuckian.

"Everything," was the gloomy reply. "Pirates, and war parties, and snags, and sand bars, and ignor'nt young fellers that jump up and holler in keelboats. It's a wicked river."

The rooster perched contentedly beside him, and

the Kentuckian eyed him thoughtfully. There were such things as good and bad omens. Hadn't he himself, while crossing Kentucky two years before, seen a good omen when the crescent moon had pointed exactly toward Louisville? He had gone there, instead of pursuing his plan of heading down to Eddyville, on the Cumberland. Had he gone to Eddyville, he would have run square into a big war party, and no doubt by this time his scalp would be waving before the lodge of some dusky forest prince.

"I dunno but what I'm glad you've got the bird, son," he admitted almost cheerfully.

Cap grinned.

Two nights later they anchored in a quiet little eddy below another point of land. Flatboats and keelboats of every description—some of the latter going up the river instead of down—were met there. Cap counted twenty-one craft, and gazed curiously at the crowd that had gathered on the shore. The passengers of all the boats were intermingling freely around the cooking fires, and men, women, and children were dancing to the music a bearded, one-eyed giant who looked like a pirate was coaxing from a violin. A tall backwoodsman made his way up the bank and stepped on board the *River Belle*. He eyed the red rooster appraisingly.

"Who owns that thar fowl?" he demanded.

"I do," Cap said proudly.

"I'll bet," the backwoodsman stated, "that he ain't as good as my dominicker."

"How much you want to bet?"

"A cask of terbaccy, ten beaver pelts, and a ham."

The red rooster was better than the dominicker.

THE WEATHER BECAME HOT, and the river dropped a little. The banks that it had flooded bore mute testimony to all the cargo besides boats that this mighty water carried. Trees, wrecked boats, buffalo carcasses, great fish, small fish, drowned deer and elk, and all the other flotsam that a river will carry lay drying on the muddy, cracking banks. Watching it, the Kentuckian's gloom deepened.

"You'll see many a thing cast up there," he said prophetically. "Mebbe, before it's finished, all the men and women who've come to settle above us will be there, too."

"Don't be so happy about things," Cap Gitchie admonished. "You're such a gol-darn optimist, Kentucky, that a man would think nothing bad ever happened to you."

The Irishman guffawed and the Creole chuckled, while up on the cabin roof, even Abijah Crabbe smiled to himself as he stood with the steering sweep in his hands and studied the river ahead. He had been down it many times, but it was never the same river twice in succession. There were always new islands born where none had been before, and islands swept away that had stood for years. It was a changeable river, a restless and ever-searching one that was continually trying new patterns and new directions. It was as changeable as life itself, thought Abijah. And, while he stood on top of the cabin, steering the *River Belle,* he reflected on the course of his own life.

Back in Philadelphia, so many years ago that it now seemed as though it never could have been, he had been a school teacher. Before the war, his world had been a safe, well-ordered place wherein he had made the sons and daughters of the well-to-do ready to further their education in England or France. Every morning he had started out from his own modest little home, and every night he had returned to find his wife and three children awaiting him there. But that had been before the plague. . . .

Then had come the war for independence, but he had seen little of it. With his family gone, he had had to go. He could not stay in any place that reminded him of what had been. The frontier, a whole world away from Philadelphia, was where he had found forgetfulness. And there seemed to be nothing taken away without at least partial compensation. In the years he had been travelling up and down the western rivers, he had seen a continent come to life.

First there had been silent, buckskinned men who

would never even venture out the door without their long rifles. Then had come wild and roaring men, sober and industrious men, shiftless men, men with initiative, men stained with every crime in the calendar. But regardless of their other characteristics, the men who had opened this raw western country had had one thing in common—the courage to try something new. And they were not only trying it, but were doing it. They raised their crops, and gathered their fruits, and trapped their furs, and sent them down the broad rivers, down to New Orleans. Down there the Spanish sat across their outlet to the sea, but if they tried to impose too many restrictions. . . . The river would have to be open and free to all men. And it would be, sooner or later. He had even heard that there were already negotiations between Gayoso, the Spanish Governor, and the infant government of the United States.

Abijah Crabbe looked down at his crew, his lined face softening. If the men who came here were courageous and daring, they were also simple. That youngster with the game cock who had been in such a hurry to get away from Louisville, the glum Kentuckian, the easy-going Creole, the gay Irishman . . . their fetish was a red rooster, their aim to see what happened when and if they reached New Orleans. The day was the thing, and so long as the sun rose, all was well.

Yes, they were a simple breed of people, these folks who had gathered from every corner of the earth to make a highway of this broad river. The wilderness had never seen their like, and probably never would again. Simple they were, but they still had their smoldering passions that a careless word or gesture could fan into leaping fire. Then God help whomever or whatever got in their way. They stood by themselves, and never dreamed of asking anyone else to help them. And, if they wanted something, they would never count the cost of getting it.

A smile twitched the corners of his lips as he listened to their heated discussion of the rooster's good and bad points. No doubt the bird would fight again at New Madrid, and at Chickasaw Bluffs, and at Walnut Hills, and at Natchez, and at whatever settlers' cabins were near where they tied up. If he won all these fights, he would become a mighty creature, part of the river tradition, and boatmen would boast about his prowess as long as any of them might live.

The rooster did fight, and win, until Abijah Crabbe steered his craft into the bustling port of Natchez. He saw the Governor's ornate barge anchored beside a heavily armed gunboat and two supply ships. A small boat with Spanish soldiers in it put out from the barge and came toward the *River Belle*. Five uniformed dragoons and a dapper young officer boarded the keelboat to look over her papers and cargo.

WITH ONLY A CURSORY GLANCE at the Spanish ships, Cap Gitchie had repaired to the *River Belle's* cabin to sleep as soon as they tied up at Natchez. The cabin was musty with the odor of baled furs, and the aroma of the previous cargoes it had held still mingled faintly with this newer, stronger one. Cap stretched out in a cleared space, and drowsily listened to the Spanish soldiers board the boat. For a moment he hovered halfway between sleep and wakefulness, wondering if it would be worth his while to go out for another look. But the soldiers would be there in the morning, and the *River Belle* was going to New Orleans anyhow. There he would see more than enough of Spanish soldiers. He dropped off into dreamless and untroubled sleep.

When he awoke it was dark, and he went on deck to see the lamps of Natchez shining palely in the distance. Tonight he would go into town with his red rooster and let him fight the best the Spanish, or the French, or whoever was in control, had to offer. His eyes sought the stern of the *River Belle,* where the Kentuckian, the Creole, the Irishman, and Abijah Crabbe were gathered about the cooking pot that hung over the sand-heaped fire box. Cap walked toward them.

"What's the matter?" he asked. "Ain't there any inns in this Natchez, where we can get a civilized meal for once?"

"Ho, ho," the Creole said softly. "You are indeed *l'enfant*, my friend."

"He jest don't know about Natchez," the glum Kentuckian amended. "Sure, we could find a place to eat. And they'd bring us a stinkin' mess of slumgullion a dog wouldn't eat. Then they'd say, 'Twenty reales, see-nyors,'—that's what they call folks down in this neck o' the woods—and when we wouldn't pay it they'd call their sojers to have us thrown in jail."

"Well . . ." Cap looked wistfully toward the shore. "There's five of us, ain't there?"

"I've got a cargo of fur to look out for," Abijah Crabbe said sharply. "I can't risk it."

"All right, cap'n. But I'm goin' to take the rooster over there tonight and see what we can stir up."

The Creole's white teeth flashed in the darkness, and the Irishman chuckled with anticipation. Cap walked over to his shipped oar, upon the handle of which the rooster had been in the habit of spending the night, and reached down in the darkness so the bird could step onto his hand. Nothing moved. The customary little rustle of feathers was missing. Surprised, Cap straightened up, then tried the handles of the other oars, one by one. He walked back to the cooking fire.

"What happened to the rooster?" he demanded.

The Kentuckian, noisily chewing a succulent bit of meat, stopped eating, his mouth half open. The four boatmen looked at each other, the ruddy glow cast by the fire outlining in sharp relief the hard, intent features. The Irishman spoke up.

"I ain't seen the bird since the Spaniards left. I thought he was with you."

Cap Gitchie stood still in the darkness, while anger crawled the length of his spine. He looked at the Governor's barge, riding softly at anchor while wavelets lapped her heavy hull. Without a word he entered the cabin to pick up his tomahawk, and when he came out the Kentuckian, the Creole, and the Irishman gathered about him. Abijah Crabbe looked steadily over the rail. He turned once, but did not speak when the four men drew the *River Belle* in to the bank and stepped ashore. Nothing that he could say or do would hold them now. Their luck had gone.

For a moment they stood on the dark shore, looking vengefully toward the Governor's barge, then started down the river bank to where half a dozen pirogues were drawn up. Slowly, so as to make no noise, they launched one and climbed in. The Creole, handling the stern paddle, dipped it as softly as a cat flicking out a sheathed claw to catch a mouse. The dark mass of the Governor's barge loomed above them, and a sharp, Spanish voice broke the silence.

"Hola?"

The Creole worked the pirogue up to the bow of the barge, keeping in the shadow of the hull. Cap silently climbed up the anchor chain and peeped over the deck. Just before him, scarcely a yard away, a uniformed sentry stood with one hand on his cutlass, peering toward the dark stern. The night was hot, and he had taken off his helmet. Cap swung the flat of his tomahawk, and with a soft little thud the sentry melted down to mingle with the shadows on the deck.

From the other end of the barge a questioning voice demanded, "Juan! What is happening?"

Running softly on moccasined feet, the four intruders entered the dimly lighted cabin and swung the door shut behind them. The Creole dropped the heavy latch into place, and stood with his ear to the door, an excited grin on his dark face. The Kentuckian wrapped his long arms about another soldier who suddenly appeared before them, then released his captive quickly, and swung a fist to his jaw. The Spaniard bounced back, then his sword licked forth and blood stained the Kentuckian's shirt. The Irishman swung the flat of his tomahawk, and the soldier dropped heavily. They raced through the cabin into a larger one with a closed door at the far end. Before they could reach it, five soldiers rose from their card game, reaching wildly for weapons. Cap jumped on the nearest man. . . .

INSIDE THAT CLOSED DOOR, Governor Gayoso had for the past hour been in conference with four of his staff officers, and was just finishing a speech.

"The interests of Spain must at all times be nearest my heart. But how shall those interests best be served? Señor Pinckney, of the United States Government, has lately sent a courier to me, saying that he upholds the claim of the American settlers on the upper river for an open, duty-free port in New Orleans. He insists that the traders who bring goods down must have whatever rights of trans-shipment they desire. Acceding to his wishes would deprive Spain of much revenue, and I do not think this infant American government is prepared to use force. I do not greatly fear the United States, nor anything they may do. The real problem is, if we continue to operate this port as a source of royal revenue, and charge such duties as we see fit, will those half-civilized frontiersmen on the upper river take matters into their own hands?"

"They would not dare," a bulky, scar-faced Colonel of Guards said contemptuously. "But suppose they do? We'll drive them back soon enough."

"My good Colonel Perez," Gayoso said, "have you ever fought Kentuckians?"

The Colonel's face flushed. "No. But it would be a pleasure to——"

At that moment the thudding of the gun butts of those soldiers who were trying to break down the outer door rumbled through the room. An excited voice shouted in Spanish, "Open up! I command you." A second later four blood-streaked Americans with tomahawks in their hands burst through the door of the conference room. As one man, the assembled officers rose and drew their swords.

"Keep your shirt on, Governor," said the tallest of the Americans, "and tell your pals to do likewise. There ain't any sense in gettin' yourselves massa-creed."

"This is an outrage!" Gayoso sputtered.

"So's stealin' roosters!" Cap Gitchie snarled. "Do I get him back? Or do we bust up your meat house?"

"Do you get what back?"

"My red rooster. The one one of your tin-horn

soldiers swiped off the *River Belle* this afternoon."

"Do I understand that one of the Spanish soldiers who boarded your boat today stole from you?"

"Yup. Make up your mind, Governor. We ain't got all night."

"Lieutenant Montez," Gayoso directed, "investigate the boarding parties who were out this afternoon. Find the soldier who stole this man's property. Have it returned, and see that the soldier is punished."

GOVERNOR GAYOSO sat for a long while after the boatmen had gone. It had taken him some little time to reassure himself that this was not the long-feared attack by the backwoodsmen. For it had seemed scarcely credible that four madmen, alone, would dare board the state barge of the Governor of Louisiana. But four men had done it, and if an army composed of similar men ever came. . . .

In his mind he began to construct phrases for an official report to be sent to His Majesty Charles IV: "In the light of recent first-hand observations . . . it is my considered opinion . . . for the promotion of friendly relations . . . recommendation for free trade along the lower Mississippi, and the opening of the port of New Orleans . . ."

Cap Gitchie's rooster had won another fight.

THE
FIFTH FRIEND

1808 By 1800 the new country had reached the Mississippi, and controlled it. Then came the Louisiana Purchase of 1803, adding an unknown section so vast it doubled the size of the nation. The Lewis and Clark expedition of 1805-6 reported that it was a great, treeless, rolling plain, cut by mighty rivers and bounded on the west by tremendous mountains.

That sounded like furs, and the free trappers plunged into the unknown—tough, fearless, far-ranging men to whom distance and hardship meant nothing. In no time they had penetrated clear to the foothills of the Rockies, and their furs were coming down the Mississippi's western tributaries to the raw, roaring, frontier boom town of St. Louis.

Typical of these indestructible trappers was John Colter, whose exploits are an American saga. A Virginian, better educated than most of his fellows, he fortunately left a first-hand account of his greatest experience, which is presented here as he lived it, virtually unadorned.

A STORM was gathering over the valley of the Big Horn. The black clouds that rolled up in the sky nudged and shoved one another as each sought for a place of precedence, and all mingled in a great, threatening mass of thunderheads. A streak of lightning flashed like a crooked sword blade beneath them, and a rolling peal of thunder rumbled through the sky. A herd of buffalo outside Fort Raymond began to mill about, snuffling uneasily, and formed a circle with their heads pointing toward its center. The two men who were riding brown and white Indian ponies over the plain spurred their mounts, and the little horses broke into a mile-eating gallop. The buffalo separated to let them run through, and a few seconds later the rain fell.

It came down in great, misty sheets, hurling itself at the short prairie grass as though it were an enemy upon which the rain had to pour down its pent-up vengeance once and for all. Depressions and buffalo wallows filled with a sluggish, roily flood. One of the horses slipped and almost went down, but the superb horsemanship of its rider averted catastrophe. Looking sullenly back over its shoulder, a drenched coyote slunk from beneath the bit of brush where it had found partial shelter. The coyote crouched low to the earth, waiting until the horsemen had gone by. Then it crept back to the brush and began to smooth its wet fur.

Side by side, the horsemen rode into Fort Raymond and pulled sharply on the single reins that ended in a loop through their mounts' jaws. As they dismounted, they drew their rifles from the buffalo-skin scabbards that covered them and examined the priming. As indifferent to their own soaked condition as they were careful of their powder's, they reinhaltered their horses, and strode toward a long, squat building whose door was surmounted by a bleached buffalo skull and horns of enormous size. Flinging open the door, they brushed past the clerk at the counter, and disappeared into a room at the rear.

The little clerk eyed the retreating backs and the wet trail of moccasin tracks with frank disapproval. He had come out to this God-forsaken Fort Raymond from a good position in St. Louis, only because Manuel Lisa had offered him four times the wages he had been earning there. But he did not have to like either the place or the people living in it. St. Louis had been civilized, at least, although in the five years since the Louisiana Purchase there had been more and more of these wild trappers fighting and carousing in its streets.

But at this desolate juncture of the Big Horn and the Yellowstone, where Manuel Lisa had built his trading post, there was *nothing* but trappers and Indians and buffalo. And the two men who had gone in to see Lisa were the wildest of them all—little better than savages. The clerk sniffed. Perhaps it was true that these men had accompanied Lewis and Clark on the expedition people said had crossed the mountains to the Pacific. Almost anything could be expected of men who seemed to prefer the wilderness to civilization. For himself, he wanted no part of it. When he had saved enough to go back to St. Louis, ruffians like John Colter and John Potts could have this wild, barren land, for all of him.

The clerk resumed his entries in the big ledger, and when they were finished, he ran his goose quill down the double column of figures. Seventy bales of beaver pelts had been brought in, as had a variety of fox, deer, bear, wolf, and sable skins. Trade goods had gone out to pay for them, and the books must balance exactly. Manuel Lisa, the trading prince of this western fur empire, had as keen an eye for trade goods as he had for sighting his long rifle. A half-pound of blue beads, over or under what should be, would not escape detection. The clerk triple-checked his entries, sighed, and with the ledger under his arm walked to the small door at the rear which had been so unceremoniously opened by Colter and Potts. He knocked, then waited until a soft, Latin-accented voice spoke.

"Come een."

The clerk entered, and with an outward show of respect stood silently waiting, while he looked at the three men in the office. Manuel Lisa, his Spanish employer, sat behind a heavy desk, his dark face an impassive setting for bright, businesslike eyes. The other two men had about them a certain cramped look, as though the small office was an uncomfortable and unfamiliar place. Their long rifles leaned against the wall, their knives and tomahawks lay on the desk. Their soft buckskin clothing, still damp, outlined lean, hard figures.

"The accounts of the shipment for St. Louis are ready, sir," said the clerk.

Manuel Lisa swung around and extended his hand for the ledger. The clerk gave it to him, and Lisa ran his eye down the columns of figures. Without speaking, he handed the ledger back. The clerk stood irresolutely, and flushed when he caught John Potts' amused eye. Lisa said, "That ees all," and the clerk gladly left the room.

John Potts jerked his thumb at the closing door. "He'd make a good pet for a Blackfoot squaw, Manuel."

Manuel Lisa shrugged, and his lips parted in a white-toothed smile. "Were there none to keep track of the furs you wild men bring in," he said, "trading would be an es-sorry tangle. What? So my leetle pet ees necessary."

"There's all kinds of buffalo in a herd, I reckon," said the other man in buckskin.

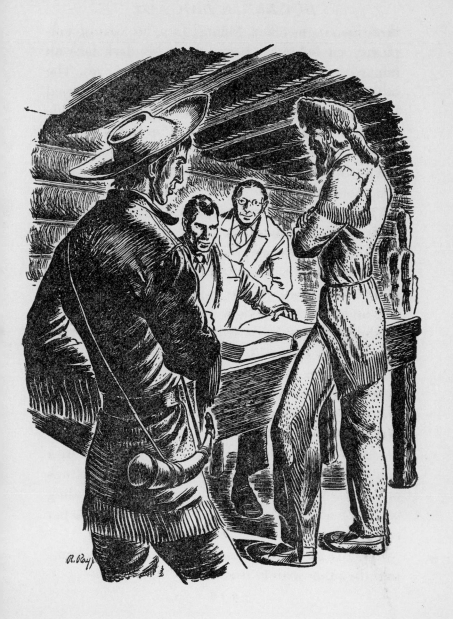

Lisa swung to face him. "Now then, my frien', tell me more."

"It's simple enough," replied John Colter. "We're aimin' to go up the Yellowstone to where it makes the big bend to the south. Then we'll hit overland to the three forks of the Missouri—I got a couple of canoes hid there. There's a million little cricks in that country around the Jefferson, and none but what's got its beaver lodges. It's Blackfoot country, but the Flat-heads and Crows is already tradin' into here from when you sent me out last summer. Mebbe we can open this country, too. That's all."

"That ees all, eh?" said the Latin trader. "Do you forget that you'll be three hundred miles from the nearest white man and the help he can give you?"

Colter shrugged. "If there was white men there wouldn't be fur. And we don't need help."

"That may be so." Manuel Lisa's eyes sought the floor. "But the las' time you went out you joined the Crows in a fight against the Blackfeet. Blackfeet do not forget, my frien'."

"We'll travel at night."

"And run your traps, and do your cooking and hunting at night?"

"Sure. Why not?"

"Well, eef you want to be crazee——" Lisa shook his head hopelessly.

"Then we can draw on you for the stores we need?"

"That was never the question," the trader said with quiet dignity. "Eef you wanted to set traps for El Diablo himself, you could draw on my stores. You come back, you pay me. You don' come back . . ." He spread his hands expressively. ". . . Manuel Lisa don' lose so much as you. But the point ees—we want trade, not war. I do not trust thees Blackfeet. But you find a really good fur country and we build a fort in it, eh?"

"We'll look around some," promised John Colter. He rose, thrust his knife and tomahawk into his belt, and held out his hand. "So long, Manuel. Be seein' you."

"Adios, my frien'. Don' eat any Blackfeet."

"Jest a couple of small ones," grinned Potts. He picked up his rifle and walked out of the room, pausing to grip the trader's hand as he went by.

Manuel Lisa walked with them to the door. A smile was on his lips, but at the same time a sadness lingered in his eyes. He had seen many go out thus, and a great many had never returned. But it was men like these who would make his dream possible. As he looked out over the rolling prairie to where the Big Horn curved to meet the Yellowstone, his mind's eye could see that watery highway carrying his flatboats and keelboats, loaded with furs, on past the Milk, the Cheyenne, the Platte, on and on, fifteen hundred miles to St. Louis, the heart of the new American trading empire. This was 1808, only two years after Lewis and Clark had brought back word of this region, and he, Manuel Lisa, already had a trading post in operation. In another two years . . .

JOHN COLTER stood for a moment beside the river, looking back at Fort Raymond and mentally checking their preparations. Unconsciously, his hand strayed to his belt to check the knife and tomahawk hanging there. A man had five good friends when he went into the wilderness beyond the point where other men ventured, and three of them were his rifle, knife, and tomahawk. The fourth was whoever travelled with him. But the fifth, and the one upon which he could depend to the greatest possible extent, was himself. A man might lose his rifle, axe, and knife. There might be no one willing or able to stand by his side just when he most needed someone there. But no matter what happened, or what desperate extremities he might encounter, ultimate reliance would have to be on that fifth friend.

Potts was stowing their beaver traps in the canoe, being careful that they laid on a bed roll so that their sharp corners and protruding edges would not puncture the fragile bark covering. John Colter steadied the craft, and cast an expert eye over the various goods within it. But they were arranged all right.

Potts was a good man in a canoe, and as much at home in the wilderness as Colter himself. But he was also possessed of a quality that would be anything but an asset should the wrong set of circumstances arise. He had a fiery temper that was aroused to fever pitch for the slightest reason. Only three days before he had nearly killed another trapper in a knife fight that had been stopped only by Manuel Lisa's interference.

But this trip did not promise anything unusual, and there should be no reason for Potts to become aroused. They were going only a few hundred miles, and that was a mere excursion. Of course there were Blackfeet there. Colter grinned faintly, remembering Lisa's fears that the Blackfeet were ready to kill any white man who ventured into their country. True, there seldom was a time when the Blackfeet weren't at war, and Blackfoot country was any place at all where they had a war party consisting of as many as four men—though of course the tribe did have its regular hunting grounds and villages.

Potts straightened up and squinted his eyes at the sun. "Time's a-wastin'."

"Yup."

Potts stepped into the canoe, settled himself in the bow, and picked up a paddle. John Colter took his place in the stern, and they dug their paddles deeply in unison. The little craft shot smoothly into the sluggish current and turned upstream. They had turned their backs on civilization.

They paddled steadily up the Yellowstone, hour after hour, through country as open as the palms of their hands. From time to time flocks of ducks took to the wing at their approach, and a diving muskrat or jumping fish would occasionally ripple the water ahead of them. Once the body of a big pike, white belly up, floated by, and they could see the huge gashes torn in its side by some rapacious bird that had been unable to lift its victim. But they saw no sign of men, red or white, although they kept a sharp watch on the treeless banks between which they were passing. Not that they could tell too much by looking at the banks, or noting the actions of the animals along them. Animals might act any way at all, and the fact that they were peacefully grazing or resting did not necessarily indicate that there were no Indians about. An Indian could crawl right in among a herd of buffalo before they even knew he was around, and antelope might start at anything at all, They were flighty beasts.

But even Indians were not infallible, and to keen eyes they were bound to leave some sign of their passing wherever they went. A buckskin thong, a broken paddle, or almost anything on the river that did not belong there would be ample evidence that Indians were upstream. They were past masters at hiding their tracks, but hiding tracks was a real job, even for Blackfeet, and they seldom bothered to do it unless they knew enemies were around. And it was just as well to see Blackfeet before they saw you, if you valued your scalp.

Toward late afternoon John Colter said, "Do you reckon it would be all right to build a fire tonight?"

"Reckon it would," his companion answered. "We ain't seen a thing all day."

"It won't be all right tomorrow night. And mebbe we'd best be careful how and where we shoot after this. But we could cook a passel of buffalo meat tonight, and eat it until we get out on the cricks."

"Pshaw!" Potts scoffed. "You're scarin' yourself jest thinkin' of them Blackfeet!"

"I've fought agin the Blackfeet," John Colter said soberly, "and I ain't scared of 'em. But neither are they scared of me. It's best to take no chances."

"Think they'll be any Blackfeet along these cricks of yourn?"

"There's no tellin' where they'll be. I even saw signs of 'em around the lake this river rises in—a hundred miles south of the big bend."

Potts snorted. "You mean the lake where you said the water shoots up outa holes? I suppose the Blackfeet was takin' baths in them boilin' springs you told about!"

"I've been there," Colter replied calmly, "and you

ain't. What's more, those hot springs soaked the soreness out of the leg wound I got in that fight between the Crows and the Blackfeet, and it's as good as it ever was."

Potts grunted incredulously. "Did the Blackfeet have guns in that fight?"

"Jest a few. There ain't been any tradin' with 'em so far, and they've jest picked up a few from the Flatheads and Crows. But they sure know how to shoot them bows and arrers."

"They won't shoot far's a gun."

"They kill jest as dead."

A half hour before sunset they swung in to the bank, and landed in the shelter of some low-hanging willows. Potts stayed with the canoe, gathering dry sticks for a fire, while his companion stalked cautiously up the bank. He halted just within the screening willows and looked all about. Nothing showed except a half dozen antelope and a herd of stolid buffalo that were bedding down for the night near a clump of cottonwoods. Colter slunk back into the willows and threaded his way upstream through them. When he emerged he was within a hundred feet of the buffalo herd. Taking aim at a fat cow, he squeezed the trigger and watched her thump heavily to the ground. The rest milled curiously about, but raised their tails and stamped stiff-leggedly away when the hunter approached.

He cut the succulent hump from the cow's back, and left the rest for the wolves and coyotes.

FOURTEEN DAYS out of Fort Raymond they came into the maze of little creeks that formed the headwaters of the Missouri. After careful exploration Colter found the nameless, deep little stream where he had concealed a canoe on his previous trip with the Crows. The canoe was intact, and apparently undisturbed. It was no wonder, for the country was a dense labyrinth. Low hills that supported a thick growth of aspens hemmed in the stream, and feeding into it, within easy trapping distance, were a dozen or more smaller creeks, all of which were choked with beaver dams. The region was a trapper's paradise, but a nightmare for anyone trying to cross it in a hurry. The only practicable route was down the little stream, which pursued a long course before it emptied into the Jefferson, one of the three forks of the Missouri. Farther downstream, the hills were mere scantily forested knolls that were covered with prickly pear, and gave way in many places to open, level stretches.

To the west and north the hills were higher, and the winds that blew from them down into the valleys carried tidings of the cold weather that would soon come to lock this region in winter's grip. But they should get out, with a good load of pelts, before freeze-up. They could divide whatever their catch brought in, pay Manuel Lisa back, and have a tidy sum left over. Then they could go trapping again; there was a lot of the western country that they had never seen, and the first-comer got the best pelts, as they knew from experience.

Although they had neither seen nor heard any Indians, they had travelled by night since leaving the Yellowstone to make the last, overland leg of their journey. By the light of a waning moon they had found Colter's cached canoe, and were now surveying the neighborhood before launching it. Pale moonlight, slanting down into the valley, struck the face of a stone ledge, exposed and vertically split by some mighty upheaval of past ages. A small evergreen grew directly in front of the three-foot crevice, and John Colter parted its branches to reveal a spacious cavern that extended back into the heart of the rock. He spoke softly.

"A Crow showed it to me the last time we were here. He says the Blackfeet don't know about it. What do you think about keepin' our plunder here?"

"Looks like a bad place to be caught in," Potts said doubtfully. "I'd rather sleep back in the brush, myself."

"So would I. And we'll have to keep the canoe out, too. But we can stow our grub in here, and our pelts."

They carried the blocks of pemmican, and the flour and salt, to which Manuel Lisa had staked them, into the cavern. And, with each trip they made, they carefully crawled under the branches of the little evergreen, so that no breaks or marks would show. Prowling Indians needed no more than a broken twig to tell them that enemies or strangers were near. But, after they had cached their food, no eye could have told that anything foreign was in the cave. Lastly, with a dead branch they brushed over the path they had made.

"Now let's go set a few traps," Potts said impatiently. "Them beaver ought to be thick enough to walk on."

"Good idea."

They launched the canoe, and paddled downstream to where a trickling little rill emptied its waters into the stream. Twenty feet back from its mouth, the streamlet pitched over a beaver dam that stretched across it. While Potts handled the canoe, Colter waded ashore, three of their twelve traps in his hand. He set one at the foot of the little path made by beaver coming down the side of the dam, and two at freshly worn trails near the edge of the water. Going on down the stream, they spotted the rest of their traps in three other little rills that dribbled into it. Beaver did not seek big water. Even if it was only a foot-wide trickle, so long as it was suitable for a dam and there was food about, beaver would live in it.

As they paddled away from their last set, they saw the dark shape of a swimming beaver, and the curling V-line it left as it started for the safety of a burrow under the bank.

"Bank beaver!" Potts jeered. "All these dams around, but he has to be different! He has to live in a bank!"

"Beaver do what they dang please," John Colter observed quietly. "Looks like our traps will be full afore mornin'. But keep your voice down!"

"Aw, there ain't any Blackfeet around here. What are you so nervous about?"

"I'm aimin' to keep my hair a spell longer," replied Colter, "and there's only one way to be sure of doin' it. Let's go. We ain't finished yet."

He put the canoe in toward a thick clump of young willows, and Potts waded ashore to make his way to the center of the thicket. He cut a dozen long, lithe shoots, trimmed the twigs from them, and carefully shoved all the cut wood under the roots of another willow. With no Indians about, it seemed a senseless precaution, but he knew that Colter would insist that nothing at all should appear out of place. He returned to the canoe with the trimmed shoots, and they started back upstream, toward their traps.

The moon was low, but dawn would soon be sending its stealthy light creeping down the little, shadowed valleys. A deer on the bank of the stream snorted, and plunged into the underbrush. A bull elk, surprised at its morning drink, lifted its head to stare, and stamped its forefoot threateningly. Out in the forest an awakening flicker rattled a sleepy song.

They stopped at the first dam, and took two big beaver out of the traps they had set there. Passing between high, rock-studded banks, they came to the next dam, and found two more. By the time they got back to the cavern there were seven beaver in the canoe.

Potts skinned them, cutting them up the belly and peeling the skins off over legs and tail. Then he bent the lithe willows so that their ends met and formed a circle. Piercing the edges of the beaver pelts with his knife, he laced them to the willow hoops and put them in the cave. They would be dry within a few days. Then they could be taken off the stretching hoops and baled.

Meantime Colter had been building a cairn of rocks in the shallow water at the edge of the stream. As soon as it extended above the surface of the water he built a fire on it and roasted the fattest beavers' hind quarters. They ate, chewing the stringy flesh with all the gusto of hungry men, and then carried the rest of the beaver carcasses five hundred feet back into the sheltering trees, where they would be nothing but picked bones in a few hours. They lifted the canoe out of the water, carried it into the forest, and cached it where it had been hidden before. Lifting the rocks on which they had built their fire, they dropped them back into the creek, smoked side down. Separating, careful to leave no tracks, they went into the woods and slept all day.

That night they went down to the stream again and set traps in the tributary creeks just below the ones they had worked the night before. Night after night they followed the same procedure, trapping down the stream until they began to work into more open country. The pile of pelts in the cavern grew steadily higher.

One morning the first gray streaks of dawn were again appearing in the sky when they started back upstream. A light mist was rising from the water, curling its tenuous fingers toward the tops of the trees. Out in the forest a great horned owl sent its fierce hunting cry rolling over the still reaches. Far away a gray wolf howled. The whistling snort of a buck sounded from the bank. A fox yelped, and then yelped again.

Suddenly John Colter tensed. From somewhere upstream had come a faint sound that did not blend in. Silently rocking the canoe in warning, he dug his paddle deeply into the water and with a dozen powerful strokes sent the canoe shooting from between high banks that might conceal an enemy into a stretch where they could see better.

The east bank was covered by a horde of blanketed Blackfeet!

Before they could turn, more Indians appeared behind them, with drawn bows. There was no escape. Colter saw an eagle-feathered warrior motioning for them to land, and put in to the bank. As he stepped out of the canoe, he heard a bowstring twang, and looked around to see an arrow slither through the loose part of Potts' shirt.

"Don't shoot!" he cried warningly.

But Potts' face was livid with rage. He raised his rifle, took point-blank aim at the brave who had loosed the arrow, and fired. Almost before the Indian fell, fifty bowstrings snapped, fifty arrows hissed through the air.

The canoe drifted slowly down the stream, its dead occupant pierced by so many arrows that he was almost hidden by the feathered ends.

THE INDIANS watched it go, standing ominously quiet until the drifting canoe had passed between the high banks and out of sight. Then, at a guttural command from the warrior who wore the eagle feathers, evidently a chief, there was movement among the Indians downstream. Colter guessed that orders had been given to bring in Potts' scalp and the two rifles in the canoe. At the same time, his own knife and tomahawk were plucked from his belt and thrown on the ground.

Knowing that any sudden move would mean instant death, he stood silently, without expression, while his thoughts worked for him. He was surrounded by a horde of Blackfeet, who had only hatred of white men written on their scowling faces. He had lost his rifle, tomahawk, and knife, and the friend who would have stood beside him. But in the last resort and desperate extremity he always had himself. A man could never abandon himself until death stole in to take all.

A young, hawk-nosed warrior came up to stand before the white man, and to spit squarely in his face. A brave with a swinging tomahawk slashed it viciously down, and the flat of the blade brushed John Colter's nose. He took half a step backward, and immediately felt the keen point of a knife bite through his clothing into his back. He stood still and studied the Indian who had spit at him. A man could not rightly call himself dead until he *was* dead, and if by some miracle he escaped from this, there was a young Blackfoot he wanted to remember. Some time he might see him over the sights of a rifle. He didn't have Potts' fiery temper, but he had a long memory.

A battle-scarred veteran who had been standing

beside the dead Blackfoot stooped and picked up Colter's knife from the ground. His lips were a tight line across his face, and venom glowed in his eyes as, with slow and purposeful tread, he approached the captive. He raised the knife, but almost instantly another warrior struck it down. They began to quarrel back and forth, and John Colter's tongue licked out over dry lips. Half a dozen more warriors joined the argument, their voices heavy with anger.

The white man looked once more at the little stream, down which the canoe had carried Potts' body. Potts, the ready fighter! If all the Indians west of the Mississippi gathered together, and one shot an arrow at him, Potts would have to shoot back. But it had not been good sense. Had he submitted, and let himself be taken prisoner, they might have gained a little time, or even have talked the Blackfeet into a friendly attitude. But now there was no chance. The braves were arguing as to who should have the privilege of first striking down the victim. Three more warriors joined the argument.

A coyote slunk through the brush behind them, and crouched very low to the earth while he fixed his eyes on the scene ahead. The coyote licked his chops, and waited patiently. He had followed war parties of the Blackfeet before, and seen them take prisoners. There was always much for him to feast on when the warriors finally departed.

The chief with the eagle feathers strode to the center of the quarreling group and let his blanket fall about his hips. He pointed to the east, and spoke firmly and rapidly. A delighted chuckle rose from the rest, and spread to the outer circle as the word was passed on.

John Colter folded his arms across his chest and stood very still. The Blackfeet were past masters at hatching up hellish schemes, and no doubt were now in the process of evolving another one. He would know in time, and if they were planning to take him anywhere, which he doubted, there was always the hope of escape.

The chief stopped talking, and a slim warrior with a long, ragged scar across his chest began to guffaw, until he was so overcome by his own merriment that he rolled helplessly on the ground. A brave with a steel-tipped lance in his hand, and a red blanket over his shoulders, walked in front of the victim. He let the blanket drop to the ground, pointed with obvious pride to his long, well-muscled legs, then gestured at Colter with his spear. Two of the Blackfeet closed in from either side, and threw the white man to the ground. He was aware of the point of the ripping knife that sliced away his clothing, and felt the knife slide into the side of his foot when the Indians cut off his moccasins.

When they let him up he was naked, and the morning wind from the little stream cut icily about him. As though it had been prearranged, those Indians standing in front of him drew back to form an open lane. The captive looked that way, across the prickly-pear flats, toward the Jefferson, five or six miles away.

The chief came to his side. He pointed across the flats, then at Colter's legs, and grunted inquiringly.

Now, at last, the victim understood, and the tip of his tongue scraped against the dry roof of his mouth. The warriors could not agree as to who was to have the honor of killing him, so the chief had decided for them. He was to be turned loose, naked and weaponless, and the first brave to run him down could claim him as a rightful quarry. He thought fast.

The chief was still pointing at his legs. Colter shook his head, showed the cut in his naked foot, and indicated the angry red welt on his leg that marked the

arrow-wound he had received from the Blackfeet
the year before. He put his weight on that leg, and
let it buckle slightly. Actually, there was nothing
wrong with his leg, and he could outrun any white
man west of St. Louis. But a little false confidence on
the part of the Blackfeet might give him a chance.

An impatient, bloodthirsty murmur came from the
waiting Indians. The chief grunted again, and pushed
Colter toward the open lane. He walked slowly forward, carefully limping a little, trying to breathe
softly and deeply, to pull as much air as possible into
his lungs. He kept his eyes straight ahead, his ears
alert for the first sounds of beginning pursuit.

No doubt the savage who killed him would go back
to whatever lousy lodge he had come from, there to
render a suitably embellished story of the white man
who had tried to escape him. Probably the feat would
be inscribed in paint on the sides of the tepee, blessed
by the medicine man, and the victor from that time
on would be known by some name that would forever
call to mind his remarkable run. Well, if they'd give
him a start, the brave who caught him would have
something to boast of.

The autumn wind played coldly across his naked
body as he walked through the lane and out toward
the flats. He did not look back, and only slightly increased his pace. This was a game, all the rules of
which were made by the more powerful players. But

anyone in any game had at least a chance of winning.

He did not begin to run until he heard the war cry burst from a hundred throats. Then he drew a tremendous breath, and leaped into action. Even so, he ran easily, saving his strength, trying to pay no attention to the sharp prickly-pear thorns that entered his feet. He would challenge any Indian to any race if he were wearing moccasins. But he was not wearing moccasins, or anything else, and blood was spurting from his cut foot.

He sped over a little hillock and down the other side, and when he passed a wide-trunked cottonwood he dodged behind it so that it was between himself and his pursuers. He was running well. He knew that. But he had to run well, because death was the penalty for doing otherwise. With that certain knowledge he knew also that he could not permit one split second of hesitation or panic. He still did not look back, because there was no use in looking back. A man could, for a flicker of time, feel the slash of the arrow or the thrust of the lance that cut into his back, but there was no point in looking around to see if it was coming. He had been given his chance, the only one he could hope for, and every desperate faculty must be devoted to making the most of it.

A medley of disappointed yells came to him as the slower and more easily outdistanced of the Blackfeet dropped behind, where all they could do was watch the finish of the race. But as the panting minutes went past, a sense of utter futility and helplessness overcame him. It seemed that his straining lungs could not admit another breath of air, his pounding heart must burst. Blood was flowing from his nose and he could taste it in his mouth. Every step on his bleeding, thorn-filled feet was agony. Despairingly, he turned his head for one fleeting glimpse over his shoulder.

Still racing on his trail, a dozen of the Blackfeet stretched for half a mile behind him. Far behind them the rest of the tribe were trotting slowly along, without hope of the kill but wishing to be in on it. There was only one very close pursuer. Twenty yards behind, the Indian with the long slim legs, who had dropped his blanket but was holding his spear ready, pounded desperately in pursuit. The brave increased his speed, closing the gap to fifteen yards. It was about over. When the Blackfoot thought to throw away his spear, he could close the distance.

Colter stopped suddenly, whirling in his tracks and throwing out both hands. It was a ruse, a last, desperate gamble tried more through instinct than reason. But it worked. The Indian tried to stop and dodge, involuntarily reacting to the impulse that bade him watch out for the weapon that might be cast by this unarmed, naked white man. He stumbled, tripped on his spear, and fell jerkily to the earth.

The spear's wooden handle splintered. The white man raced toward the fallen brave, snatched up the broken lance, jabbed it into his pursuer, pulled it out, and turned to run on.

He had counted on distraction here, and he received it. The following warriors paused for an instant by the side of their wounded comrade, and when they resumed the race, Colter was only a few hundred yards from the Jefferson River. Before they could close with him, he had reached the bank.

Ahead of him was a small island, whose upper end had caught and held a tangled debris of floating tree trunks, branches, and weeds. Drawing one last agonizing breath, he dove into the icy water, and came up beneath the tumbled mass of driftwood. He clawed his way up through the center of the wood until he could breathe again, and waited.

STARK NAKED, carrying the broken half of spear, John Colter walked into Fort Raymond eight days later. He paused by the staring clerk, and gravely dropped the broken spear across the ledger. "Souvenir, Junior," he said, and walked on into Lisa's office.

"Hello, Manuel," he croaked. He dropped into the same chair he had occupied the day they had planned the ill-fated expedition.

Manuel Lisa's questioning black eyes gave the only evidence of his astonishment. He went to a cupboard and poured out a stiff drink of brandy. Colter sipped it slowly, feeling warmth flow back into his numb, stiff body.

"You guessed it, Manuel," he said. "The Blackfeet caught us. Potts is dead, and all I got left is what you see." He finished the brandy. "But there's lots of beaver on those little cricks—more'n I thought."

"So-o? And what would you suggest, my frien'?"

"That I go back," John Colter replied shortly. "There's a pile of pelts cached up there, and plenty more to be took. But we need a fort, I reckon." Then, as though it were an afterthought, he added, "Some of them Blackfeet are a mite unfriendly."

FREIGHT
FOR SANTA FE

1833 *While the fur trappers were busy pushing the northwestern frontier steadily back, and paving the way for the Oregon pioneers who were to follow them a generation later, an equally hardy breed was performing a similar service in the southwest. These men were the bullwhackers, muleteers, and traders who slogged the eight hundred weary miles of the Santa Fe Trail.*

In the 1820's and 1830's, St. Louis was still the great western trading center. But steamboats had pushed west, across what is now Missouri, to the spot where the Missouri River makes its big bend to the north. Here Independence was built, as the eastern terminus of the Santa Fe trade. Cotton goods and hardware from New England, brought down the Ohio and up the Missouri, were freighted by wagon train to the Mexican city of Santa Fe. Mexico had thrown off the yoke of Spain in 1821, and welcomed both American trade and settlers to its provinces of New Mexico and Texas. Thanks to the brawny, sweating bullwhackers who cursed their stubborn teams over the Santa Fe Trail, the Southwest inevitably became part of the United States.

A BRIGHT, deep-yellow moon hung in the sky, painting roofs of the scattered houses a startling, unreal silver, and dimming the few oil lamps that still glowed within the windows. Independence, Missouri, the terminal point from which the Mexican Santa Fe trade started, was a raw, sprawling, frontier town, and law-abiding citizens shut themselves in early.

Ryder Jackson strolled down the board walk that ran along the side of the dirt road that served as the main street. Moonlight revealed in soft outline the heavy black hair that covered his head like a mat, the strong face and square jaw beneath it, the deep chest, and the slim waist and hips.

"Independence, Missouri," he murmured to himself. "Well, here I am."

The town wasn't much to look at, but at least it lacked the placid, rural atmosphere of Red Branch, Illinois, the place from which he had started two months ago. Red Branch was a little country community, where the farmers came in every Saturday to smoke their pipes and sit on the steps of the country store. It was all right for those who liked it, but Ryder Jackson had decided that he didn't. You could hardly turn around there in these settled times of 1833 without kicking some neighbor's pig out of the way, or way-ing his cow back home. So he'd sold his farm and dairy cattle for five hundred dollars in gold, shaken the dust of Illinois from his restless feet, and hit the trail west. Now here he was, at the end of the line. He still had his money, but not much idea of what to do with it, or himself.

He stopped suddenly. Just ahead, in the semi-darkness, a bull whip had snapped like a pistol shot. An angry yell rolled down the street. Ryder Jackson edged cautiously forward, letting his jacket fall back so his knife and revolver would be immediately available. A happy grin played across his lips. He knew a man was a fool to break in on somebody else's fight, especially in a strange town. But that was the next best thing if he couldn't start one of his own. He came to a road that slanted across the one he was walking, and stopped again.

The bright moon sprayed down into the middle of the dusty road, and its light at the intersection almost matched that of day. In the center stood an old man dressed in baggy trousers and a flannel vest. A flowing beard hung from his cheeks and chin, and uncut hair dangled below his shoulders. He was short and fat, but when he moved he did so swiftly and silently. Five other men, gliding shadows in the semi-gloom that surrounded the bright patch of moonlight, moved cautiously about the embattled figure. The old man raised his hand, the long bull whip cracked again, and one of the lurking men yelled in pain.

Ryder Jackson's grin widened. He always enjoyed

watching a real expert work, and obviously the old codger was a past master of the bull whip.

"Drop the whip, Grandpa!" one of the waiting men yelled. "Drop it and fight like a man!"

"Come git me, you scum!" the old man rumbled.

"Grandpa Dancer don't dast fight man to man!" another called.

The old man braced his feet and shifted his hold on the whip stock. The men in the shadows retreated a little, but continued to yell taunts. Ryder Jackson's eyes narrowed. There was purpose in their retreat, and in their yelling. While four continued to hold the old man's attention, another of their number had slipped around and was approaching from behind. A short knife gleamed in his hand. Jackson made a swift little run forward, curled an arm about the neck of the knife-wielder, and spun him about. He cracked his fist against the man's jaw, and watched him stagger back into the darkness.

Just then, a big collie dog glided in from the shadows to stand beside the owner of the bull whip.

"Where you been, Alec?" The old man said plaintively to the dog. "Chase 'em out of here!"

The big collie snarled understandingly, and stalked stiffly forward with his teeth bared. The five men grouped to meet him, then thought better of it, and melted silently away. Curling the lash of his bull whip, and catching it in his hand, the old man called back the dog, then turned to face Ryder Jackson.

"Why horn in on my fight, stranger?" he asked.

"Why—uh—I figure five against one's too many, especially when the one's an old man——"

"Who you callin' an old man?" the grizzled bull-whacker snapped. "I'll have you know that Joab Dancer kin fight twenty times as many prairie dogs as that, even if he is sixty-eight years old."

"My mistake, Grandpa," Jackson said soothingly. "Sorry I spoiled your fight."

"Pshaw!" Joab Dancer snorted. "'Twouldn't of been much of a fight. But them scum thought I had tradin' money on me, I reckon."

"Why didn't you tell 'em different?"

"And admit I was scared of 'em? Not me! Say, you're a likely enough young feller. Where'd you come from, anyhow?"

"Illinois."

"Ow-w!" the old man growled. "You younguns are all fools! I know your story; you had a good job in Illinois, but it wan't enough for you. You had to go some place else. I bet you're thinkin' of tradin' into Santy Fe?"

"Maybe."

"Well, forgit it, and go back to Illinois. Nobody but a be-danged fool would hit the Santy Fe Trail."

"What do you know about it?"

"What don't I? I started as a bullwhacker four

248

years ago. Now I own two teams, and am takin' my own wagon this trip, soon's I git goods to fill it. What's your name, anyhow?"

"Ryder Jackson."

"From now on, you're Ride. Now, Ride, you go back to Illinois, where you belong."

"Did you ever milk cows?"

"Not me!" Joab Dancer snapped. "And nary I will. Milkin' cows would be even wuss than whackin' bulls!"

"That's what I think. And I aim to see this Santa Fe Trail. What's wrong with it?"

"Ain't nothin' right about it," the old man grumbled.

"You made money, didn't you?"

"Yeah, even after the Mexicans has took their hunnert per cent duty, you kin make six times what you start with. But you earn it, by the time you chivy a team of oxen eight hunnert miles. Then you come back to Ind'pendence and start all over agin. You git in a rut. This is my last trip. Me and my grandson are goin' to buy steers in Santy Fe, and move to Texas, where we kin jest sit and watch 'em grow."

"I'm still going to do it."

"Now I know you're crazy!" Joab Dancer groaned. "Where's your team and wagon?"

"Thought I'd buy 'em here."

"You'll buy 'em *here*? What you'll buy is a set of

foot-sore oxen, or wind-broke mules, that couldn't walk from here to Council Grove! And, when you're done, you won't have the price of trade goods left." The old man squinted at him thoughtfully. "You got money, eh?"

"Some."

"Whyn't you say so! Well, if you're idjit enough to throw it away, mebbe I kin help you do it. Leastways, I won't rob you—much!" Joab cackled silently, then grew serious. "Looka here. I got a wagon and teams, but I ain't got enough money for all the trade goods I kin haul. Come along and bunk down in the wagon. We'll see if we can't make a dicker."

RYDER JACKSON awoke in the soft light of early dawn. The first thing of which he became conscious was the white tops of the prairie wagons that were scattered through a grove of young trees just outside the town. He sat up and counted them. There were sixty or seventy of the big cargo wagons and a sprinkling of smaller carts. A few early rising men, wearing everything from the corduroy coats of city-bred merchants to the linsey jackets of farmers and the leather hunting shirts of frontiersmen, walked among the wagons or squatted by cooking fires. The cool morning breeze brought the smell of smoke and the fragrance of boiling coffee.

A bull-necked, red-faced man wearing blue jeans crawled out of the back of the next wagon and bellowed out, "Gus! Gus! Where the blazes is that man? Hey you, Gus! Come 'er! Who taught you to load a wagon, anyhow? The way you got it piled, these goods will be a mess afore we git to Council Grove. Can'cha do nothin' right?"

A squawking rooster leaped from the seat of another wagon and flapped across the prairie. A lean man dressed only in red underwear set out after him, and the early risers dropped everything to watch and offer sarcastic comment.

"Yip-ee!" shouted a frontiersman with a long rifle. "I'll bet twenty dollars on the rooster!"

"Whyn't you let him go, Red?" a burly bullwhacker shouted. "You shouldn't ought to steal chickens in Ind'pendence, anyway."

A small brown mustang, with Joab's collie frisking happily beside it, drew up by the Dancer wagon. The rider was about twenty-three, Jackson's own age. He was tall and supple, with the softest brown eyes Ryder Jackson had ever seen on a man. The whimsical curve of his mouth, beneath the drooping, silken mustache, matched the gentleness of his eyes. This man seemed as far removed from the hard-bitten bullwhackers as Red Bank was from Independence. But beneath his gentle appearance was both physical and mental hardness; he looked as if he could hold his own. As he swung from his saddle the little brown mustang nibbled his arm with soft lips.

"You're Ride, aren't you?" he asked in a soft and musical voice.

"That's right."

"Grandpa said to look for you. I'm Carson Dancer."

"Glad to know you. Where is Grandpa?"

"You'd better not call him that," Carson Dancer admonished with a smile. "I can, because I'm his grandson, but he won't take it from anybody else. He's gone to Independence to buy goods."

"But I thought he was going to buy *my* goods this morning."

"He is. He took your money."

Ryder Jackson's hand went to where his money belt had been, and touched nothing. His face flushed angrily, then a sheepish grin spread over his face.

"Joab's got light fingers, I'll say that," he admitted ruefully.

"I know you mean no offense," young Dancer laughed. "So I'll take none. Grandpa figured he'd do better alone. The dealers know better than to try to cheat him. You haven't got a horse, have you?"

"No. I came by steamboat from St. Louis."

"Grandpa'll get you one. Well, I've got to bring in the stock. You might be starting breakfast. Grandpa will want to load your stuff as soon as we eat."

He mounted the little mustang and, with the collie

dashing beside him, rode away. Eight or ten other men were headed in the same direction, toward the grazing teams. The wagoneers waited expectantly, eating breakfast or making last-minute inspections and adjustments of their equipment.

As Ride busied himself with breakfast preparations, a youth with a scatter gun held awkwardly in his hand strolled slowly past. Jackson turned to take another look at this tired-looking young man who was wearing a tall silk hat and a corduroy business suit. His face was thin and pale, his arms and legs seemed pitifully inadequate to the task of supporting and assisting the body of a man.

"My name's Dorrance Crispell," the stranger remarked. "You're new here, aren't you?"

"Just arrived," Jackson grunted. He began to shave kindling with his knife. "You a preacher?"

Dorrance Crispell shook his head. "Up until a little while ago I was a school teacher. But my good doctor has exhausted all his resources. He said that if I cared to live beyond thirty, I'd have to try another cure. Life on the prairies was recommended."

"I didn't know sick men travelled with caravans."

"There's more than one of us with this one. I have already met and talked with five who are making the trip, in hopes of ridding themselves of mortal ills."

"Well, I hope you do it." As he dumped coffee in the pot, Ryder Jackson reflected that the Santa Fe

253

Trail would be strong medicine for this frail youth.

Dorrance Crispell shrugged. "It's a last chance. And, even if we gain no benefits, this will be a last adventure in living. I've read all available records of the Santa Fe trade, and it really is adventurous. Did you know that Captain Zebulon Pike visited both Taos and Santa Fe over twenty-five years ago, and that his excited reports of possible trade with the Spaniards really started all this?"

Ride began to slice bacon. "No. I thought it began after Mexico threw out the Spanish."

"It's true that it didn't amount to much until then. Spain didn't encourage it, and the first traders were even jailed—for nine years. But after Mexico declared its independence, in 1821, Captain Becknell blazed the route directly across the desert, and thirst killed nearly all his party. It's still very dangerous in spots, I believe."

"Is it true that the Mexicans will give land in Texas to the Americans?"

Crispell nodded. "The Mexicans want both American trade and settlers. They passed an act in 1825, giving acreage and other privileges to Americans who want to settle. It's said that there are at least twenty thousand Americans there now, and that Mexico is beginning to regret its offers."

"How's that?"

"The settlers do not look kindly upon Mexican

rulers, and there's even talk that they may try to throw off Mexico, as Mexico threw off Spain."

"Do you think they will?"

Dorrance Crispell shrugged. "I do not pretend to wear a prophet's cap. But Texas is not dependent on Mexico. Almost everything the colonists need—or Mexico itself needs, for that matter—comes from the States. Texas is a vast country, hard to govern. Mexico is weak . . ." He gave a tired smile. "Two and two usually make four."

He wandered off, leaving the dissatisfied Illinois farmer staring into space. Texas was vast . . . no neighbors crowding you. Trade already established with the States . . . a market for beef cattle, that didn't have to be milked, or babied . . .

"Here come the bulls!"

Ryder Jackson turned to see a great herd of milling, lowing oxen approach the wagons. The horsemen rode among them, breaking the herd into small groups and in turn breaking those up. Some of the oxen, trained, submitted without protest to the yoke, and within twenty minutes after the herd first appeared two lumbering wagons were already rolling westward. But at least half the herd were either untrained or unsubmissive. Sweating, swearing bullwhackers went among them, and the cracking of their whips sounded constantly as they sought out the animals that belonged to them.

One by one the big wagons trundled off across the prairie. They would all stop at Council Grove, some ten or eleven days' journey to the west, and the caravan would organize there. No hostile Indians ever came farther east than Council Grove, and until they passed that point it was not necessary for the wagons to band together for protection.

Driving sixteen huge black oxen, Carson Dancer came up on his brown mustang. As he swung off his horse, the biggest ox, evidently the leader of the group, broke back through the trees. The rest began to follow.

"Get 'em, Alec," Carson ordered.

The big collie's tail streamed behind him as he leaped happily away to the head of the fleeing animals. He jumped at the nose of the lead ox, and snapped his teeth together. The ox halted, head down and front hoof pawing the earth as he rumbled angrily. Alec dashed around and nipped his heels. The ox turned, and started running again. But always the trained dog was at his head or heels, barking, nipping, and worrying. Finally the sixteen bewildered oxen were brought into a compact little herd.

"Hold 'em, Alec."

Ryder Jackson looked at the animals with an expert's eye. All were big, strong, and in the best of condition. He said so, admiringly.

"None better," Carson agreed. "Most of them have

made the trip before . . . Here's Grandpa now."

Joab Dancer was riding a big-boned bay. Tied by the bridle reins, a neat little black mare walked behind it. The old man drew up beside them, and indicated the extra mount.

"She's yours, Ride. Let's see you live up to your name." He winked at his grandson.

Ryder Jackson swung into the saddle, and the little mare went into a vicious pitch that almost unseated him. But he rode her to a sweating standstill, and the Dancers looked at each other with approval.

THEY STARTED WEST in company with four other wagons, three of which were drawn by oxen and one by mules. Some of the loose stock, which would be called into service when those pulling the wagons became footsore, tired, or lost, had gone on in a herd attended by four riders. But some wagons preferred to take their alternate stock with them. The watchful Alec was herding their own oxen and two extra saddle horses.

Mounting the little mare, Ryder Jackson rode ahead up the trail. He overtook a few wagons, whose drivers waved at him as he rode by. But there was, so far, nothing of interest to be seen, and after a couple of hours he rode back. Carson Dancer had tied his brown mustang to the tailboard and was sleeping inside the wagon. With his bull whip cracking at regular intervals, old Joab was walking beside the placid oxen. Ryder dismounted, looped the little mare's reins over his shoulder, and walked along beside Joab.

"Nothing much up the trail," he reported.

"You'll git used to that," the old man grunted. "Ain't nothin' much 'twixt here and Santy Fe, neither—barrin' buffalo wallows, dust, rivers, snakes, mudholes, stampedes, rain, hail——"

"Hail, on the prairie?"

"Big as eggs. And I forgot lightnin'. Why, when you git a real prairie storm, with rain comin' down like a solid thing, and lightnin' strikin' all around, you don't dast to stand up for fear of gittin' hit by lightnin', and you don't dast to lie down for fear of gettin' drownded."

"How about Indians?"

"They ain't nothin' much. Oh, now'n agin you'll meet a party of Pawnees, or Gros Ventres, or some other heathen tribe. But it's skassly ever they fight, 'specially if you let 'em know you're ready for 'em. I suspicion there ain't been a dozen men kilt by Injuns on this trail in the last two-three years."

"Not much excitement, eh?"

"Naw. Same old thing year after year. Like I told you, this is my last trip; then I'm headin' for the Texas country. There's grass down there as is greener than green. A man could stake out a little piece, say as much as he could ride across in a couple or four days, get hisself a passel of cattle, and really start livin'. And, when I do git down there, I ain't never gonna look at another ox as long as I live."

"Why don't you drive mules, if you don't like oxen?"

"One's bad as 'tother," Joab answered sourly. "Four span of oxen'll pull heavier loads than four of mules, and they'll eat forage mules won't touch, once the grass gits high enough for 'em to git aholt of. But they're tarnal slow, and they got no sense, and they git sore feet easy. Both oxen and mules must of been put on earth 'specially to plague anybody fool enough to try to drive 'em. It's a bothersome business! Until we git in buffalo country we won't even be able to eat nothin' but dry grub."

"What supplies are we carrying?"

"For you, Carson, and me, there's a hunnert and fifty pounds of flour, the same of bacon, thirty of coffee, 'bout fifty of sugar, and a sack of salt. Some people takes real delicate stuff like crackers and beans. But they ain't fitten for a freighter's stummak. Sowbelly and biscuit's what his innards is used to."

The whip cracked, expertly flicking into the side of the off lead ox. Without changing pace, the lumbering beast strained a little harder into its yoke. Joab's forceful words, expressly designed for oxen, followed the crack of the whip. The team pulled harder.

They camped that night near the upper reaches of Cedar Creek. A man named Slaughter, who had volunteered as cook, stirred up a savory mess of bacon, flour, and a few pounds of beans that somebody threw into the pot. Each man scooped a skillet full and sat on the grass while he ate with his fingers. The simple meal was washed down with numerous cups of scalding black coffee.

After supper a drizzling, cold rain started. The stock, turned loose to graze, struck toward a distant grove of trees. Old Joab Dancer watched them contemptuously.

"Goldarn critters allus do that," he observed in disgust. "They ain't got the sense of a bumblebee—at least a bee knows enough to come home once in a while. We'll have to be out a couple of weeks afore them fool things learn to stick near the wagons. Then you can't chase 'em off. Well, let's git under cover—we won't need a night watch until we git to Council Grove."

They crawled under the wagon's hood, spread their blankets on top of the trade goods, and listened to the steady patter of the rain. As usual, Joab was pessimistic.

"Hope this rain stops," he grumbled. "If it don't, somebody's sure to git bogged down in Cedar Crick."

He tossed and turned, trying to make himself comfortable. "Doggone it, Carson, you put all the cotton goods on your side, and packed the tinware right where I got to lie on it. What do them Mexicans do with all these pots and pans, anyway?"

"Don't worry, Grandpa," came the gentle voice. "The first time the team runs away, they'll shake it down for you."

Ryder Jackson smiled to himself in the darkness. He'd left Red Branch because it was too crowded, and now he was jammed in an oversize peddler's cart, like a doll in a bureau drawer . . .

IN THE COLD, dim light of early morning the wagon rolled on, past the trees known as the Round Grove, and into the bottom land of Cedar Creek. Slaughter, driving the lead wagon, came back along the line, snapping the lash of his whip in the air as he walked.

"Bogged down in a right smart way," he announced cheerfully. "How about double-teamin'?"

"I told you," Joab groaned, stopping his team.

Ryder Jackson looped the reins of his black mare over a peg on the tailboard and walked up to the mired wagon. It was in to the hubs. Slaughter's oxen were blowing and heaving from the mighty efforts they had made to drag it out, and Slaughter himself was mud to his knees. Joab Dancer drove his eight big blacks in ahead of the bogged team, hitched them, and stood back. He cracked his bull whip.

"Hi! Gee up!"

The ponderous beasts strained against the yokes, almost sinking to their knees as they strove with every ounce of brawn and muscle to move the wagon. It rolled forward, then settled back. Jackson waded into the mudhole, grasped two spokes of a hind wheel, and strove to turn it forward. Carson Dancer took the other hind wheel, and Slaughter and a man named Maloney were on the front. The whip cracked again.

"Gee up there! Move that wagon! Step into those yokes! Buck! Bright! Dandy! Black!"

Again the linked teams strove, but the wagon barely moved. The popping of Joab's whip sounded constantly, and the oxen tossed their heads and thrust their tongues out. With a sudden, lunging heave the wagon came out of the mud and rolled onto dry, firm ground. But one of the following wagons had to be doubled through, and a mile farther on was another quagmire where three teams had to be used. On they went, crossing streams, mudholes, and endless rolling hillocks. On the eleventh day they came to Council Grove.

Some of the wagons, drawn by fleet mules, had been there several days, and their owners had estab-

lished comfortable camps among the rich groves
lining the creek bottom. As the late-comers arrived,
those with faster wagons lined up to offer unsolicited
advice.

"Well, well! Do you s'pose he could be goin' to
Santy Fe?"

"I dunno. If he figgers on gittin' there, he better
put them little oxies in the wagon and pull it hisself!"

And, as the late arrivals came, they in turn jeered
at those who were even later. It was evening of the
following day before the final wagon, drawn by eight
already footsore oxen, came in to camp. The red-
underweared man who had chased the rooster back
at Independence went about taking count.

"Where's Otterson?" he demanded of the last arrival.

"Why, does he owe you money?" the weary driver
inquired tartly.

"Don't git smart! As probable captain of this caravan I won't put up with it. I'll have you know——"

"You ain't been elected yet," the driver said sourly.
"And, when you might be, you kin take a long jump
into the clostest dust pile, far's I care. But if it's goin'
to make you sleep any better, Otterson's turned back.
He's goin' to sell his team, wagon, and load to the
next damn fool who wants to go tradin', and head for
Texas on horseback. Wish I could!"

Ryder and Carson had unyoked the oxen, turning

the big black beasts out with the grazing herd. Alec would watch his charges critically, and it was quicker to let him cut out the team than it was to try to do it with a horse. The Dancer stock always grazed with one eye ready for the collie, and started for the wagon as soon as he appeared. But many of the oxen were grazing yoked together. They were the wild ones, those which even yet had not been broken. It was far easier to leave the yokes on them than it was to beat the big brutes into submission every time they were needed.

Carson Dancer climbed into the wagon, and emerged with two axes and an adze. He held one out.

"Come on, Ride."

"What's up?"

"There's no more wood fit for wagon repairs between here and Santa Fe. We always cut it at Council Grove, and carry it along with us. Of course, Grandpa gets out of the axe work whenever he can. He claims it's squaw work, but I think he's just lazy." He looked straight at old Joab, sitting comfortably in the shade of the wagon, and grinned.

"Git that wood cut, you young whippersnappers!" old Joab growled. "And see that there ain't no knots in it!"

They went down to the creek bottom, where other men were at work, and felled a tall, straight tree. After trimming the branches, they cut the trunk into

264

two equal lengths, and squared them with the adze.

A blue-denimed ex-farmer nearby eyed them approvingly. "Ye can use an axe," he admitted, with a nasal New England twang. "There's no sense catchin' up a team to drag your logs, boys. I got a span of mules here, all harnessed."

"Thanks," said Carson gratefully. "I'll remember this, when we get to buffalo country."

The team of mules was hitched to the logs, and they were dragged to the Dancer wagon. With one lifting on either end, they hoisted the logs into place and chained them underneath the wagon. They might ride all the way to Santa Fe without being needed. But they would be worth their weight in trade goods if an axle or whiffletree cracked. A broken wagon couldn't travel.

The sudden rattle of a stick beating on a tin pan sounded above the noises of the camp, and they looked toward the source, to see the red-underweared man standing on the tailboard of his wagon.

"Come close!" he bellowed. "Come up real close! We got to organize!"

Slowly, drawn by the magnet of the summoning voice, the wagoneers drifted in. For a moment no one spoke, and the red-underweared man smiled ingratiatingly. He cleared his throat.

"Now, what about the captain of this here caravan——?"

"Not you!" a weather-beaten bullwhacker snorted, "You couldn't be cap'n of a toy boat!"

"Is that so?" The red-underweared man's voice rose to a high pitch. "I'll have you know I've——"

The stocky bullwhacker mounted the wagon, unceremoniously thrust the other aside, and looked around. He pointed the stock of his whip at old Joab Dancer.

"How about it, Joab?"

"I ain't honin' to be cap'n," the old man said positively. "Take it yourself, Billy Marsh."

"I don't want it neither."

"Aw, come on, Bill," a mule driver said, and others picked up the cry. "Come on, Bill, we want you." "Take it, Bill."

The weather-beaten bullwhacker looked around, an expression of distaste on his face. "Wal, somebody's gotta be it. Anybody as don't want me fer cap'n, speak up now."

Nobody spoke. The bullwhacker sighed, and pulled at his whiskers.

"All right; I'm cap'n. As usual, we'll have four parts to this here wagon train. You, Joab Dancer—an' I don't give a hoot if you don't like it—are in charge of them sixteen wagons nearest you. You, Tommy Malone, Greg Hartman, an' Al Garbaugh, take the wagons nearest you an' make up your sections. Everybody with a wagon list the men an' goods you carry with your lieutenant. Two men in each section to roussle the guards out. Everybody does guard duty, turn an' turn about, beginnin' tomorra night. In the mornin' we'll leave in this order: first, Al's section, then Joab's, then Tommy's, then Greg's. Git some sleep."

As usual on clear nights, they slept under the wagon. They were awake in the first dim, wan light of early morning, and gathered at the cooking pot which the tireless Slaughter had ready. They had scarcely finished breakfast when the call came from the captain's wagon, "Catch up!"

"Go get 'em, Alec," Joab ordered.

The big collie raced happily off, and returned driving the black oxen ahead of him. A cursing muleteer, struggling with a stubborn brute that braced its feet and refused to move, looked enviously at him.

"I'll trade a good span of mules for that dog," he offered.

"Huh," Joab Dancer snorted. "You could toss in your wagon and its load, and still not have enough."

Other teamsters were pursuing running beasts through the camp, swearing, sweating, and yelling. The jingle of harness chains mingled with the rattle of yokes and the creak of wagons, all punctuated by constant shouts. Finally the last vicious mule and the final stubborn ox had been subdued, and the caravan was ready to start.

"All set?" came the call from the captain's wagon.

"All set!" the various section leaders bellowed back.

"Stretch out fer Santy Fe!"

BY THE TIME they had reached the Arkansas River, their most difficult crossing, the caravan was well organized. Since they were now in Indian country, the long, snake-like line of the wagon train had been broken into a more compact arrangement of four parallel columns, one section to a column. To equalize the hardships of plodding through dust clouds or mudholes churned up by the wagons ahead, the lead wagon for each day dropped to the rear of the column the next day, to work its slow way up through the procession again. Every night, the wagons were drawn up in a protective square, and the section leaders appointed night watches, turn and turn about.

Late in the afternoon they drew up at the north bank of the Arkansas, and after consultation with his lieutenants, Captain Marsh decided to make the crossing that night. There was not only the danger of a night rain swelling the river, but teams always pulled better when they were warmed up. If they waited until morning, the wagons would have to take a turn around the prairie, to give the teams a "hot collar" before crossing, which would waste time.

The river was here about half a mile wide, with a sandy bottom and a broad, smoothly flowing current. Its brown surface was broken by sand bars and low, reed-covered islands, but the flowing water was so full of sand and silt that the bottom could nowhere be seen. While loads were readjusted to keep perishable goods high in the wagons, horsemen were sent ahead to test the ford for quicksand, and to stick willow poles in the sand bars that marked the best route.

"Lock your wheels goin' down the high banks," Marsh told his lieutenants, "an' double-team the heaviest wagons. We'll start here, an' quarter downstream, so's the wagons won't git hit broadside by the current. Watch out fer quicksand—*an' keep the wagons movin'!*"

Ryder Jackson watched the leading wagon, drawn by six span of tough, wiry mules, slide down the five-foot bank. As it plunged into the river, the wheel span was pulled under the water. But the four leading span had found firm footing, and the wagon lurched ahead, the wheel mules blowing and thrashing as they came to the surface. One by one the following wagons bumped and splashed after them, until a long, irregular line stretched diagonally across the river. Horsemen rode or swam back and forth, shouting, cursing, prodding, encouraging. Several wagons were caught in quicksand, but only one could not be extricated. As its short-legged oxen gave up the struggle one after another, team and wagon sank from sight inch by inch, while horsemen and wagoneers milled helplessly about. Half a dozen wagons were overturned, and much of their precious cargo swept downstream. But the Dancer wagon, thanks to old Joab's expert handling and the power of his big blacks, came through without a mishap.

As the wagons straggled up the south bank, the first section drew up at right angles to the line of march. The next section continued straight, but stopped to make a long wing on the wagons already halted. The third division swung to form another wing, and the final wagons closed the gap. When finished, the "formed" wagons made a rectangular enclosure which might be defended in the event of an Indian attack. The oxen and mules, some of which were still yoked, were permitted to graze for a while on the open prairie, then driven into the enclosure through an opening left at one corner. But nothing was heard that night except the heavy breathing of exhausted animals, the snores of tired men, and the distant howling of wolves.

They went on the next day, trundling over the flat plains, and the constant popping of rifles and pistols bespoke the efforts of those up ahead who were trying to clear rattlesnakes out of the line of march. It was shortly after eleven o'clock when Carson Dancer rode up on his brown mustang, much excited, and pointed across the prairie.

Ryder Jackson followed his gaze. There, about a quarter of a mile away, a hundred or more buffalo were grazing on the short prairie grass. Ryder stole a glance at Carson Dancer. The other's eyes were alight, and his face glowing with excitement.

"Buffalo!" he said. "Now we'll have some fun!"

Riding up to the rear of the wagon, he reached in and pulled his rifle from its resting place under the bows of the hood. Then he touched his heels to the brown mustang's side, and the little horse was away. Almost at the same moment, four other riders cut from the caravan and bore down on the lumbering, shaggy beasts.

Ryder loosened his pistol in its holster and galloped

after him. The wind fanned his cheek, and a surge of pure delight travelled up and down his spine. This was life. This was excitement. This, as Carson Dancer had said, was the best part of trading into Santa Fe. Another rider on a steel-gray horse drew up beside him, and stayed there. But Jackson was watching Carson Dancer, the buffalo hunter.

Joab's grandson clung to the brown mustang's back so closely and so tightly that horseman and mount seemed one. Far ahead of the rest, they pressed close on the heels of the running buffalo. There came the faint crack of a rifle, and for a moment a swirl of dust hid the hunter. Ryder spurred his mare.

The dust lifted, and he saw that Carson had turned the running buffalo. The big beasts were quartering across the other horsemen now, running fast, with heads low and tails erect. But beside the leaders was the brown mustang, running with free reins while his owner held his rifle ready.

Ryder Jackson was vaguely aware of the man on the steel-gray horse, still beside him. He spurred the little black mare, and drew the pistol from its holster.

Suddenly a single tremendous bull cut from the herd, shaggy head swinging and red eyes rolling. Head down, he charged straight at the two horsemen. The steel-gray squealed and reared, while its rider fought desperately with both hands to control it. Wild with fright, the horse plunged and bucked. The

shaggy bull was almost upon it now, preparing for the upward thrust that would disembowel the horse.

Ryder Jackson spurred the mare around to the side and shot once. The buffalo seemed to hesitate and change pace, then bored in again. At that moment Carson's mustang streaked past the mare, and Ryder heard the crack of a rifle and the flat slap of a bullet striking flesh. The buffalo took two staggering steps, its legs buckled, and it rolled completely over by its own momentum.

The steel-gray calmed down, and for the first time Jackson looked at the lean, tanned man who rode it. It was Dorrance Crispell, the former invalid. He grinned across at Ryder.

"Nice shot," he said."

The brown mustang was already closing in on the herd again.

THE CARAVAN WENT ON, day after day, into the country that was variously called New Mexico or Texas. Double or even triple-teaming, they crossed more rivers and flooded creeks and stretches filled with treacherous buffalo wallows. They plodded over the hot, dry desert. They rolled over endless green hillocks splashed with mountain pink, spiderwort, and larkspur. They fought their way mile by mile over the plains, disturbing the buffalo, wild mustangs, prairie dogs, antelope, and rattlesnakes which, until white men saw fit to come this way, had held undisputed sway over these wild regions. Stopping two or three hours at midday to let the animals graze, forming their protective square at night, they travelled steadily southwest.

Ryder Jackson became bored by the slow monotony of the creaking wagons, but as day followed day in endless procession, the land laid its spell on him. The empty green earth and the empty blue sky satisfied a craving for spacious freedom that he had never fully understood before. At night, even the stars seemed bigger and more widely spaced. Room . . . room . . . limitless room . . .

THEY WERE IN the rolling hill country of the upper Pecos River when the Dancers' off lead ox was bitten by a rattler and had to be shot.

"Golblamed things!" old Joab sputtered, his face purple. "They ain't got no sense. Allus breakin' a leg or runnin' away or gittin' bit! Golblamed things!"

He strode up and down beside the dead ox, snapping his whip viciously.

"Now, Grandpa," said Carson mildly, "that's the first ox we've lost, and you know it. I'll go cut another from the loose stock, and we'll be hitched in no time."

He did, but by the time the substitution had been made, the last wagon of the caravan was a mile ahead. It was then that Ryder Jackson saw the Indians.

Apparently rising from the ground, they came flowing over a little hillock, leaning over their horses' necks as they swept forward.

Joab cracked the bull whip again and again, sending the long lash flicking sharply into the backs of the oxen as he strove to make them run. At the same time Carson pulled his rifle from the wagon and fired a hasty shot. The Indians were too far away to hit, but the report might warn the wagon train.

The Indians swerved, breaking their tight formation and racing along on a course parallel to the wagon's. An arrow soared out, imbedded itself in the rump of an ox, and the wounded animal lunged forward. Then the team really began to run. From his jouncing, swaying wagon seat, Joab used his whip continuously on the straining oxen. Ryder and Carson rode alongside, prodding the beasts into still greater activity.

The Indians changed their tactics again, rushing closer now and shooting. Arrows thudded into the side of the wagon, and another ox was hit. If they were able to cripple the team before it could reach the safety of the wagon train, they could loot the wagon. But they would have to work fast. The caravan had formed up, and the Dancer wagon was travelling as fast as sixteen terrified oxen could run.

Carson's rifle cracked again, and an Indian's horse crumpled, throwing its rider twenty feet through the air.

"Keep workin' 'em!" he shouted to Joab. "We're nearly there!"

The old man needed no urging. He was standing up now, wielding his whip like a Roman chariot driver. The running oxen reached the square, and raced into the hole that had been left open for them. As they went through, the left hind wheel hooked into the next wagon, tearing off the wheel and dropping the wagon box to the ground so hard that Joab was thrown off his precarious perch. But the off-balance wagon slowed the oxen, and brawny wagoneers had them under control before the old man could catch his breath enough to curse.

Then another horde of mounted Indians, so many that they seemed to pop up like blades of grass, swept over the rise. A few rifles cracked from among them, and a volley of misdirected arrows fell far short. The word of the wagon train's captain was passed down the line.

"Shoot when I give the order!"

But nobody paid any attention to him. They were hard-headed men, rugged individuals, each of whom had property to defend and each of whom was capable of defending it. And, to every wagoneer, his own method was by far the best. A variety of conflicting orders went down the line.

"Let 'em have it!" "Hold your fire!" "Charge 'em!" "Stay here!" A nervous trader fired, and a scattered volley of shots followed.

The advancing Indians stopped short, then began to retreat. A few lingered within sight of the caravan, but the majority disappeared as suddenly as they had come.

Inside the formed square a tethered horse snorted, and pulled back on its tie-rope. The rest of the animals were uneasy, milling about within the enclosure. One sweating teamster grasped the tether rope trailing from the bridle of a wheel mule and yanked it up short. The mule braced its feet, and strained in the other direction. A passing bullwhacker lashed the stubborn beast's rump with his whip, and the mule's heels flew into the air. Rearing and bucking, he was finally led to the wagon and harnessed. Similar scenes were taking place all through the embattled square. A horse screamed. There sounded the steady thud-thud of the frightened mule's hooves as it steadily kicked the wagon to which it was tied. But several minutes passed before someone shouted, "I smell smoke! They're goin' to burn us out!"

Ryder Jackson became vaguely conscious of smoke in his nostrils, and he squinted against the breeze as he strove to see it. Then it appeared, a light blue, snake-like thing that curled above the top of the hill and slowly crept down it.

The oxen stood stupidly, with hanging heads. But the horses and mules were panicky now, rearing and plunging as they sought to get away from this unknown new terror that was stalking them. Men ran among them, catching tie-ropes and snubbing them short to wagon wheels.

"Who's got plows?" the captain's voice bellowed above the confusion. "Git 'em out an' git a trench dug! Garbaugh, your section back-fire this side of the trench. Hartman's section, look after the stock. The rest of you stand guard right here!"

In spite of the initial attitude of every man for himself, the weeks of organization and the captain's bull-like voice had their effect. The steadiest mules were hitched to bright new trade plows, and driven through holes in the defensive square. Back and forth, through the approaching smoke, they made a widening path of turned earth. On the near side of the path fires were started and allowed to burn over small, controlled areas. By the time the prairie fire reached the plowed safety strip, plowmen and firemen were back in the square, on the alert. But no Indians were to be seen except a few disappointed watchers in the distance.

Smoke was everywhere now, and the rearing, kicking animals needed constant attention. There was a moment's searing heat, then a great crackling and hissing as the fire reached the plowed furrows and burned itself out.

Through the settling smoke, Ryder Jackson saw three mounted Indians riding over the horizon. But in his mind's eye the horsemen were not red, but white, and he was one of them. Carson and Joab Dancer and Ride Jackson had hit the long, hard trail to Santa Fe, had put up with and conquered everything that had tried to stop them. In a few days the wagon train would reach Santa Fe, and trade its goods. And then . . . ?

Then three would ride to Texas.

END OF THE

TRAIL

1844   While Texas was winning her freedom and becoming a state, Independence had become the terminus of another great overland route. In 1841 the first wagon train of emigrants set out over the Oregon Trail. From Independence this trail led up the North Platte, crossed the mountains through South Pass, and wound on to the Snake River in what is now Idaho. Here it split, northwest for Oregon, southwest for California.

The "Great Emigration" of the 1840's was made possible by the fur traders and trappers who had first blazed the trails and then, when beaver hats went out of fashion and the demand for furs fell off, turned guides for the wagon trains. These mountain men—Kit Carson, Jim Bridger, Jedediah Smith, Tom Fitzpatrick, Jim Clyman, and the rest—were the last great group of Americans who lived their lives in the wilderness. Their knowledge and resourcefulness completed the long trek from ocean to ocean. The job was done. They had come to the end of the trail.

So, in 1844, twenty years after he and Jed Smith and Tom Fitzpatrick had first discovered South Pass, old Jim Clyman saddled his horse at Fort Bridger and set out for the west again. . . .

THEY LAY TOGETHER by the trail, a broken axle, a dead ox, and an elaborately carved chest of drawers filled with household goods. Jim Clyman swung off his horse to examine them. The little brown dog that had been running beside him edged curiously up to sniff at the ox, and the horse blew through its nostrils. Jim Clyman reached up with his left hand to scratch the gray stubble on his chin. He looked westward, where the ominous spears that were the peaks of the Sierra Nevada Mountains arched endlessly to reach the sky, and studied the nest of clouds that were gathering over them. A broken axle, a dead ox, and a chest of drawers. . . . The little brown dog wagged up to him, and Jim Clyman spoke as he would have to a man.

"There's gonna be trouble ahead, Bub."

The brown spaniel reared with both front paws against his master's thigh, and shoved his nose into the cupped hand. The old mountain man stroked the dog's ears absently, and spat into the rutted trail. There was going to be trouble, sure enough, although not this time from the Indians. The Arikaras, Arapahoes, and Blackfeet had been tamed back in the early twenties, when the mountain men and the trappers had been the only ones to hit the trails west of the Missouri. Tenderfeet now travelled those paths which the feet—and the blood—of the mountain men had marked. Now tenderfeet needn't fear the Indians—

anyhow, not very much. But they didn't take into proper account the much more savage enemies of mountains and distance and weather with which they had to cope in this year of 1844, when every tenderfoot, all his brothers and sisters, sons and daughters, uncles, aunts, and grandparents seemed to be either on the way to California or Oregon, or obsessed with the idea that they must soon start.

A broken axle, a dead ox, and a chest of drawers filled with household goods. . . .

Jim Clyman spat again into the rut, and did some thinking. There had been six wagons in this party ahead of him when he left Fort Bridger, back in Wyoming. Their trail had freshened considerably just after he left the Humboldt Sink. Now five of them had gone on, and might already be over the divide above Truckee Lake. The sixth had broken down, its occupants had taken time out to make another axle, and the cow that had been tied to the back of the wagon had been yoked in to take the dead ox's place. The team that now pulled this wagon was a very tired one. Women, Jim Clyman reflected, would hang on to their household goods until the last gasp. They'd keep the chest unless it just had to be thrown out so the wagon could be lightened and half-dead cattle could still stagger on toward the land of promise, the milk-and-honey land of California.

The old mountain man looped the horse's reins

over his arm and started to walk along the trail, his eyes on the ground. Trotting placidly beside him, the little brown dog waved his tail and gave all his attention to snuffling through the rut in which he walked.

The long trail to the promised land, Jim Clyman thought, was surely marked with heartache. The path taken by these people was strewn with dead oxen, and graves, and broken wagons, and chests and tools, clear back to the old homes from which they had come. Why did they start? Why did they get themselves a yoke of oxen or a team of mules and a covered wagon, cast everything else aside, and hit the long stretch clear to the west? Jim Clyman answered his own question aloud.

"I know why, Bub," he said to the dog.

Back in New England homesteads, while battling their way through drifts to feed cattle, men thought of perpetually green fields where cattle could graze all winter. Or, while guiding a plow through stubborn, rock-strewn earth, they dreamed of soft black soil where plows never bucked. Or women in storm-lashed prairie huts conjured up images of flowers blooming at Christmas, of zephyr-soft breezes instead of blizzards. The west was a rich and sunny land where every woman was a queen and every man a king. It was thus that these people had talked to themselves and, talking, convinced themselves that they should go to Oregon or California. But they were deluding themselves and they knew it. Deep in their hearts they were aware that they had to go west for the same reason that Columbus had to sail for America. All about was sameness, and unchanging ideas, and routine, and satisfied people who were content to cope with the world they knew. But if there was something new to discover, an opportunity to be seized, a challenge to be met, *they* wanted to do it.

"That's the answer, Bub," Jim Clyman said.

He sighed and mounted his horse. People who blindly obeyed a beckoning finger that bent in their direction were always getting into messes, and this was going to be a bad one if somebody didn't come along to get them out. There were two men, a woman, and two children with the wagon ahead, and they were walking. He had found out that much while he studied their trail. Again he looked at the piled masses of clouds over the mountains, and shook his head.

It was a long, cruel trail that the immigrants had followed. Along it many a man, woman, and child, bereft of their own horses or wagon, had been refused permission to use someone else's. They had had to walk, and it was a singular thing that they had nearly always walked toward the magic lodestone that drew them to the west. They had walked until they died—except for those very few who had walked clear to California. But all the luck in the world had been on the side of those who had finally made it.

And the cruellest part of the entire trail was the divide above Truckee Lake. It was only a year ago that Jim Clyman had helped another train of six wagons get over it. They had hitched four span of oxen to a single wagon, and they had strained up the slope until some of them had died from the terrific strain. Other oxen had been brought to replace the dead ones, and behind the wagon men and women had pushed. But that had been a train with oxen to spare, and no snow had yet fallen on the slopes.

Jim Clyman spurred his horse, and the animal broke into a little trot. His old friend, Caleb Greenwood, had been guiding that other train. Most of the mountain men, now that it was no longer profitable to trap beaver, guided immigrants on the California or Oregon Trail. Caleb had been seventy-nine last year, but after they had finally come down from the mountains he had taken his gun and gone back up to get himself a mess of bear meat. The mush-and-milk food of the wagons, he had said, had run him down seriously. Jim Clyman smiled in recollection.

A day and a half later he rode his horse into Truckee Meadows and saw what he had known he would see there.

A FIFTEEN-YEAR-OLD BOY, dressed in homespun and carrying a rifle, turned to stand beside the trail when he heard the horse. The little brown spaniel padded forward to meet him, and the boy stretched out a hand to stroke the dog's ears. The mountain man reined in his horse and dismounted.

"Howdy, Son. My name's Jim Clyman."

The boy tossed back his head, to fling the long, straight hair out of his eyes, and continued to tickle the dog's ears.

"I'm Nathan Parker," he said. "I'm afraid you're in a bad way, Mr. Clyman."

"So?"

"You can't get over the divide. We tried it. We drove the three oxen and the cow up ahead of us to break a path. But the snow's too deep to go on. We stayed on the slope all night, and it snowed. The next morning we couldn't go on at all. We had to come back down and build a camp to spend the winter in."

"What happened to the oxen and cow?"

"We got the cow back down—she hadn't been hitched for a long pull. But the oxen died right there in the snow, and are all covered up now."

Jim Clyman writhed inwardly. You could always trust a tenderfoot to get himself into trouble, and then to make it worse with his own foolishness. A mountain man, knowing the divide to be snowed under, never would have taken the oxen up in the first place. A party aiming to winter had to have food, and the weather-wise game had already gone from these heights. Three oxen would have lasted five people for a long time. But they were gone, and there was only the cow left.

"Got any grub in your wagon, Nate?" he asked.

"Not very much." The boy flushed with pleasure. A man, evidently one who understood this country, had called him Nate and was asking him questions. "All we got is just a little flour and beans, and Mr. Cressman's got those."

"Who's Mr. Cressman?"

"The man travellin' with us. It was really his flour. He owns the cow, too."

"Looks like Mr. Cressman aims to have vittles for a spell," Jim Clyman muttered. "Who else is along?"

"My Uncle George and Aunt Kate—their name's Parker, too. Uncle George is out huntin'. Then there's my little cousin, Ann. She's almost four. Are you goin' to stay with us?"

"I dunno just what's to be done, Sonny. S'pose we toss a stick in the air and see how she lands? I got a few blocks of pemmican in my saddle bags, and it looks like we're goin' to need 'em."

They walked together up the trail, the little brown dog frisking ahead of them. A cold blast of air surged down from the top of the mountains. A few scattered flakes of snow trailed on the wings of the wind, and the angry brood of clouds glowered at them. Jim Clyman smelled wood smoke, and a moment later they came within sight of a broken-down wagon and two brush tepees built at the base of a huge pine. Beside one of the shelters hung the freshly butchered carcass of the cow.

"I'll bet that'll be Cressman's dugout," Clyman grunted.

"Yep. He won't——"

Nate was interrupted by a woman who came out of the other shelter. She was tall, with clear blue eyes that were set far apart. The little girl who clung to her skirt was a tiny image of her mother. Jim Clyman nodded respectfully.

"Howdy, ma'am."

"Oh—hello. I had hardly expected——"

Nathan Parker said, "It's Mr. Jim Clyman, Aunt Kate. I found him riding up the trail. Uncle George get anything to eat?"

"He's not back yet." The woman looked questioningly at him, then down at the little girl. She hesitated.

Jim Clyman understood. On the road to California you were always welcome at any camp—so long as there was plenty of food in it. He reached into his saddle bag, got one of the pemmican blocks, and cut it in two with his knife. Half of it, and the three remaining blocks, he slipped into the spacious pocket of his jacket. The little dog looked pleadingly up, but his owner looked away from him, at the woman.

"I'm right glad to know you, ma'am. Here. There's

a lot of git in pemmican. Why don't you sort of cook up a meal for the little girl and yourself?"

The woman looked down again, and when she raised her head, tears brimmed in her eyes. Clyman looked away, pretending not to hear the thanks that she called after him, and walked over to the tree where the butchered cow hung. As he reached up his knife for a piece of the meat, a warning voice came from the other shelter.

"Leave it alone."

The little dog backed against his legs, growling, and Jim Clyman stopped, knife in hand, to look at the stocky, dark-haired man who emerged from the other shelter.

"I'll bet you're Cressman."

"I'm Cressman, and that's my beef. Leave it alone."

Without seeming to move fast, the mountain man took three steps forward and dug the point of the knife into Cressman's pudgy stomach. His voice was mild but steady.

"It's camp meat and I'm takin' charge of it. I'm takin' the flour, too."

"You are not!"

"If you want to argue the point, we'll fight it out here and now, and see who's gonna be boss."

Cressman muttered belligerently, but without looking at him again Jim Clyman cut off a piece of the beef, walked past the other into the brush shelter, and picked up the small keg with the few pounds of flour in it. Nathan Parker padded beside him as he strode away.

"He'll be mad at you!" he said in an awed voice.

"Well dog-gone, I've went and made somebody mad! Take this meat and flour in to your Aunt Kate. The flour's for whoever needs it most, and I'm sayin' who needs it. Tell her to have a good hot stew ready for your uncle when he comes back."

The boy disappeared in the shelter, and Clyman unsaddled his horse. He rubbed the animal's nose a moment, then stood back and shot it through the head. An almost inaudible sigh escaped him. It had been a good horse, a faithful and intelligent horse. But when people's lives were in the balance a horse didn't count.

He sighed again. Of all the dang fools ever created, a mountain man was probably the dangdest. He and the horse and the dog could have gone over the divide. But only the most abysmal fool would think of coming into a camp of stranded immigrants, taking charge of it, and trying to take them over, too.

He had butchered the horse, and was hanging it up, when he saw a man emerge from the pine trees and walk through the steadily falling snow. Except for his rifle, he was empty handed. Clyman pretended not to see, until a voice spoke from behind him.

"Hello, stranger."

"Why, howdy," Clyman said, turning as if in surprise. "You must be George Parker."

"That's right."

He was a thin man with pale blond hair and a hesitant manner. The mountain man's heart sank. It was certainly going to be a mismated crew that left this camp to go over the divide. Kate and George Parker, two sensitive, high-strung people with a fine native courage but no experience. Cressman, a selfish man ready to turn beast whenever that was expedient. A little girl who, at the best, would be an encumbrance, and a fifteen-year-old boy. He looked again at the blond man. George Parker seemed as though he'd be all right so long as he didn't have to face any difficult decisions, and then make them himself.

"Say, George," he said, "bring your wife, Nate, Cressman, and the little girl out here, will you? We got to have a powwow."

He stood near the place where he had butchered the horse, and the little brown dog came up to nuzzle his hand. He waited until the stranded wagoneers were gathered about him, then addressed himself to George Parker.

"How'd the huntin' go, George?"

Parker flushed. "I guess I'm not very good. I couldn't even see any game."

The mountain man shook his head grimly. "There ain't any to see; it's all gone down inta the valleys, where food's easier to get. So we'd starve to death if we tried to winter here. We got to go over the divide."

For a moment there was silence, as each in turn pondered this information.

"What assurance is there that we can do it?" Kate Parker asked.

"None. None a'tall. The only sure thing is we'll starve if we don't do it."

He saw that pronouncement hit home with all the impact of a bullet. These tenderfeet wanted to go to California, not to starve. And they'd follow anybody who talked as though he were able to take them there, even though they had never seen him before today.

"I'm ready," Cressman growled.

"Well," George Parker said, looking at his wife, "well, I guess we'd better try."

"It looks," Clyman said deliberately, "like there ain't a vote ag'in it. We got more meat here than we can carry, and I want everybody to eat's much as they can before we start. Even if you got to stuff it down, do that. Mrs. Parker, save most of the flour for the little girl. George, I'll want your wagon spokes."

"What for?"

"For snowshoes. Spokes are good frames, and I'll lace 'em with hide. You and Cressman get in all the wood you can and take a big passel of meat inta the shelters. This snow's gonna fall hard, and we can't start 'til it's over."

IT SNOWED HARD for eight days, at first soft, feathery flakes, and then hard, crystalline ones that piled on top of the shelters and dribbled through the cracks in them until more snow added itself to that already there and stopped up the cracks. It piled up on the pine branches until they became overloaded and spilled their burdens. Driven by the wind, it formed long, curling drifts against every obstruction. And, when the storm finally passed, threatening clouds still hung over the divide.

During those eight days Jim Clyman, Nate, and the two Parkers had worked shaping the wheel spokes into snowshoe frames, scraping the hair from the horse and cow hides, slicing them into thin strips, drying these before the fire, and lacing the dried strips across the frames. Snow was piled high about the shelter, but the fire lit the interior, and sent its blue smoke climbing up through the smoke hole in the roof, that was kept open by poking a long stick up through it. The kettle bubbled constantly, melting snow for drinking water and simmering endless stews. Meal-time was any time anyone felt like eating. They could afford to be prodigal with their food when they could not possibly carry all of it with them, and every ounce they ate now added to their strength.

On the morning of the ninth day, probing through the smoke hole with his stick and finding no snow to push away, Jim Clyman took the shovel that he had brought in from the wagon, and began to dig. The snow, eight feet of which had fallen in eight days, was almost even with the top of the rude shelter. Working the point of his shovel up along the side of the door, he pushed the snow aside, and blinked in the unaccustomed flood of light. He continued to dig, enlarging the hole. Then, cutting steps as he went, he dug upward and outward, and emerged into a white, silent world. To one side, the shelter in which Cressman had crouched alone for eight days was only a soft mound on top of the snow blanket.

Jim Clyman slipped his feet into the harnesses of the home-made snowshoes and walked over to Cressman's shelter. He shovelled a hole down to the door, shouted, and when muffled sounds emerged, dropped the shovel down. Cressman had survived, and could dig himself out.

Young Nate Parker, who had come out of the shelter to try his first experimental steps on snowshoes, floundered over.

"Say, is this snow ever deep!" he panted.

The little brown dog frisked happily about, his big paws better support on the crystalline crust than the snowshoes of the heavier humans. The mountain man watched thoughtfully, his lips pursed. A dog was really something to have when a man was out this way. The least you could say about them was that they never worried. But then, neither did young'uns

—all Nate Parker could think about was the wonderful depth of the snow. But he could take care of himself. Ann couldn't, and it was going to be a mite of a problem to get the little tike over the divide and down the other slope.

He reached over to slash the thong that bore a twenty-pound chunk of horse meat aloft on a pine branch, and caught it in his hands as it fell.

"Take this inside, will you, Nate?" he called.

The boy carried the frozen chunk of meat into the tepee, and a moment later his uncle and aunt came out. They glanced at the shelter where Cressman had cleared a hole for himself and was working to shovel his way to the top of the snow, then set to work helping carry the rest of the meat into their shelter. With the axe, Clyman began chopping the frozen stuff into thin slices, then used his knife to pare the rest of it from the bones. He had begun to make up four packs when Cressman came down into the shelter, and stood sullenly watching him.

"Where's the fifth one?" Cressman demanded.

Jim Clyman said reasonably, "I figger we men can pack mebbe thirty-five pounds each up the slope. Nate's takin' twenty-five."

"What about her?"

"The little girl can't wear snowshoes, so somebody's got to help her all the time, and carry her some of the time. We'll take turns."

Cressman sputtered belligerently. "You know we ain't got much chance of gettin' out of here unless we haul every ounce of food we can!"

"We're takin' four packs." Clyman's voice was smooth. "I told you before I'm big buck at this lick."

Cressman subsided, and Jim Clyman went on making up the packs. He folded a portion of the meat in a square torn from the wagon cover, and formed broad shoulder straps with more of the same material. A blanket was tied to each pack, and two to his own. The little remaining flour he wrapped in a strip of buckskin and put in his own pack. Finally he hung his powder horn at his belt and put half a dozen bullets in his pocket. One rifle was enough. More would be extra weight. He rose.

"Cressman, you carry the axe."

"I'll carry it," Nate Parker offered.

"Cressman will."

He climbed up the steps he had chopped and stood for a moment in the snow on top of them. The little dog crowded close to his heels and squatted down on the tails of his snowshoes while he waited for the rest to join him. They started west toward the slope, Kate Parker and Ann behind Clyman, then Cressman, with George and Nate Parker bringing up the rear. Jim Clyman walked a quarter of a mile and turned around. Kate Parker smiled at him. But there was sweat on her face and she was breathing heavily.

The mountain man went on without slowing his pace. It was a right long way over the pass and down the opposite slope, and they'd better push it hard while they were well-fed and rested. When, and if, they got out of these mountains, they might be crawling on their hands and knees. He studied the clouds that hung low over the mountain peaks, and pushed on another mile before stopping. Then he waited for Kate Parker to close the gap that had imperceptibly widened between them. She was now carrying Ann.

"That little mite you got there," he said, "could rest easy as nothin' on top of my own pack for a spell."

"I'll carry her, Mr. Clyman," the mother said with quiet dignity.

Clyman turned and went on. Immigrants bound for California might be senseless folks who hadn't the least idea of how to take care of themselves. But there was no denying that some of them possessed courage of a sort to brighten the eye of the doughtiest mountain man. Kate Parker's baby was going over the divide with her. She might have to pant to hold up her end. But her baby was still going with her.

THE NEXT DAY they struck the steepest part of the slope and began to claw and fight their way up it. Storm clouds milled angrily above them, and it was bitingly cold. Jim Clyman stopped to turn and look back through the half-gloom, and his brown dog gladly sat down in the tracks he had made. One by one the rest struggled up and stood panting near him. The mountain man measured with his eye the distance to the top of the divide, and anxiously studied the clouds. A rising gust of wind blew a whirling line of snow around them. Not seeming to hurry, but still moving purposefully, Jim Clyman paused behind each pack-laden man and cut the blanket from his back. He spread two of them on the snow.

"We ain't goin' to make it," he said in a matter-of-fact voice. "Sit in a circle on these blankets, and I'll put the others over us. Every person's responsible for holdin' down his part. The baby goes in the middle. We ain't gonna freeze if we do it right. It's an old mountain man's trick."

They sat down on the blankets obediently enough. Clyman pulled the rest over them, tucking them in closely. He closed the last gap with his own body as the storm began to rage down in full fury. Dry snow piled on top of the improvised tent. The little dog whimpered in the darkness, and the child talked baby gibberish. All that night, all the next day, and all the next night, nibbling at the pemmican that they carried, they crouched under the blankets and kept each other warm with body heat. Then they pushed the snow from the blankets and, rising like specters, floundered on their way through the soft snow.

That day they got over the divide. Jim Clyman stood at the top of it, waiting for the rest to straggle up. First Cressman came. Then Nathan Parker appeared and, finally, George and Kate Parker, the father carrying Ann. The mountain man stared at them silently. Coming up that murderous, snow-filled slope, George Parker had thrown his food pack away to help his wife and baby. Jim Clyman could not find the heart to reproach him. He turned to start down the slope.

"I was wrong about him, Bub," he muttered to the tired little dog. "He *can* make up his own mind."

TWO DAYS LATER Jim Clyman turned off the trail into the forest. With the axe that he had taken from Cressman he chopped down four small trees. He trimmed the branches from them, and cut the trunks in half. Then he arranged the logs on the ten feet of snow that lay there, made a little pile of shaven pitch-pine sticks, and poured a pinch of powder from his powder horn. He struck a spark into the powder, and the fire flared up. The little brown dog lay near the comforting warmth, paws outspread and tongue lolling expectantly as he glanced up at his master.

The mountain man looked back up the irregular line of snowshoe tracks he had made coming down, and frowned. He and the dog could have been another fifteen miles down the slope by this time. But you couldn't travel that way with tenderfeet. Not that anyone except Cressman had hung back, or complained of the cold and hunger. They just weren't making it so well. George Parker and his wife were taking turns carrying the little girl, but they had to rest every little while. Nate, the boy, had plodded steadily along with his lightening pack—and it had been lightened because Jim Clyman insisted on using the food he carried before any other. Now that was gone, and Parker's was gone. He would start using Cressman's tonight, and save his own for the last hard stretch. He had rationed the food carefully, and they should make it if the tenderfeet could keep up and if another bad blizzard didn't hit them.

As he threw more wood on the fire, the dog rose from his bed in the snow and cocked his head up the trail. Nathan Parker appeared, stumbling down the snowshoe tracks with his head bent and his eyes streaming. The sun had shone brightly all day, and the Parkers and Cressman couldn't seem to get the knack of avoiding snow blindness by squinting properly. But there was no point in exaggerating burdens, or of stressing them.

"Dog-gonit, Nate," he said, "I thought you'd took off on another track."

"Nope." The boy gave a tired grin and sat down to slip the blanket from his shoulders. "I'll stick."

"Reckon you will. Well, fire's ready. Where's the others?"

"They're comin'."

Kate and George Parker, with the little girl riding on her father's shoulders, staggered along the trail and threw themselves wearily down by the leaping fire. Tired as she was, the mother took the child and cradled her in her arms. Jim Clyman petted his dog, and watched them reflectively. Once, when he was out with Ashley, a mountain man had come stumbling into camp. He had travelled almost seven hundred miles through hostile country, he said, and for the past nine days he had had nothing to eat. Many times he had been tempted to give up and die, but he had kept himself alive by thinking of the buffalo steak he was going to have as soon as he got into somebody's camp. That man had lived on hope. Hope was a wonderful thing, a sustaining resource when all others failed. The Parkers had it in large measure.

Cressman came in to the fire and sat with his head hunched over his chest, staring with vacant eyes at the flames. Clyman looked keenly at him. Cressman, the laggard, who had been hanging back more than anyone else the past three days, seemed more fit and ready to go on than any of the others. His face was fuller; his color better. But his expression was becoming more beast than human. The old man's eyes narrowed.

"Let's have your pack, Cressman. Time for grub—such as it is."

"My pack? *My* pack . . . ?"

Cressman raised his head, and glanced crookedly about. He dropped the pack, and the mountain man stepped forward to unfasten the thongs that bound it. But even before he did he knew that it was empty. He took a step forward, his knife in his hand. A deep anger leaped within him, and red shapes wavered before his eyes.

"You ate it!" he snarled. "You ate it, didn't you? That's why you hung back!"

The hot cloud of rage slowly dissolved, and he again became the leader of the little group. Dimly he saw the rest looking at Cressman, saw civilized eyes glowing red in the reflection of the fire, betraying a deep, elemental passion that went far, far back. They were primitive people, cave people who had seen their food stolen. Cressman did not notice them. His eyes were rolling, a vacuous grin played about his lips. The trail was driving him mad.

"Eat the dog," he babbled. "We c'n eat the dog."

Jim Clyman stuck his knife in a log, drew his pack to him, and pulled out a small piece of frozen meat. He saw the eager eyes of the Parkers fixed upon him now, the greedy eyes of the half-mad Cressman. Cressman started to rise, his hands twitching. Clyman reached for his knife.

"Sit down!" he growled. "Mebbe you eat tomorrow, but not tonight. You've had your'n!"

He cut two thin slices of meat for each of the others, impaled them on sticks, and put them over the fire to cook. Melting snow in the kettle, he stirred a little flour into it, flavored it with a tiny piece of meat, and handed it to Kate Parker. The baby ate hungrily, but when the mother was given her own ration, she shook her head.

"Can't I save it for tomorrow?"

Beneath her question was a deeper and more penetrating one. There was tomorrow, and the next day, and the next. . . . The baby had to eat all those days. The future generation must survive.

"Eat it now," Jim Clyman said gruffly.

She did, tearing the meat into tiny morsels with her teeth and devouring them reluctantly. While they ate, Clyman never took his eyes from Cressman. But the man was apathetic, mumbling to himself and smiling foolishly. When they had finished, the mountain man spoke as cheerfully as he could.

"I been in such fixes before, and I'll be in 'em ag'in. We're gonna get through. But if anybody touches my pack, I'll kill him."

"Eat the dog," Cressman raved. "Kill and eat the dog."

Clyman glanced across the fire at him, and said nothing. But when he rolled up in his blanket that night, the dog was beside him.

JIM CLYMAN HIMSELF was not exactly sure as to what took place the next few days. He knew only that the two slices of meat were cut to one, and that when they finally came out of the deep snow they cut the lacings from their snowshoes, boiled them, and drank the gelatinous soup. The last of the meat he carried had been eaten yesterday morning, while starved eyes had looked at the little brown dog and then guiltily away again. This morning the baby had had the last of the flour.

He walked on, the spaniel dragging wearily at his heels. On either side the tall pines rustled, and the racing little brook he was following cast itself furiously over the ice-sheathed rocks and boulders in its path. It seemed that he was back with Ashley's men

when the starved hunter had wandered into camp. That memory was very plain and very sharp, and he caught himself glancing around as though looking for the bountiful fare that Ashley's camp had always offered. That hunter, he remembered, had lived entirely on hope, on the hope of a meal of buffalo meat. But tenderfeet weren't mountain men. They wouldn't believe that they were going to get anything unless they could see it before them. And all they could see was his dog. . . .

He forced himself back to reality. Behind him were people, hungry people, each of whom, in his own way, thought of the things nearest and dearest to him. Cressman, in his insane wanderings, had gone back to his farm on the Fox River and was enjoying all the things it had once offered him. Nathan Parker thought of going on, of continuing to follow this man who had dared suggest coming over the divide when it was impassable. George and Kate Parker thought of the child in her arms, and of all the life that was to be.

But their whole minds, when they were at either the morning or the evening fire, centered on the little brown dog and the salvation he offered. Here was food, and food was life, and they had to live. They could not be lured this far, then die within reach of their goal. He turned aside, and gathered wood for a fire. He poured a little gunpowder under the wood and lighted it. Tonight they would camp out of the winter snow The little dog lay down before the fire with his head on his paws.

Nathan Parker appeared, and almost as soon as he sat down beside the fire his eyes fastened on the dog. Carrying the little girl between them, Kate and George Parker came stumbling out of the semigloom. Cressman crawled up, babbling of fat sheep that had grazed beside the Fox River and of the many meals he had eaten there. Then he, too, fell silent, and all eyes were fixed on the dog.

Jim Clyman edged his knife out of its sheath. An animal was not supposed to mean anything when human lives were at stake, but the little spaniel was more to him than any person. He was a friend, one to whom he could confide his innermost thoughts and troubles, one who had always been satisfied to share his fortune. The knife point stopped at the dog's throat, and Clyman held it there while he looked at the eager people about the fire. They had been led on by tangible hope, by the certain knowledge that, when their last food gave out, they had a final resource in the dog. And they could go no farther without food. The dog would feed them tonight, tomorrow, and perhaps the day after. It would see them through. He touched the knife against the dog's throat, and the spaniel whimpered in his arms.

"Well, by God!"

It was not a curse but a prayer, and it came from

outside the circle of fire light. A tall man with a rifle in his hands stood there, a strong, well-fed man with a pack on his back.

"You came over the divide?" he asked incredulously.

They struggled to their feet, staring in disbelief at this man who had brought them salvation. The caveman had gone from them. They were once again civilized, thinking people.

"Got caught out on a long survey," the stranger explained, "and saw your fire. Our camp's only a piece down the trail, but I reckon you'd better eat right here." He swung his pack to the ground.

Jim Clyman slowly slipped his knife back in its sheath, and tickled the little dog's ears with a bony finger.

"We made it, Bub," he said huskily. "We made it. This here's the end of the trail."

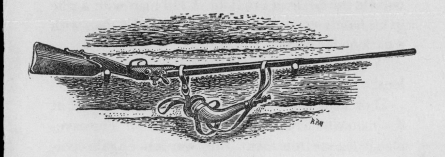

That's how it was. From the Gulf of St. Lawrence to the Golden Gate, foot by foot, mile by mile, through forests and plains and mountains, the frontier was pushed steadily back by unpretentious, unknown, unsung heroes: seamen and scouts, traders and trappers, boatmen and bullwhackers, missionaries and mountaineers. Through three centuries of expansion and across three thousand miles of wilderness, America's destiny followed the trails blazed by the buckskin brigade.